MW00799724

Blame it
on the Moon

Blame it on the Moon

Lou Pugliese

BLAME IT ON THE MOON

Copyright © 2024 by Louis Pugliese
All rights reserved.
loupuglieseauthor.com

No part of this publication may be reproduced, distributed, or transmitted
in any form or by any means, including photocopying, recording, or other
electronic or mechanical methods, without the prior written permission of the
publisher, except as permitted by U.S. copyright law. For permission requests,
please use the contact form on the website at loupuglieseauthor.com

This is a work of fiction. Names, characters, businesses, places, events,
locales, and incidents are either the products of the author's imagination
or used in a fictitious manner. Any resemblance to actual persons, living or
dead, or actual events is purely coincidental.

Library of Congress Control Number 2024907447
ISBN 979-8-9900726-1-9 (hardcover)
ISBN 979-8-9900726-0-2 (paperback)
ISBN 979-8-9900726-2-6 (e-book)

Book Cover by Chris Holmes
Interior Design by Autumn Skye
Editing by Jennifer Ellen Cook

First edition 2024

Every man is like the moon, both sharing a dark side
Unseen, unspoken truths of them
where sin is stuffed to hide
Ever changing, waxing, waning, full, and even gone
It drives the tides of Earth and man
through dusk and day and dawn
Seen or not, it's always there and fills our nighttime air
Some say that when it's New and dark,
it's lurking in its lair
While restless souls come out and play,
New moon remains concealed
Until the time when secrets drop and all will be revealed

Richard Eugene Craft

M y name is Richard Eugene Craft. I'm sixty-something as I write this, and I live alone in a haunted house. I came here to write the great American novel. The house is in Northern Virginia, Arlington. Today it's an unusually quiet setting. The land and house are almost an eerily sheltered piece of history. Wandering through the buildings or grounds, a person could easily be back in the mid-1800s.

It's a typical large farmhouse, with three floors, including the attic. A concrete pad was poured out front in the middle of the gravel driveway in the 1960s. A basketball rim and hoop still stand there as a nod to half-court games between my brother and me. I keep a basketball by it ready to go for those few and far between times when I pretend I'm exercising.

The house has absorbed the deaths of many family members over the years, including my wife Gwen, and my infant son. It also served as a field hospital from 1861-1865.

The original flooring in the house is planks of elm wood, saturated in the DNA of untold numbers of soldiers as they bled out and died there during the Civil War. Those floors have been sanded, sealed, and polished in subsequent upgrades to the house, but the blood in their grain will always be there. No doubt this is why the house is presumed to be haunted. How could it not be?

Tom

It was a dark and stormy night. I'd never use that in my writing, but it was a dark and stormy night when the house relationship entered a new phase. It wasn't raining, but the thunder was booming and the lightning was flashing when I heard the ping, ping, ping of the basketball out front. I was back in one of the downstairs rooms preparing to turn it into an office. My desk was currently active in the main hallway of the house, and I was hoping to move that clutter in case I ever hosted visitors.

My brother's gun was in the top desk drawer, and I picked it up as I passed. It was an impressive piece, a Ruger .357, six-inch barrel, nickel plated. It hailed from 1976 and had an engraving on the barrel: "Made in the 200th Year of American Liberty." Surely that would scare off any ghost.

The switch for the outdoor floodlights was located in the canning kitchen behind the small kitchen. I turned on the lights along the way, the hall, the small kitchen, and the canning kitchen. I could still hear the basketball at play as I turned on the floods, and then, aside from the brewing storm, things went silent. When I walked back through the small kitchen and main hall to the front of the house, the basketball court was empty, with the basketball lying right where I always left it. Situation normal.

I decided to return to my chores in the future office room. I also decided to take the gun with me. I couldn't imagine using it, but it seemed like the right idea at the time. I was taking apart one of two twin bed frames when I heard a new sound. I could swear someone or something was fumbling through the drawers in the kitchen. The gun and I stepped back into the hall. The lights from the kitchens and the outdoor floodlights weren't on. I hadn't turned them off, and the switches were all inside the house.

I was uncomfortable that I was having one of those high-anxiety moments as I moved forward in the dark with a gun in my hand. I kept my finger off the trigger.

The kitchen noise, the basketball, and all of the thunder and lightning had ceased. I don't think I had known a moment so completely absent of light and sound since I had been here.

I felt the presence before I saw it. A figure was slowly emerging from the darkness of the kitchen area, his bare feet shuffling over the stained planks of history. As it grew closer it appeared as a Black man wearing only tattered shorts. He had a small kitchen knife in his right hand. He hadn't seen me yet. I was petrified. Should I run? Should I shoot? Should I play dead? I chose to speak, loudly.

"Who are you and what are you doing here?" I shouted. My eyes had adjusted to the dim light by now, and I saw a young man jump at the sound of my voice, obviously as terrified and surprised as I was. "Why do you have a knife?" I continued. "If you think you're going to kill me, I promise I'll shoot you dead right where you stand." I was shaking badly. I hope he couldn't read the fear behind my bluster.

"Oh my God, Dr. Craft, please don't shoot, it's me, Tom. I'd never kill you."

"I don't know who you are Tom, or where you came from, but if you don't get rid of that knife, I'll be taking it from your dead hands." I don't know where I found the guts to go all Dirty Harry at this moment. I was so scared I thought I would shit myself.

"No knife," he said as he moved very slowly to place it on the desk in the hallway. "No knife" he repeated as he raised his hands.

"Sit in that chair." I didn't want him on his feet, able to quickly make any moves.

"I'm sitting, Dr. Craft, I'm sorry if I scared you. I was just going to peel an apple in the kitchen. I'd never kill you, but others are coming, one that would kill you."

"How do you know who I am?"

"Dr. Craft, are you okay? It's me, Tom. We've been knowing each other for years."

"Where are you from?" I asked.

"Right here, Dr. Craft. I live in the root cellar. I've been staying there since the war let up and sister Betty died."

I was suddenly very dizzy. Dr. Craft, the war, Tom and Betty.

"What year is it, Tom?" I asked, afraid of the answer.

"Why, it's 1866," Tom said as he evaporated before my eyes.

I started a journal that night.

Lincoln

The next morning, I visited our local animal shelter. It seemed a dog might be good company, especially with the uncertainty about last night's visitor.

"Good morning," a pleasant young lady greeted me. "I'm Amy. Can I help you find a friend?"

"I've been debating about getting a dog partner. I live alone, and it might be nice to have someone to talk to."

"We have a full house of candidates that would be great companions. Would you be interested in a napping partner, a hiking partner, or maybe a protective partner?"

"All of the above, I think. Not a giant wild snapping guard dog but someone of a manageable size that's pretty alert would work."

"Do you mind a barker?"

"Not if there's something that needs to be barked at."

"Do you have space for running and exercise and play?"

"Twenty acres of open wooded land. Lots of trees to pee on. None of it is fenced, but it could be."

"I may have a perfect fit. Are you familiar with shelties? They're a herding dog, especially alert, really smart, easily trained, loyal, and great frisbee players."

"Who wouldn't want that?"

"The previous owner that turned this guy in hated the barking and the high-activity needs of the breed. They thought they were getting a cute Lassie miniature who would only act up if Timmy was in the well."

"I do have a well on the property but no Timmys."

"I think young Atlas may be a perfect fit for you."

"Do you think he could learn a new name? I have a desire to call the dog Lincoln. I'm hiring him to help me free some slaves."

She didn't ask, I didn't elaborate.

"Once you're his bonded person he'll be happy to learn any name or command. The breed is a hard-working people-pleaser, sometimes distracted by outside influence but mostly just wanting to hang and play with his peeps."

"How long does it take to bond with one of these shelties?"

"You'd likely be lifelong friends by the time you show him his new home."

"Then let's meet my new napping partner."

Atlas, soon to be Lincoln, was a strikingly beautiful fawn sheltie, and happy to see us. We hung out for a bit in one of the shelter's play areas. He was a little barky, but I thought it would be nice to have some noise in the house that I knew the source of. We filled out the paperwork and set up a home visit for the next day. The shelter insisted on checking the place out to make sure their dogs ended up in safe spaces.

"Should I pick up some dog bowls, food, toys, and bed on my way home?" I asked. "Or would that be premature?"

"From the little I know about his potential home, it sounds like a perfect environment for this guy. I think you're safe to make a small investment."

I went shopping from there. My new friend, Lincoln, would have all the comforts of home when he came to stay.

Linking with Lincoln

Amy and Atlas, soon to be Lincoln, showed up early the next morning. Atlas was crated in the back of her car.

"He is crate trained, and the crate comes with him," said Amy. "If there are times you would need to lock him up. He doesn't mind it. It can be comforting to him as part of his routine."

"I lean to a free-range existence for Lincoln. There's a lot here for us to explore together, and I want him to feel like an unfettered part of the family. I'll find a spot for the crate, and it will be there if he chooses it."

"Sounds good, let's do our checklist on the house and grounds. If there are no showstoppers, I can leave him with you today. I'll keep him on the leash for the tour. We recommend that all dogs stay on a leash when not in a confined area, but obviously, that will be up to you and Lincoln."

Lincoln seemed to bond with me from the start. He remembered me from the day before and was all happy and tail-wagging this morning. The walkthrough of the house was surprisingly uneventful. I had expected the legendary dog senses would pick up every spirit in the history of the place. Lincoln was inquisitive and interested throughout but not tentative or fearful at all.

He stayed close by my side as we did our outside survey, and Amy even let the leash drop in many areas since he was so focused on me. I showed them the pump for the well. It was working today, and Lincoln took a drink. He was both curious and cautious around the outbuildings, like he had some sense of occupancy, likely the rodents and squirrels that he would come to love chasing and herding.

Amy kept up the small talk as we roamed. She was a cute young thing and more than a little flirtatious. I was flattered by the innuendo. I was also acutely aware that she had some serious baggage and daddy issues if she was trying to hit on me. I would have welcomed female company in my life, but I was happy to let the ball drop on this one.

Her focus became business when we got to the orchard.

"Are these apple trees?" She asked.

"Pears," I said

"Pears or apples could both be a problem for you and Lincoln. A bite or two of either is fine, but if he were to decide to make a big meal here, he'd wish he hadn't. He'd have some intestinal distress at the least. That would be followed by some pretty violent illness, the kind you'd prefer not to have to clean up. He's not a big dog at twenty-five pounds, so potential rapid weight loss and dehydration are quickly problematic. Not to mention that apple and pear seeds also contain cyanide."

"Showstopper?"

"Not necessarily. He'd always have to be on a leash in this area, but that pretty much means you can never turn him loose outside if there's fruit. Life would be open and easier for both of you if you had a fenced area."

"I can do that, but it could be several weeks to get it installed. How long can you hold onto him?"

"We can do all the paperwork now, including a clause that he'll not be off-leash on the property until the fence is complete. Are you willing to do leash training with him?'

"I've already contacted a trainer to get us started on come, sit, stay, and all of the social niceties."

"Richard, I think we can do this. I think he's the right dog for you and I think you're the right human for him. You'll need to agree to leash-only outings until a fence is completed. That would give the two of you some great bonding and training time. By the time the fence is done, he'll be your best companion ever. The fence will also give him other protection from stray animals and other areas he shouldn't dig in."

"The house was a field hospital during the Civil War. There's a burial pit of the hospital waste, unclaimed bodies, amputated limbs, etc. at the property's edge. I suppose that would be a bad digging spot," I said, laughing.

Amy laughed with me on that one. "The mental picture of what Lincoln might emancipate from that spot is not good," she said. "Okay then, I now pronounce you dog and human on a probationary status. We'll add the fence and training conditions to the paperwork. I think I can trust the two of you to follow the instructions, and I'll schedule a follow-up visit for a month from now. If all goes as the three of us hope for, he'll be yours unconditionally. If not, for any reason, I'm afraid I'll have to take him back to the shelter."

"I understand," I said, "and I appreciate your trust and leniency. We won't let you down."

"I believe that."

"I do have one last question before we wrap up here."

"Yes," she said, looking expectant. I think this is the part where she thought I was going to hit on her.

"How long have you been in the humane trafficking business?"

I could swear Lincoln laughed with us.

Lincoln Learns

Atlas accepted becoming Lincoln seamlessly, responding to his new name right away. That first evening he was already at home, jumping into bed with me and sleeping through an uneventful night.

We booked the fence project the next day. The contractor promised a completed area within two weeks. Lincoln was becoming a little bit larger investment than initially anticipated, but I had some real work lined up for him. Just having an understanding housemate would be worth the cost.

"Lincoln," I said after our first morning breakfast together, "Let's get you acquainted with your surroundings." I took him into the out-buildings where he had expressed curiosity on his first walkabout. Two of these were original to the first construction. Those are the outhouse, a two-holer, and the smokehouse, which still has some hams hanging in the rafters. Those hams have been there for as long as I can remember. They're probably still edible today. Lincoln seemed to think so, taking in the permanently smoky smell of the place. The other building is a large utility shed, added much later as an addition to the horse stalls, for storing the landscaping and farm implements. Lincoln seemed sat-isfied with his new yard.

We graduated training in two weeks. Lincoln was pronounced exceptional in his role. I was pronounced less than exceptional, but the trainer allowed that perfect leash skills weren't a necessity. They only really mattered in competition, and it wouldn't hurt our relationship.

The fence would be complete in a couple of days. Working with the contractor's advice, I chose an open-view wrought iron design that complemented the architecture. It covered about half an acre on the left end of the house. We planned oversized gates on three sides for easy access in mowing. Concrete and posts were already in and the final construction was easy to visualize. It would be a real treat for Lincoln to have a free run spot for his pooping pleasure and ready access to water from the pump.

But first, Lincoln and I had work to do. The house had been unusually quiet since his arrival, just the normal creaks and groans expected for its age. Maybe his presence alone would keep the poltergeists and the night talkers at bay. I think I'd be okay with that.

It was time to look into the one spot I had avoided on my own since I'd been here. The root cellar was dug under the canning kitchen to the right of the front porch. The entrance is hidden by shrubbery and azaleas surrounding the house foundation. Lincoln and I walked behind the shrubs and down the four stone steps to the underground sanctuary. Access was through a short door with no windows. There was a hasp on the door but no lock. I thought I might add one depending on what we found. I brought a flashlight and the gun. I don't know why I had the gun.

The door opened easily. I didn't expect that. It should have been blocked by built-up sediment or rusted hinges, but it wasn't. The initial view was a dark deep space, just the first few feet visible from the sun. My brother Bob and I used to play here many, many years ago.

I turned on the flashlight and extended the leash so Lincoln could go bravely before me. I had to duck through the doorway but could stand fully past that. I shut the door behind us and let him off leash to explore on his own. I was somewhat encouraged by his lack of trepidation.

It hadn't changed since my childhood.

The chamber was about seven feet high, probably eight feet wide, and forty or so feet deep, lined with shelves still holding canned goods and labeled preserves from who knows when. A couple of workbench areas were built in. Forgetting for the moment why we were there, I was envisioning the amazing hobby space/wine cellar tables that this could become. I could fill the shelves with my own private Lego Land.

I heard Lincoln making some rustling sounds ahead. Moving forward with the light I could see that he was digging in something at the end of the space. It was a large pile of fresh hay. It had been a very long time since a horse or hay was on this property, but this looked like it could have been laid in yesterday. Even with the flashlight, it was difficult to see the contents of the dusty unlabeled jar in the bowels of the cellar. At a dim glance, it appeared to be some sort of sausages and maybe pickled eggs.

The unique feature back here was an interesting collection of Civil War artifacts, belts, buckles, buttons, and even a sword in its sheath. They all looked new. A chair at the back workbench had no dust on it, odd. There were also paper, ink, and a quill pen. And several mouse-chewed wrappers from cheese and snack packages that I knew had disappeared from the kitchen.

My mind was spinning by now, but Lincoln showed nothing other than normal curiosity. "Let's go, Link," I said, suddenly fearing a flashlight failure. "I'm not ready for this." I wasn't emotionally prepared for another Tom encounter.

I put a lock in the hasp that afternoon.

I Now Pronounce You

As promised, Amy returned at the one-month mark to check on her probationary students.

"I love the fence," she said as she slipped out of her little car in her short skirt, seemingly oblivious to the exposure of stocking tops and garters. I didn't know women dressed like that in real life, but I didn't mind the view. "What do you think?" she said.

Briefly flustered, I came quickly to context. "Oh, the fence. I love it, too. I wasn't initially keen on the idea, but I think it does enhance the house and landscaping, and it's great for Lincoln. If you have frisbee skills, he'd love to show off for you."

"Nice," she said "I'm always up for playtime." I tried not to read anything other than frisbee into that comment, but it was difficult.

Amy did have frisbee skills. She and Lincoln chased around for about twenty minutes. He caught and returned every throw until he let her know that he was done. On the last catch, he dropped the frisbee by the pump and took a long drink before lying in the cool puddle.

"Let's take him for a little walk outside the fence and see how you guys did with the trainer," she said.

"I think you'll be impressed," I told her as I had Lincoln step into his halter. I secured the leash.

We walked the grounds near the house, stopping regularly for a sit-and-stay and some hand-shaking. She seemed pleased with his progress. I took us to the pear orchard. The pears were just beginning to come into season. None were on the ground yet, but some edible specimens clung to the branches.

She had a great laugh and smile. I was beginning to wish I was much younger. "Oh, what's this? I didn't notice it on the last visit."

It was a granite marker with two words, "Yellow Cat." "Family tribal knowledge says that great granduncle Craft was adopted by a feral cat after his wife died. It looks like they were pretty close, as he chose to give it a proper burial and a memorial when it expired. Just another little oddity here."

Back to the house, we wandered with Lincoln through every room. He balked at the attic entrance. "That's odd," she said.

"I haven't introduced him to that level yet, but we'll get there soon. It's just some old stuff left over from my brother, but there's probably some resident rodent population as well that he's heard. I haven't been quite bored enough to get into serious cleaning out. I'm sure he'll be okay with it once he gets to explore." I failed to mention the exploration Lincoln and I had done in the root cellar.

"Can we go up there now?" said Amy.

"Sure, why not?" The attic had a flat door at the top of some steps. I raised it and leaned it back on an upstairs railing as I climbed the stairs. The attic had pretty good daytime light from the windowed dormers so it wasn't at all dark or scary.

"This a nice space," said Amy. "You could have a very cool library or study here."

"That's a good thought. The house is so big I hadn't even looked up here much, but it is a uniquely nice spot."

Lincoln had followed us up and was sniffing around. He loitered at a pile of my brother's army stuff, footlocker, and duffel bag, when I noticed something missing. There had been one of those heavy, scratchy army blankets on top of the duffel bag the last time I was up here. It was gone. I particularly noticed its presence because previously I wondered why they'd issue such a thing to a soldier in tropical Vietnam. At that moment, I sensed a sudden chill and Lincoln backed away. Amy didn't seem to notice.

We worked our way back down through the other rooms. Amy sat on the bed in one room again, seemingly oblivious to the upskirt skin she was displaying. "You have a lot of bedrooms here," she said. "Do you get many overnight guests?" She winked. Maybe just something in her eye.

"No, it's pretty much just Lincoln and I hanging out. Do we have paperwork to finish?"

"Just a little to make everything official."

We made it to the kitchen table, signed off on the county forms, and she pronounced us dog and human.

"Now this doesn't have to be the end of the relationship," Amy said. "If you need anything from me — and I do mean anything — " she winked again. "Give me a call, and I'll be here for you and Lincoln."

We parted at the car. The ingress was even more revealing than the egress had been. We waved goodbye, and I felt a real urge to relieve myself in her wake. I was now certain I was right about Amy and those serious daddy issues that I was not going to look into any further.

School Days

W ell before the appearances of Tom and Lincoln, I had put in a teaching application at a local college. I had been enjoying my faux career as an author, but after Gwen was gone, I realized I needed to get out more and have a routine for my days.

When I was in California as a corporate guy, I finished my MBA and a doctorate in HR. That set me up for a change in my livelihood by becoming a college professor. Northern Virginia Community College (NVCC) was always looking for experienced adjunct professors in a variety of business categories. I felt a real calling to teaching in general, and community college in particular. I had done my first degree, an associate in Administration of Justice, at NVCC many years before.

I liked that community college students tended to be there for a reason. They were more motivated and less entitled than their fancy school peers. They also tended to support a great cross-section of careers and ages, some hoping to change their lives, some just broadening their outlook, but all there for a reason. The veterans and working adults were often well-traveled and experienced in the world, which opened up some great class discussions, and I could always learn more myself.

Lincoln was a great new companion, and the two of us hunkering down in this particular house was interesting, but probably not the best choice for a 24/7 pastime. It wouldn't hurt my writing to add some outside stimulus. And it wouldn't hurt my soul to interact with other live human beings on a social level.

My acceptance notice from NVCC came back, to begin with the fall schedule. I started with NVCC in the fifteen-week term from August to early December. I'd be teaching three classes, Introduction to Business, Marketing, and Human Resources. That meant Lincoln and I were apart for only about a few hours at a time, three days a week.

NVCC also supported a lot of continuing education offerings and unique hobby classes in their evening schedule for working adults. One of those was a paranormal research class, complete with a field trip to a nearby ex-asylum. I had the time and more than a vague interest in such things, so I signed up. So would begin my clandestine search for reinforcements on the ghost hunt.

The instructor was a thirty-something woman named Audrey Welsh. The first class was syllabus, outline, expectations, and introductions, the usual drill. Our instructor was a partner in a New Age store. I wasn't familiar with the world of crystals and incense, but I wasn't familiar with anything paranormal either, so I was intent on keeping an open mind.

I hung around after the first class to introduce myself as fellow faculty at the school.

"Hi Audrey, I'm Richard, can I call you Audrey?"

"Sure, we're an informal lot here." She laughed, always a good sign.

"I'm fellow faculty here. I'm a retired corporate guy teaching business classes."

"Nice, perhaps we can quid pro quo. I'm a probably never-to-be-retired small business owner. Right now, I have another commitment, so I need to get going."

She seemed unimpressed, but she also seemed like the type that would be initially guarded. On the misogynistic Bo Derek scale, Audrey had all of the foundational features of a 10. In plain clothes with no makeup, she was still a solid 8 or 9. I wasn't offended by her initial response, accepting that really attractive women who haven't put themselves on the open market are probably tired of getting hit on by creepy strangers.

"Before you go, I wanted to share the reason I signed up for your class. I happen to live in a haunted house, and I'm hoping to better understand my roommates."

She perked up a little when I told her that. She said, "You just might be in the right place."

Paranormal Education Part Deux

The second class got deeper into introductions.

Audrey said, "If we're going to be an effective paranormal team, we should know our teammates' strengths and leanings in the paranormal pursuit. How many of you believe strongly that ghosts are real?"

Three hands went up.

"How many are skeptics, but curious?"

Four more hands, including mine.

"And then there was one," said Audrey, looking at her class roster for a name. "How would you identify, Chuck?"

"I'm a full-time electrician and a part-time pastor in a local church. I'm a non-believer in the occult, but I do encounter churchgoers that are strong believers. I'd like to have more understanding of their thinking so I can be of better counsel."

"Interesting, and a very noble open-minded purpose for an otherwise closed mind. An electrician, eh? It's a shame that the sites we'll be visiting this weekend don't have electricity. Lights going on and off and changes in lighting intensity are very commonly reported paranormal phenomena. Your skills would be invaluable in sorting those out if we were on an excursion where they occurred.

"To share my position on the topic," she continued, "I would probably fall a little into the skeptic camp. In my day job, I'm an owner/partner in a New Age store. I encounter a lot of true believers in a variety of mystical and spiritual fields, including my partner, Vicki. As an offshoot of that, I developed my interest in paranormal studies years ago as a hobby. Much like Chuck, I wanted to be able to identify with my customers' thoughts. I'm also an artist. I do believe that much of my art is a revelation. Often, without a plan, it simply flows through me onto the canvas in a surprising, and usually pleasing, way. I'm not a psycho-believer in the occult, but I have come to accept there are some things out there that we may never fully understand or explain."

I was good with that approach, having experienced that dilemma personally in both my residence and my writing.

The second part of the class introduced us to an array of instruments popular in ghost hunts and what we might hope to find in our field trips.

Audrey started, "I know that some of you have been on these types of investigations before, but we also have several novices. I want to go over the equipment we'll be taking with us so everyone is familiar with the tools of the trade.

"Number one is the electromagnetic field detector, or EMF. Some people may try to tell you these are ghost detectors. Not true. What they can do is give us a baseline of EMF activity in our search area and let us know if there are any unusual changes in that activity during our time there. A thermal imaging camera will help us similarly with temperature changes.

"Number two will be our hot spot cameras. These are essentially night vision trail cams that hunters and hobbyists use. We'll spread a few around in areas that strike us as likely haunts. Don't be too disappointed if the only images we capture are us." She laughed.

"Wear your pants, everyone," I said. I don't think they got it.

"We'll carry digital recorders for potential EVP, or electronic voice phenomena, as they call it in the trade.

"We'll scatter around some cat balls. These are simple pet toys that light up with the smallest of movements. Like the hot spot cameras, we are likely to find ourselves to be the key influences on these. They also respond to animals and even large insects."

"I understand cat balls can be difficult to harvest," I commented. They didn't get that one either.

"Lastly, we have access to a couple of REM pods. A REM pod, or radiating electromagnetism pod, sends out an electromagnetic field wherever it is placed. If the field is disturbed, it emits both a light and sound alert. We'll put these in a central spot of interest and keep one of our hot spot cameras with it. In theory, a triggered response with no visible image could indicate a supernatural presence. In practice, we are once again the most likely culprits, so don't get over-excited if it goes off."

"I believe I had the GI Joe REM Pod when I was a kid. Or was that the space capsule." Three strikes.

"There are only eight students in the group, which is a good number for investigative jaunts. Per your syllabus, we are going to dive right into field research this Saturday with a trip to the former Western State Asylum in Staunton, Virginia. There are multiple sites of that historic facility. We'll have access to two of those. One is the completely abandoned main facility. This building was self-sufficient, with its water, heat, and electricity provided by its own power plant. Our second stop will be a set of buildings that are being converted into condos and apartments. We won't bother the living residents, but we will prowl through the large cemetery there.

Let's all be here promptly at 7:00 p.m. on Saturday. That should get us to our destination around 9:00, with plenty of darkness to begin our work. Bring your flashlights. Expect to spend three or four hours in Staunton, getting us back here around 3:00 a.m. Sunday. I've arranged for a driver and a small bus so we can travel together and share our experiences on the way there and back. Or nap if you prefer. If there are no burning questions or concerns, I'll see you all Saturday evening."

An older woman in the front row raised her hand.

"Yes," said Audrey.

"Have you been to this place before, and if so, what have you experienced?"

"I've made the trip several times. I have to admit it was very creepy and scary on my first visit. I'd encourage you to look up the history of the Western State Asylums and the activities that happened there. I'll be sharing some of that on our ride down Saturday."

"Did you have any ghost sightings on your visits?"

"Plenty of spooky weirdness but nothing I would say was a definitive ghost sighting. It's certainly an environment for such things if they are real. If there are no more questions about our pending trip, I look forward to seeing all of you on Saturday."

"One last thought to remember," I said. "What did one ghost say to the other ghost?"

No response.

"Do you believe in humans?" I chuckled alone.

Everyone groaned as we started shuffling our notes and books to head out when Audrey called my name. "Richard, have you got a minute?"

"Sure."

"I do have an interest in what you said about living in a haunted house. I'd like to talk more about it but I'm up to my ears with the shop, teaching this class, and finishing the final semester of my MFA at George Mason."

"Yikes, you are whelmed."

"I have an extra interest in your experience because the building our store is in is also allegedly haunted. Vicki and I live over the shop, and we do hear and see some odd things. I'd love to compare notes."

"Do you ever have downtime at the shop?" I asked. "Maybe I could swing by to see you there."

"We get good traffic in the mornings and evenings and a few folks at lunchtime, but the afternoons from 1:00 to 3:00 are usually fairly quiet. That's when we catch up on restocking, inventory checks, bills, and the business stuff. We could probably get in an hour or so to visit then. Are you sure that wouldn't be out of your way? It's here in Annandale."

"No problem at all. I have nothing on my schedule tomorrow after my morning HR class. Give me the address, and I'll see you around 1:00 tomorrow."

She gave me the address and I was so excited I pre-tripped it on the way home. I had to laugh when I passed by. I knew the building well.

A Piece of History

I pulled up in front of New Age Renaissance right at 1:00 p.m. the next day. As I walked in I was greeted with "Namaste," to which I unconsciously and stupidly responded with "Konnichiwa" which had been the standard afternoon greeting on most of my business trips.

"You must be Vicki," I said to the woman at the desk, a petite, really cute young lady with a pixie haircut.

"Good guess," she said. "Since you don't appear to be a random Japanese tourist. you must be the Richard that Audrey was expecting. She warned me about your dad humor."

"Guilty," I replied.

"Welcome to our world, Richard. She was taking a break to work on some school stuff. I'll ring her up and she should be down in a couple of minutes. Feel free to browse. Can I get you a water or a cup of coffee?"

"No, I'm good for now. I'll take a look around while I'm waiting, thanks."

I had been here many years before but I couldn't remember what the layout was then beyond the main counter area where my friend Ricky had bought his first bong. I started my wandering to the right of the front door where there was quite a library of what appeared to be research and self-help books. Deepak Chopra and Marianne Williamson were the dominant sections. Not being a New Age aficionado, I chuckled at a couple of the titles.

I walked quickly through a room of crystals of various sizes and colors. I don't get that at all.

The next area was all yoga. The shelves were full of rolled-up mats, pool noodles of various sizes, and foam bricks. A large selection of videos and more books completed the display as I wandered into the next cubicle of incense and powders. That's where Audrey joined with a shushing warning when she found me laughing out loud at one of the displays.

"What is wrong with you?" she said, trying to sound stern but smiling at my weirdness.

I had tears in my eyes as I pointed at a large wooden rack. It held jars of different colored powders and a sign that said "Scents of the Universe." The shelves were labeled with the names of the planets. There were many gaps in their inventories, except one.

I almost couldn't speak as I tried to choke back my laughter and said, "How come no one has bought the scent of Uranus?"

Still crying, I said, "Do you happen to stock that new perfume made with holy water? It's called Eau My God."

She smiled again as she said, "I see we need to get you away from this room. Would you like to see the rest of the place, maybe with less boisterous commentary?"

"Lead on, my sensei."

We passed through a doorway into the world of massage. "I like this spot," I said, impressed by the array of oils and creams and how-to resources. One whole wall was dedicated to the largest array I've ever seen of personal massagers aka vibrators. I picked up a squeeze bottle of a "Fire and Ice" labeled cream and commented that it sounded stimulating.

"It is," she said. "Maybe if you're a very good boy you'll get to find out someday." Another smile, I think we just flirted.

The last large room of the store was a gallery with lots of paintings and pictures. Most were very peaceful settings. Landscapes and seashores were abundant. There were also several images of reflective people portraits. "These are beautiful," I said.

"Thanks," Audrey replied. "Most of them are mine. I have the ones I'm working on for my MFA show upstairs if you'd like to see them."

"Absolutely."

We circled back to the main counter space. "Have you met Vicki?" Audrey asked.

"Oh yes," said Vicki. "You didn't tell me he was Japanese." Audrey looked puzzled.

"When she gave me the 'Namaste,' I responded with my best 'Konnichiwa.' I don't think it impressed her."

"Au contraire," said Vicki. "Audrey and I both find men with linguistic talents to be very attractive." Pretty sure that was a flirt from Vicki. I like it here, I thought.

"Do you ladies know the history of your building?" I asked.

Vicki spoke, "We found it as an abandoned old house but visitors have told us it had a hippie history, also that it was supposedly haunted."

"I can't speak to the haunted, but in the '60s and '70s this was the great and mighty Peacock Plume, a record store and headshop of renown. My friends and I would swing by here to pick up obscure albums, yes vinyl albums, of little-known artists like Rare Bird. We also bought our rolling papers and various other paraphernalia during our visits. The place was iconic back in the day."

"Vicki" Audrey said, "Are you okay with the shop if Richard and I park upstairs for a little while?"

"Certainly. Take your time. It's been ages since you've had a man up there," Vicki laughed. I think Audrey blushed.

I'll Show You Mine if You Show Me Yours

I followed Audrey up the creaky stairs to the apartment. Nice view. It was a surprisingly bright and open space, with a large living and kitchen area and a bedroom suite on either end. Everything was modern and neat with comfortable contemporary furnishings.

"Would you like something to drink?" asked Audrey.

"Water would be good."

"Sparkling okay?"

"Preferred, actually."

She got me a big bottle of Pellegrino from the fridge.

"Before we settle, let me show you my MFA gallery works. I'd love to get an objective outsider's opinion on the display."

"Lead me on," I said, wondering if that qualified as a flirt.

I followed her to the bedroom, another nice view. I hoped they didn't have security cameras that would record me staring at her butt with less-than-noble intent. The bedroom suite was almost as large as the living room. Paintings were everywhere on the walls and stacked neatly in vertical groupings on the floor around the room.

She gave me a moment to let it all sink in and said, "Well, what are your thoughts?"

"I'm nobody's qualified expert, but I'm truly amazed at your talent. I love all of it."

"Thanks. Do you have any sense of theme?"

"What struck me downstairs and also here is serenity. I'm especially drawn to the seascapes. It's like I can feel every grain of sand and see right through each crashing wave. There was an Outer Banks artist I loved many years ago. He went by M. Charles. I always wanted to own one of his works but could never afford it when it was available to me. Your work is at least equal, and some stronger, to what drew me to his art."

"Do you see a favorite?"

"This one here with the waving sea oats and the darkening sky. I can feel the cold wind of an autumn walk in the dunes before a breaking storm. It's just incredible."

"Take it with you." She said.

"Oh, Audrey I couldn't. You can't be serious."

"I mean it. From my haunted house to yours, I want you to have it, but you must promise to display it prominently and speak highly about the artist when you have guests." I was growing to love hearing her laugh. "Okay then, let's take it with us to the living room so you don't forget when we're done talking about ghosts."

She sat on the couch and I picked a big chair, a little afraid to be too close to her. The same peaceful music from the shop also played up here in the living quarters. I stared at my new painting in awe as we got to the business of our visit.

"Why do you think your house is haunted?" she started.

"It's an old place, the mid-1800s, which lends itself to creaks and groans, much like your staircase here, but there are other sounds, murmuring voices, an occasional muffled scream, and shuffling objects, that I just can't find an explanation for. The house was used as a hospital for several years during the Civil War. Who knows how many people passed through and passed on there? Lights sometimes turn on or off on their own. Maybe I need Chuck the electrician/pastor to stop by."

"Maybe we do, too," she said. "The mystery lighting scenario happens regularly, both here and in the store downstairs. Do you ever find things moved? We get that here a lot."

"Oh yeah. Food disappears from the kitchen all the time. I recently discovered a blanket missing from the attic. I haven't found it yet. I'm afraid it might be in the same spot the food goes to, but I'm honestly scared to check on my own. I've also been visited by either a bad dream or a real ghost. He seems to be a basketball fan."

Audrey stared at me a little too long. "That we haven't had. My skeptical paranormal DNA alerts on that one."

"It was very real. I heard a basketball dribbling in the driveway, and it stopped when I turned on the outside lights. Seeing nothing, I went back to what I was doing. The lights turned themselves off, and a man appeared from the kitchen. He thought I was my great granduncle Dr. Craft, and he told me the year was 1866."

"Wow, have you kept notes on what you've seen and heard?"

"I started a journal that night and write down what happens every day."

"Is there any pattern to what you see and hear?"

"Oh yeah. The strange sounds and small poltergeist-type activities are fairly constant. The basketball scenario happens once a month consistently."

"That's way powerful," she remarked thoughtfully. "Do you track the dates?"

"I keep the journal on my phone." She took notes as I went through the calendar. "It's been three months since the first time."

"These dates are the nights of the new moon." She said with conviction.

I broke up laughing. "How in the hell would anyone know that?"

She laughed back. "Duh, I'm a part owner of a haunted New Age store. We'd have no credibility at all with our supernaturalist customers if we didn't stay on top of our astrology and moon phases."

"I forgot to mention that my property also has a large mound that was a communal pit for unknown bodies and associated medical debris during the war years. Do you think that could be a source for strangeness?"

Another "Duh" and another laugh. We were finding camaraderie in our dark humor.

"Then there are the family deaths. Dr. Craft and his wife, my brother, and my wife and son all died in that house."

"Your wife and son?"

"Yes, just six months apart. That was a tough year for me."

"I'm so sorry."

"It's okay. Getting back into the world with the school stuff and working on my writing has helped me deal with it. The best therapy has been Lincoln."

"Lincoln?"

"Lincoln the sheltie. I found him at the animal shelter the day after my apparition. I thought some company would be good to help me fend off ghosts." I laughed. "He's been great, and he's willing to go with me when I search out the oddities of the place. He used to be a little shy about the attic, but now he goes everywhere. Lincoln has been the perfect companion. He's always happy, and he's made me happy, too. He was my greatest therapeutic step in recovery from depression to some sense of normalcy."

"That's good," she said. "Everyone needs a companion. I want to talk more about all of this on our Staunton trip this weekend. Right now, I do have to get to some shop chores and my art exhibit. Thinking about your hauntings, I have a favor to ask."

"Anything," I said.

"The week after we get back from our group outing is another new moon date. Would it be okay if I came to your place that evening to hang out and look around?"

"That would be very cool," I said, wondering why I used the word cool in this century. "I have a blanket I'd like to find, and the dog and I aren't up to the task on our own."

"Then it's a date," she said. God, please let that be another flirt. "It's also a good excuse for me to meet Lincoln."

We gathered my new artwork and headed down to "Namaste" Vicki on the way out. "Konnichiwa," she responded.

I picked up a picture frame and some hanging hardware on the way home.

The Ride to Staunton

We all arrived on time for our class field trip. The two duffels of research accessories were quickly loaded and everyone was checked for flashlights. Chuck gave us a brief lesson on lumens. The standard household flashlight, which is what most of us brought, puts out 100–400 lumens. "Those are good enough to keep you from tripping over doorways and random stuff on the ground," he said, "But if you really want to see what's going on, I brought a high-end tactical LED model that puts out 9600 lumens. It will be daylight wherever I am."

Duly impressed, and deeply embarrassed by our lack of lumens, we loaded into the van. I liked that Audrey put her purse on the seat next to me. I was hoping she would join it.

"Buddy up and get to know each other before we get to our destination," Audrey announced. "These are old buildings with no upkeep. You should always be in pairs at the minimum. If you choose, we're a small enough group to stay together. Let me know what you prefer when we arrive. When we're about an hour into the trip, I'll give you a little background on the history of the facility and answer any questions."

Joy of joys, she did sit next to me as the driver exited the parking lot.

"Whew," she said as we started. "This is a good group. Usually, we have latecomers and silly requests and an atmosphere of herding cats. I hope we all remain as compliant when we get into the building."

"Let me help," I said standing up to make my brief announcement. "Okay everyone, as the momma ghost said to the baby ghost, 'Fasten your sheetbelts.'" I sat down to boos, also appropriate.

It was a quiet group at first but soon everyone was chatting excitedly. Only two of the party had done this before, so there was much nervous speculation. The veteran spookers held court with the freshman spookees as we headed down the road.

"I'm looking forward to the new moon visit at your place next week," said Audrey.

"Lincoln and I are too. We don't get a lot of company, except those that rouse us during our hauntings. How did you develop your taste for the occult?"

"It was Vicki that got me curious. She believes this stuff is real."

"How did the two of you meet?"

"We both had shops in the same strip mall. She had her New Age thing, and I had a small gallery. We hit it off from the first time we commiserated over barely eking out our meager livings. The work of being the only employee in your business is a lonely journey, so we soon took to closing one or the other store each day at lunch. We'd put up a sign pointing to the other shop during that hour so we didn't miss any potential business, and we now both had time with enjoyable company to break up our days."

"Nice," I said. "How did you end up in the Peacock Plume?"

"Vicki found the place through a realtor customer. It needed some renovation, of course, to become what it is now. We both had some savings, and our current stores had enough credibility to qualify us for a business loan. We were also going to be able to give up our individual apartments when the store opened and drop our leases at the strip mall. It was a no-brainer financially, and it's worked out better than planned."

"Can I ask a personal question?"

"Maybe. Try me."

"You two seem to have a great business arrangement. Does your partnership together extend beyond that?"

A briefly puzzled look turned to an outburst of laughter that woke up the whole bus.

"Sorry for that," she said to the group. "Richard said something that was actually funny for a change." Everyone chuckled at that one and I looked into my lap to hide my bright red face.

She turned back to me. "I'm not sure whether to be offended or flattered or just tickled by that. I do love Vicki, and I know she loves me. From the time we met, we've been convinced that we're sisters separated at birth. We have slept together often, as women can do when one or the other needs comfort during a bad time, like a loss or a breakup, but our pleasure perspectives are definitely found in men. Vicki's boyfriend stays at our place regularly, and I can assure you the sounds are louder and spookier than any of our poltergeist encounters. I've been in a drought for a couple of years, consumed by the MFA, the teaching gig, and the store, but I'm hoping to re-emerge soon."

"I apologize for asking," I said. The break out of the drought comment was encouraging, but I still hoped she'd wink or flash skin like Amy so I knew for sure if she liked me that way.

"Don't be sorry," she said. "I'm happy to remove that potential roadblock for you."

I took that as a wink and an upskirt. I'll move cautiously, but I eventually will move.

"Time to go to work," said Audrey. I almost muffed by jumping on that line when she stood up and addressed the bus.

"As promised, here's some backstory on our destination. The building we will tour started as a utopian 1800s model of care with a vision of fresh air and mountain views deemed to be therapeutic for its residents. Good thought, but one that changed with the times. By the mid-nineteenth century, the asylum morphed into an overcrowded warehouse with many residents locked up and restrained by shackles and strait jackets.

"The darkest years were 1906 to 1943. A man by the name of Joseph DeJarnette was the director of the hospital in those years. He also happened to be a noted eugenicist. Followers of the eugenics movement believed that you could improve the genetic quality of a total population by altering or excluding those judged to be inferior. Forced sterilizations, electroshock therapy, and lobotomies became common practice there. Women inmates were a big part of this. The only requirement for their incarceration was a declaration by men that they were 'hysterical.' If there are ghosts haunting buildings, you might expect some disgruntled, confused, or even pissed-off former residents hanging around this place."

A hand raised, one of the women. "What was the definition of 'hysterical' that would get a woman imprisoned?"

"Basically, a declaration by a man, often the husband, supported by the director of an institution. Not surprisingly, there is a large body of research, mostly by women, that has studied and documented the practices of that period. Common reasons for referral were PMS, depression, defying gender roles, being unmarried, and being oversexualized, which means they were caught masturbating."

"We're definitely going to find some pissed-off lady ghosts," said one of the men.

I'm glad he said it. I was going to throw in one of the misogynistic jokes from my repertoire, and he reminded me how stupid that would be.

And Then We Were There

The bus seemed to draw into a nervous reflective state as we drew nearer to our destination. As we exited I-64, Audrey spoke up. "If you look to the hill on your left, you can see where we're going. It's that large dark building. We'll meet with someone from the local police department to get our clearance and access. They should be expecting us."

Officer James Gearhart was standing out front next to his cruiser when we pulled up and started unloading.

"Audrey," he said, greeting her with a hug. "Always a pleasure. Do you have some fresh prospects for our lockup?" He laughed.

"We have a couple of experienced trackers in the group but mostly first-timers," she responded.

"I've opened up the gates and the usual haunts. I've got some perp hunting to do on my own, but I'll be back to release you and lock up in two hours, per our regular schedule."

"Thanks, Jim, I appreciate it." Why did I tingle when she knew his name and he greeted her with a hug?

"Okay gang," said Audrey. "This is the place. Before we go in, I want to point out a couple of exterior features. The big building on the left was the power plant and pumping station that supplied all the infrastructure. Notice the cages on either end of each floor. In the beginning, those would have been the balconies for the fresh air and mountain

33

views. In later years they became the pens where attendants wheeled out the zombie patients to get them out of the way. It was much easier to do maintenance and cleaning if the wards and rooms were empty."

"That's so sad," said one of the women.

"Load up your gear," said Audrey. "There are sadder things to see inside."

Each buddy team took some cat balls, a digital recorder, and a hot spot camera. Audrey had the EMF detector and the thermal imaging camera. She let everyone know that they were welcome to use those if they thought they were on to something.

The large, once impressive entryway was filthy and covered with graffiti. We wandered through the two floors we had access to as a whole group with people commenting on the various rooms we discovered. Wards still had steel bunks in place. Some individual rooms had ripped padding on the walls, others were just bare. An REM pod and camera were centrally placed on each of the two floors.

The creepiest rooms were the treatment areas. Several looked like operating theaters or autopsy and science labs. Again, all were filthy, cluttered, and graffiti-laden. Very depressing, especially by flashlight. We picked out the most ominous-looking spots and left trail cams and cat balls in our wake. Old degraded knob and tube wiring could be seen in many spots, probably abandoned and left in place when upgrades were made. Electrician/pastor Chuck kept muttering to no one in particular, "Not to code, not to code."

Small groups broke off to travel with their digital recorders. This was not the first rodeo for our three strong believers. They took the EMF and thermal camera from Audrey and disappeared into the bowels of darkness. As the groups scattered, Audrey and I were left as a team.

"I've seen all of this many times," she said. "It never fails to depress me to think of this place in action. Is there anything in particular you'd like to explore?"

"I think the treatment rooms and labs were the spookiest to me. I'd also like to step out into one of those balcony cages. The view should be spectacular, even at night."

"It is. Let's finish up there."

"Sounds good." Really good, I thought as we headed to the labs.

Walking past a padded room, I got my first real fright when I could see the moving light of a cat ball. Like a sissy, I grabbed Audrey's arm for protection, and she laughed out loud.

"Did you see it?" I asked, a little scared.

"I did, I've seen it many times."

"What do you think it is?"

"Let's walk in and find out."

I was even more creeped out and Audrey was even more amused when we saw two large rats peering back at us.

"Holy shit," I exclaimed.

"Comes with the territory. I've never seen a cat ball light up that wasn't triggered by some animal or one of our classmates. First-timers get anxious about these, so I throw them in the bag of tricks for a little excitement. Did you notice that our three experienced trackers didn't even take any of those? They focused on the EMF and heat sensor camera. I'm not convinced that those are any more effective, but I'm also not convinced that ghosts exist so I may be biased."

"I'm pretty sure I encountered a real one at my place."

"That's why your place intrigues me. I think you're a pretty normal guy and I also believe you've seen something. I want to believe in something paranormal, and maybe you have just that."

I hope I have more than that to offer, I thought.

We dutifully carried our digital recorder through the lab rooms. I was getting attuned to the rat scurrying noises and I didn't think I heard anything more unusual than that.

I stood by a metal table in the middle of one of the rooms. "Lobotomies, forced sterilizations, probably other weird tactics like leeching. What were these guys thinking, and why were they allowed to get away with it?"

"They thought they were saving the population into a better future race. They got away with it because it was government-supported almost worldwide at the time. These men were gifted heroic pioneers in their day. It wasn't until after the Second World War that everyone came to know the horrors."

"I think I've seen enough of the Frankenstein rooms. Take me to your balcony."

"Let's go!"

As we walked to the other end of the building, we saw traces of our class, heard an occasional gasp, and always knew where Chuck was as daylight came and went.

The balcony view was beautiful. It's a shame it was broken up by thick steel bars. We both stared out into the night, pointing out the stars as well as the fast-food joints right off the highway exit. We stood close and I placed my hand on the small of her back as I pointed out a constellation I thought I knew over the mountains. She didn't pull away. It was a glorious moment.

Our two hours were almost up, and we had agreed to regroup in the main entry.

Audrey spoke, "How did my fellow explorers do?"

No one was displeased with the trip. They all spoke excitedly about the cat balls and the sense of occupancy. The three seasoned veterans volunteered to gather the digital records for further study over the weekend. Apparently, they had some secret tools and methods to draw out the unknown. I was thinking about when I was young and stoned and listening to "I Am the Walrus" in reverse. The supposed "I buried Paul" line blew us away. I couldn't wait to hear what they would produce, but my expectation was maybe a muffled "not to code, not to code."

"When we're done for the night, you're welcome to gather any of the recorders or cameras and keep them until the next class," Audrey told the pro team. "I've never had students with your level of experience and interest before. I'm pretty interested in seeing what you come up with. No doubt we'll all learn something from your efforts. For now, let's gather up our tools. We still have a haunted cemetery to visit."

Jim the cop was waiting for us. "Audrey, I did a drive-by at the cemetery before I came here. Your regular lot is open, and I let the concierge know that residents shouldn't get spooked by flashlights on the hill. Of course, we know they will anyhow," he said, smiling.

"Thanks again, Jim, for always being a gracious host. I'll let you know when the next outing is scheduled."

"No problem, this always gives me a nice break in my shift. Nothing else is going on in Mayberry but some drunks peeing in alleys."

Cemetery

W e seemed quite loud on the bus exchanging stories of individual experiences from the haunt. I'm not sure if we were loud or if it just sounded that way since we'd all been whispering for two hours. The trip to the cemetery was only a few minutes. The restored buildings at that location were very impressive. These were now high-end condos and apartments. Audrey said the initial purchases were very slow, but after a year or two without any reported apparitions or deaths it was now a desirable address.

"When we leave here," Audrey said. "We will make a rest stop a mile or so up the highway. If anyone has an urgent need before that we can swing by the main building." No hands went up.

"Speak now or forever hold your pees," I shouted. Tough room.

We pulled into a parking lot to the right of the main campus. At this end, beyond the beautifully restored buildings was another large structure still untouched. It was reminiscent of the abandoned asylum we had just left, a stark contrast. This was the backdrop for our destination, a hill behind the property.

We gathered our gear and headed up the small climb to a garden of gravestones, mostly flat markers in an unkempt field.

"What you see is what you get," said Audrey. "Take as much time as you want to visit the remains of the Western State legacy. I'd suggest breaking out of groups and taking this one in individually. I've always found it to be a deeply personal spot. We'll meet back here in an hour to talk about your experience before we head home."

The eight of us classmates spread out and wandered the acreage as single travelers. I don't visit cemeteries often, but when I do it's to see my dearly departed in their final rest. There are great memorials to loved ones and lots of flowers marking visitation. There was none of that here. It was striking, a field of the unwanted and unknown. I turned off my flashlight and stood in the middle of it, hoping to channel some spiritual force. It was lonely. I didn't hear any voices from our group or otherwise, and I didn't see any ghosts, only the wandering daylight of Chuck and his torch. I've got to get one of those things.

By the time our hour was up, we were all back at the van.

"Thoughts?" asked Audrey.

One woman spoke up softly. "There are no names."

"There are just a handful of the official state markers that have a name. Many have just a number, but that's still very few of the total assembly. There are over 2,000 totally unmarked graves in the Western State Cemetery."

"But why?" another woman asked.

"Remember that these people were not locals. They were strangers sent here from all around the state. Mental health issues were stigmas and embarrassments to their families. Out of sight, out of mind."

Chuck had turned off his electrician's accessory and slipped into pastor mode. "Would anyone mind if I said a prayer here?"

No objections were voiced.

"Dear Lord, we're saddened by the loss here. Beyond the lives snuffed out go the souls that died alone in vile and twisted conditions. Allow us to stand in for the one-time families and friends who abandoned them here. We know that every life comes from you and belongs to you. We also know that you welcome the broken and damaged and make them new again. Thank you for letting us see this sadness and know that you will raise all again, this time in your perfect glory. To you and to us these are not lost souls. They are vessels of your love. We take comfort that they will not be forgotten by you and that we will all meet again in the greatest of reunions. In the name of Jesus, we offer this prayer."

A few soft "Amens" and a couple of tears closed our night here. We shuffled onto the bus in silence.

As promised, we made the much-needed rest stop a few miles up the road. People were talking excitedly again about what they saw, heard, and felt. There had been much to both mourn and respect in our few hours, and I doubt anyone left without some value in personal reflection.

The chatter on the bus quickly descended into soft snores as we traveled home. I fell asleep myself and had a dream that I hadn't had since childhood. I dreamed that I was at the edge of a forest. A young girl appeared in an old-style long dress with lace trim. We never spoke, but I knew her name was Elizabeth. We stood and looked at each other until I woke up.

When I did wake it was to discover Audrey's sleeping head on my shoulder. Nice. I was careful not to move for fear of disturbing that moment. I closed my eyes and enjoyed her warmth.

Back at school, the driver beeped the horn a few times to wake the sleeping and let us know we were home. The various paranormal tools were collected and sent off with our pro team. Everyone went to their cars and drove off, as did the bus. It was Audrey and I alone in the parking lot.

"Sorry I dozed off," she said.

"I'm not, you needed the rest."

"Very true. Tomorrow, I start back with the MFA project. The next couple of months will be the most time-consuming until that's over."

"Will I see you at the new moon?"

"Those nights may be the only break I get for a while. I look forward to it."

"See you in a few days," I said, and we went our separate ways.

The New Moon

They say (whoever "they" are) that the most active periods of the poltergeists seem to occur in the day or two of the new moon when the night sky is completely dark.

"Do you believe that, Lincoln?" He gave me that cocked-head stare as if he fully understood the words and was pondering a response, but, as is his custom, he never shared his deep thoughts. We were getting the house tidied up for company. I'm an "everything in its place" kind of guy, so cleaning up after me is pretty simple. Lincoln, however, has a habit of distributing fur balls everywhere in his wake. Lincoln was out barking in the yard while I Swiffered. I looked out to see what he saw, a yellow cat running past the fence line and into the woods. "You're new around here," I said to myself.

Audrey arrived at 5:00 p.m. so she could see things in some daylight. Lincoln acknowledged her presence with a little barking, a dance, and some of his excited and impressive vertical leaps. Show off.

"Welcome to our humble abode," I greeted her.

"Hardly humble" she replied. "I almost got lost in the driveway. I never would have believed such a secluded and gorgeous spot existed in the clustered suburbia of Northern Virginia."

"All of the clustered suburbia around here was once part of my great granduncle's farm almost two hundred years ago. Over the years the family reduced it to the twenty acres you see today."

"It's beautiful," she said. "How do you keep it up? Everything looks so well-maintained and perfect."

"I've got a guy, as they say. Buck. I hardly ever see him, but the grass is always mowed, trees and shrubs trimmed, leaves and limbs removed, and the driveway maintained with fresh gravel every year."

"That has to be expensive."

"Actually, quite reasonable for all he does. My brother Bob set him up in the landscaping business when Buck was only a teenager. I inherited the house when Bob passed away but Buck actually lived here for twenty years and kept the place up until my wife Gwen and I moved in. When I do see him, he's always telling me how much he likes the place and considers it a privilege to do it. He almost makes me feel guilty for paying him," I laughed. "But he does cash the checks."

"I'm impressed. I can't wait to see the inside."

"Come on, Link, let's show the lady your house. Anything in particular you'd like to see?"

"Everything. We can get to our supernatural business when it's dark, but I'd love to get the lay of the land in daylight."

"Let's take a little walk before we go in."

I left Lincoln off leash this time. No problem, he was attached to Audrey, such a lady's man. We wandered through the pear orchard, where I let Audrey give Lincoln a treat, and poked our heads in the outbuildings. I pointed out the area of the burial ground. Back inside the gate, she pretended to enjoy a little frisbee time with Lincoln and we headed inside.

"Where would you like to start?" I asked.

"You mentioned that Lincoln had an issue with the attic. Let's start there and work our way down."

We climbed all the steps to the top floor and I raised the door to the attic.

"Wow," she said. "Look at that light. This is a perfect art studio."

"I hadn't thought about that." I was thinking about the missing blanket.

"No, really. This is a rare find for an artist. I'd kill to have a place like this to do my painting."

"You're welcome to it. It would be a small token in exchange for my signed Audrey Walsh."

Back to business. "Why do you think Lincoln had reservations about the attic?"

"Not sure, but you see that pile of army stuff my brother left behind? That's where the blanket disappeared from, so someone or something had to have visited."

"Interesting. Let's see everything else."

Down to the second level, we wandered through the four bedrooms and the bath. She sat down in the same place where Amy had flirted with me. This must be a lucky spot, I thought.

"This room has an interesting vibe. It feels welcoming and threatening at the same time."

I hoped I wasn't the threatening element. I had been thinking about her in the Amy position. Audrey was not only beautiful, she was also more age-appropriate for me. We wouldn't be able to discuss where we were when Kennedy was shot, but she'd understand Jim Jones, classic rock, and 9/11. Unlike Amy, Audrey and I could have actual adult conversations if and when the magic of sex wore off. Come to think of it, I guess I am the threatening vibe.

"One more floor," I said as we descended and went to the great room. "This was the operating room of the hospital during the Civil War. Oddly, it's never seemed to be the source of our unknown disturbances. I would have thought this would be ground zero for troubled souls."

"Well, I see you have a signed Audrey Walsh on the wall here. That's probably as good as a Virgin Mary statue to scare off the ghosts."

Darkness was setting in and we made our next plans.

"I want to do the root cellar tonight," I said. "The ghost Tom said he lived there. Lincoln and I found food wrappers from the house and what looked like a bed there. I put a lock on the door after that and started keeping my journal. I have a strong premonition that the missing blanket is there now."

"Even with the door locked."

"I don't know that the door is still locked. I've been afraid to go near it."

Ping, ping, ping

"Do you hear that?" I asked.

"I hear something. It sounds like it's out front."

"It's the sound of a basketball dribbling on the concrete. That's what I've heard every month on the new moon. Let's go turn on the outside floodlights. I bet it will stop."

We did, and it did.

"That is spooky," said Audrey. "I guess the root cellar is the place to go if we're going to face it. I'm game if you are."

"Should I bring the gun?"

"No," she almost shouted and I could see her stiffen. Quieter now, "No guns ever. Someone very close to me was killed with a gun."

"I'm so sorry. I didn't know."

"Why would you even own a gun?"

"I don't. I mean I didn't. It belonged to my brother. It was left in the house after he died."

"I never want to see it."

"You won't. Honestly, it scares me too. I'll get rid of it. One of my students is a cop. I'll ask him how to dispose of it."

"You promise?"

"I do. It means nothing to me and a lot to you. Having a ghost-hunting partner beyond Lincoln is much more important to me. It will be out of the house and gone for good tomorrow."

"Thanks," she said softly.

"So, we're good?"

"We're good." She didn't smile but she did seem to relax. "Let's go visit our basketball-playing cellar dweller."

I left Lincoln inside this time. We were going to throw a cat ball on the hay pile just for fun, and he would have messed that up. I think I was also feeling a little jealous about his attachment to Audrey. Not really, but I didn't mind the excuse to be alone with her in a dark place. God, maybe I am a creep.

Into the Cellar

The lock was on the door just as I left it. I had given her a description of the cellar, and everything initially looked the same. Our flashlights were sufficient, but I vowed to get one of Chuck's tactical jobs before we did this again.

"This is another great feature of an old house," she said. "I love hidden nooks and stairways. Have you ever been to the Winchester Mystery House in California?"

"I have. That's the hidden nook and stairway capital of the world," I laughed. "Maybe I should adopt that owner's solution of continually building to keep the ghosts confused and at bay."

When we got to the rear of the cellar, I saw it. The blanket was lying on top of the hay. It was still neatly folded. It was also joined by a pillow I had gotten for Lincoln. I hadn't noticed it was missing because it had been hidden in a closet, waiting to be a Christmas present. Little Lincoln is an avid pillow humper, and this one seemed appropriate for the task. The Christmas-themed embroidery was "Feliz Naughty Dog."

"I'm still not sure I believe in ghosts, even after I think I might have seen one face to face. But that blanket and pillow were in the house since I locked the cellar door. How could we explain this?"

"I try to keep an open mind on the occult," Audrey said. "But I also try to plug in things like dreams and sleepwalking as possible explanations for the unexplainable. Let's put up a couple of cameras, including the thermal sensor, set out audio recorders on the workbenches, drop a cat ball, and settle in to watch and listen."

"First, I want to show you another unexplainable. Look at these Civil War artifacts. They have to be over 150 years old, but they look new."

On closer inspection, there were some marks and nicks on some of the articles, possibly battle-worn scars. The leather on the belt was also worn and had what looked like sweat stains. Aside from that, these could have been issued recently.

"You need to show these to an expert," said Audrey.

"Definitely. That's my next research project."

We moved on to the distribution of the paranormal tools and settled in on the floor of the room with our backs to the cellar door. We weren't touching, but Audrey did choose to sit pretty close to me. She didn't have to do that, and I liked it.

It didn't take long for the cat ball to light up. We had a camera on the hay pile, so we knew we should have an image of the source.

"Don't get excited," she whispered. "Remember what I told you about cat balls."

"Animals and people."

"You're a good student."

After more than an hour of sitting in the quiet darkness, Audrey spoke. "There is certainly a feeling of presence here. There is also nothing going on that we can sense in the way of paranormal activity. I vote we lock it back up and check our equipment."

"Good call," I said. "My butt went to sleep a long time ago. I wish I had some of that Fire and Ice to revive it."

We packed up the gear, locked the cellar door, and settled at the kitchen table.

"Would you like a drink, some wine perhaps? I happen to have a box of Costco's finest pinot grigio in the refrigerator."

"That sounds great but I have to pass. I'm driving, and I have an early morning ahead of me. I will take a bottle of Costco's finest water if you have some."

She started going through the cameras while I went to the back kitchen to get the water. When I returned, she had a shocked look on her face as she stared at the small camera screen.

"Oh my God, Richard, we did capture something. You have to see this."

I have to admit I was more than a little scared by her reaction. I moved around the table to stand beside her. What I saw on the screen was a mouse with a cat ball. Audrey laughed.

"You're playing with my emotions," I said, also laughing.

"You're an easy mark," she said, still laughing. "We'll have to play cards sometime. But right now, I need to pack up and hit the road. I'll see you on campus and we can plan our next explorations of your haunted house."

Lincoln and I walked her out to the basketball court where she was parked. The basketball sat right where I always left it.

Next Steps

The September new moon was in the books and documented in the journal. It was a fairly quiet one. We did have the basketball, the blanket, and the pillow to ponder but no new overt sightings. Maybe they have to get used to Audrey before they make their presence known. Or maybe she's right that everything could be dreams and sleepwalking. All I know is I have another new moon date with Audrey in October, and that's good enough for now.

I brought the gun to school the next day, locking it in the trunk of my car. I wanted to check with Sergeant Darrel Metz of the Arlington County Police Department. He's an interesting guy in my 10:00 a.m. marketing class. Darrel is forty-five years old and has been with Arlington County Police since he was twenty-one. He did his associate's degree in Law Enforcement years ago at NVCC, just like I did. He then went straight into police work, like I did not.

He and I had met a couple of times in the cafeteria. He finished a Bachelor of Arts in Applied Behavioral Sciences a few years back and he has his eye on an MBA program that he'd like to finish before his retirement to open up more second career opportunities. He needed to rack up a couple of more essential business credits as prerequisites for the MBA, which is how he ended up in my class. Sharp guy. I snagged him after class.

"Darrel, have you got a few minutes to talk?"

Mid-term grades were coming up soon. "I'm not failing, am I?" he asked with a chuckle.

"Hardly, and you know that," I said, also laughing. "This has nothing to do with school."

"I've got some time, what's on your mind?"

"I have a gun in my car."

"No shit, me too." He laughed out loud.

"Well, I want to get rid of mine. Is there a proper way to do that?"

"Several, let's take a look and see what you've got."

At the car, he seemed duly impressed. "Nice Ruger .357, especially with the six-inch barrel for target shooting. I'd buy it myself but it's too nice for me. I shoot my guns and this one looks like a virgin. The bicentennial lineage is probably highly collectible. Would you like me to see if I can sell it for you? I can think of several places I can list it where it might move fairly quickly."

"Can you take it with you to do that?"

"I was going to ask if I could. I need to post some pictures on the gun sites to promote it."

"It's all yours," I said, happy to be rid of it. "If it doesn't sell, I don't want it back. It belonged to my late brother and I just want it out of the house."

"A wise decision. A handgun isn't a good thing to just have lying around without a real purpose. If you want home protection against intruders, a can of Bear Mace is far more effective, and it won't accidentally kill you or someone else. That said, I'm pretty sure it will sell quickly, and I can handle the legal transfer with the new owner for you."

"Thanks, Darrel, I would appreciate that. Can I buy you lunch?"

"Not today, I do have some things on my schedule. When it sells you can take me out for a fabulous feast. You'll have the money for it."

"That's a deal," I said. "Oh, one more thought. Would you happen to know anyone who would be an expert on Civil War memorabilia?"

"Funny you should ask. A lot of older cops are into that. I know a guy in Pennsylvania who's quite knowledgeable. Don Weston. He's retired from the Philadelphia Police Department. We met years ago at a convention for regional task force coordinators, and we still stay in touch."

"Can I get his contact information and use you as a reference? I've found some stuff at the house, and I'd like to have it verified. The condition is too good to be true."

"I'll email his info. I'm sure he'd love to see what you've found. He lives in York, so he's only a couple of hours' drive. You could do the drive or send a couple of pictures his way. Maybe he'd even come to you and join us for our feast."

"I'll let you know how it goes. Thanks, Darrel." We parted ways, gun gone.

Classes went well that day, as always. I've found teaching to be more of a fun hobby than a job. I like the students and the classroom atmosphere. I constantly hear other teachers complaining about the workload and the hassles of grading. I don't get it. I have a spreadsheet for each class. There are points for attendance, which I enter every day. I also record homework, quizzes, and tests as they are done. Coming up on mid-terms, I already have a running score and grade for every student. I must be doing something wrong, this is too easy.

In Audrey's class, we reviewed the results from the Paranormal Pro Team. They were excited to show us shadow images from the cameras and the enhanced audio purporting to be the muffled speech of the ghosts. "I buried Paul" was a much cleaner recording. Most of the group seemed equally excited about the findings. After class, Audrey and I had a quick dinner in the cafeteria and agreed we were unimpressed. I also told her about Darrel and assured her the gun was gone for good and that I had a good Civil War connection. She gave me a genuine "Thanks." Except for our October date and class time, I wouldn't see much of her at all until her MFA work was done and gone. I look forward to our December new moon, when that will all be behind her and she can relax. The box of Costco wine will surely still be good, and maybe improved with aging, by then.

October's New Moon

Time at school flew by this month, and our next excursion into the occult was upon us. No doubt we'd find ourselves in basketball season again in a few hours.

"Welcome back," said Lincoln and I in our own ways. "How are your semesters going?"

"I have to confess I'm pretty whipped," said Audrey. "And glad to be here. We're doing a holiday transition at the shop, which is always extra work. I normally enjoy the decorating and the new inventory coming in, but this year it's work."

"Hang in there, your big goal at Mason is in sight soon, and things should lighten up when that is done."

"I know that logically, but I won't know it emotionally until it's over."

"Can I give you a hug?"

"I think I'd like that." I think she did. I know I did. It was the closest we'd been since the bus trip and it felt great.

"Thanks, I needed that," she said when we broke the embrace.

"Me too," I said. "There are plenty more of those available if you need them getting through the next couple of months."

"Good to know," she said. "I made a plan for tonight, if it's okay with you."

"I'm sure it will be," I smiled.

"Since my school schedule is going to kill our November new moon and December will likely be bitter cold, I think we should set up outside tonight by the burial pit. The thought of everything that went in there in the war years is even sadder than the Western State Cemetery. At least the anonymous dead there got their own plots."

Suddenly we all jumped at the sound of a loud crash in the house. I jumped again when Lincoln started an obsessive barking and ran off to the great room. We quickly followed and found him zooming everywhere, back and forth, and over furniture, still barking like he'd lost his mind.

I loved that Audrey's first response was to Lincoln. She quickly calmed him down and hugged him but he was still shaking in his alertness and still making noise.

I was searching the large room looking for the source of the crash and seeing nothing. When I turned back to where we had entered, I saw the cause. Audrey's painting had fallen from the wall. It was still attached to the nail I had hung it on but the wire had pulled out of the hardware on the back of the frame and allowed it to slip all the way to floor level. It was standing on edge on the ground with a mighty crack in that corner of the frame. A large puddle of liquid seemed to seep from the seascape.

While Audrey was still comforting Lincoln, I kneeled down to look closer for damage. The frame would need to be replaced, but I was glad to see the picture seemed to be fine. Turning my attention to the puddle, I instinctively dipped a finger in the liquid and smelled it. It had no scent, but why would plain water be here? I tasted it, and it was salty. I cringed.

"Audrey, it's salty, it's leaking seawater," I said ominously.

She initially gave me a blank look and then burst out laughing. "What?"

Laughing harder now. "I'm pretty sure you just tasted dog pee."

Having a hard time shifting from my occult assessment to potential reality, I said, "What about the picture mysteriously falling?"

"I'm attributing that to your less-than-stellar handyman skills."

"What!" I blustered, my manhood punctured.

"Pardon me for having some expertise in mounting artwork. I can see from here that you double-looped the picture wire, which is fine, but you twisted the ends together without a ferrule or even tape to hold them. I'm surprised it hung for this long."

"Okay," I said, humbled. "What's a ferrule, maybe I need to get one for the next time."

"It's a small metal piece that you loop the wire ends through and crush with pliers, very dependable for hanging heavy objects with wire. I have them at the store."

"I guess I need to get a new frame and do this over. Thankfully your artwork is undamaged."

"Do us both a favor. Go ahead and reframe it but leave it there on the floor until the next time I'm here. I'll bring the right stuff and teach you how to do it. This mystery will never happen again. Or, if it does, it will be a mystery for real."

Ping, ping, ping. It was dark now, and the basketball had started.

We turned on the outside floods on our way out the door. As always, the basketball stopped, and we carried our lawn chairs out to sit by the burial pit. In an attempt to reclaim my manhood, I fired up my new tactical spotlight. It was an Amazon special with 200,000 lumens. The entire side yard from the orchard to the pit was instantly sunscorched.

"Think you used enough dynamite, Butch?" She laughed again. I love her laugh.

"I must admit it's overkill, but I had flashlight envy from Chuck," I joined the laugh.

We settled in at the edge of the pit. We didn't take Lincoln with us so there would be no distractions. It took some time for our eyes to adjust to the darkness after I turned off the torch. When we did adjust, we were met with an amazing clear sky of a million stars. Very romantic for a night by a mound of dead bodies and medical waste.

Our chairs were close together, and I purposely touched her arm as I pointed out various things in the sky and the layout of the surrounding ground. She never shied away from my touch but she also hadn't overtly initiated touch between us on her own. I remained cautiously optimistic, knowing how many other tasks she had on her mind and understanding that a relationship would be an unnecessary added burden at this time in her life.

Yellow cat wandered out from the tree line behind the grave and sat on the mound staring at us. "That's a new one," said Audrey.

"It is fairly recent. Lincoln and I started seeing it in passing just in the past couple of weeks. If I lived anywhere else, I'd say it was just a neighborhood stray, but remind me to show you something in the pear orchard that might add it to our mysteries."

After an hour or so of no bodies emerging from the ground and the cat slinking back into darkness, Audrey said, "I probably should get going." We packed up our chairs, I declared sunlight with my magic ray, and we walked back to the house, passing through the middle of the pear orchard.

"That is spooky," she said looking at the small granite stone etched with "Yellow Cat."

"A comrade of great granduncle Craft," I said.

"Why do I think of Stephen King's *Pet Sematary*?"

"Me too, can't help it given the surroundings."

"We need to add that to the pile of Civil War stuff, moving blankets and pillows, basketballs, and your Tom apparition. I'll miss taking a break from this in November. I do think there is a 'more to be revealed' something here," she said.

"Don't forget the falling picture."

"That one's on you, Tool Time." That great laugh again.

We parted with another hug. "I'm going to work on the Civil War guy while we're apart. I will see you on campus but my November nights will be dark without you."

"There's always your new flashlight."

"Funny girl. How about if I make a date with you and Vicki to bring lunch to the shop one day in the next couple of weeks? I really wouldn't want to wait until December to see you outside of school again."

"Sounds like a plan," she said and then drove away into the night.

Lincoln was still a little tentative, staying close by me as I wrote the October new moon into the journal. He was a real spooner when we went to bed, and we slept well, dreaming of yellow cats and Audrey.

November

Audrey and I will trudge through our individual and collective classes through November, waiting for the December date when finals are posted and it will all be over. I'm hunkering down in November to get back to my writing. I've read that "real" writers turn out a minimum of 1,000 words per day. I probably hadn't put down a fresh 1,000 words in the past year. If my writing never succeeds, I'll always have the teaching. It isn't a trudge for me. I like my students, and I like the hobby.

I'm also diving into the Civil War for November. I started by exploring the websites of collectors and how to tell if an artifact is real. There are a lot of fakes, and some are quite good. I determined that I couldn't tell on my own, and all the sites recommended getting expert advice, so I fired off my first email to Darrel's friend, Don Weston.

"Hi Don, my name is Richard Craft. A mutual friend, Darrel Metz, sent me your way. I've recently inherited a family property that dates back to the mid-1800s. My great granduncle was a doctor, and this home was used as a hospital during the Civil War. I've found several war-era artifacts, belts, buckles, etc., and even a sword in a root cellar. They are all in exceptional condition for their presumed age. I'm attaching some detailed pictures and my contact info. Darrel says you're the guy to ask if they may be real. I'd greatly appreciate it if you could take a look, see what you think, and let me know. I look forward to hearing from you. Thanks, Richard"

I had a response early the next morning.

"Hi Richard, even though you're hanging out with that rat bastard Metz I thought I'd help you out anyway :) Just kidding, Darrel and I go back some years and I always enjoy an excuse to stay in touch. I'm glad he sent you my way. From the images, I have to say I was initially puzzled. You got some great pictures and all the right details in your shots. You probably already know that there are more fakes in circulation than real artifacts these days. These certainly look real in all aspects but the condition is too good for that to be the case. Having said that, I've never seen such authenticity in counterfeits.

"I suppose it's possible that some unique combination of conditions from the place of storage could have dramatically slowed the aging process but that's not something I've encountered or read about in my research. I wonder if we can arrange to get the pieces to Churchville University where I am. We have a unique and extensive collection of known original pieces for comparison and some additional expertise on campus to look them over. Let me know if that's something you'd like to pursue. Thanks, Don."

One more round to seal the deal. "Don, I could run up your way this weekend if that works for you. Thanks, Richard."

"Richard, my schedule is open and I would have cleared it anyway to see this particular collection. Tell me when you'll be here and I'll arrange for the other resources to be available. Thanks, Don."

Back at school the next day, Darrel Metz grabbed me after class. "Congratulations, you are about to be $709 richer."

"You sold it that quick?"

"I put in on several sites and initially got some lowball offers, which is normal. I also listed one auction that usually gets more realistic bids. That one hit with a guy from Richmond who quickly bid your Ruger up to $799.00, which was enough to shut down the other bidders. He'll be here next week. I'll meet him at a locally licensed firearms dealer that will handle the paperwork. The auction cost is $40 and the transfer is $50. With my finder's fee of an extravagant feast, you'll still pocket a few dollars."

"Thanks, that was easy. Do you have any plans for the upcoming weekend?"

"I don't. What's on your mind?"

"I contacted Don Weston, and he wants to see my Civil War stuff. If you're up for a road trip, maybe we can share our feast with him."

"That would be the most fun I've had in years," he said, genuinely excited about the prospect. "But I have to warn you Don is a world-class eater. If we let him pick the venue, your profits from the gun will dwindle exponentially."

"So be it."

I was pretty jazzed about my productivity and good news for the week. I couldn't wait to tell Audrey the gun was gone for good and we were about to find out much more about our haunted house paraphernalia. I also couldn't wait to see her in person so I called New Age Renaissance to book a lunch date tomorrow with her and Vicki.

"Namaste, New Age Renaissance," answered Vicki.

"Do you have Prince Albert in a can?"

"Nice try, Richard, I'll get Audrey."

"Don't. I want to surprise her."

"With what? Your legendary wit?" A tinkling fairy bell of a laugh.

"I want to bring you guys lunch tomorrow. I have a couple of things to tell Audrey, and I wanted to see her, and you of course, in person."

"Don't tell her I told you this, but I'm pretty sure she misses you too."

I'm glad no one was around to see how red my face was. That one caught me off guard in a really good way.

"Then tomorrow is good?"

"Especially good. You'll get to meet my boyfriend, Trey. He's coming to hang out and help with shop decorations."

"Perfect. I'll swing by Jersey Mike's on my way there. Any food restrictions?"

"Veggie for me, the others are still dedicated carnivores."

"Great. I'll be by around 11:30 tomorrow. Remember it's a secret."

"We love secrets in our business."

I don't think I'm going to get my 1,000 words written today. Or any day through the weekend.

Lunch at the Peacock Plume

N ot knowing Trey's appetite, I brought two giant original Italians and a giant veggie sub. Leftovers wouldn't be a problem. That turned out to be a good call. Trey was a six-foot-seven former football player.

"Trey, meet Richard. Richard, meet Trey," said Vicki as I walked in, Lincoln in tow. "Richard is Audrey's paramour in waiting, but they don't know that yet."

I'm getting a lot of new information that I like.

"I hope it's okay that I brought Lincoln. I can put him in the car if he'll be a problem."

"Oh no," gushed Vicki, "I've been dying to meet him. Audrey tells me he's the bestest dog ever. She loves that little guy."

More good news. I dropped the leash, and Lincoln ran to meet Trey and Vicki. While they were all loving and hugging, I had to smile at the odd couple. There was Vicki, a tiny, occult-believing, hippie sprite, and there was Trey, a monster of a human being and no doubt, a real man's man. They do say opposites attract.

Vicki picked up the phone and called upstairs. "What are you doing Audrey?" Pause. "That's good that you're organizing your show work, but I need you in the store." Hang up.

"She'll be right down."

Audrey was greeted on the steps down by her bestest friend Lincoln.

"Lincoln, what a great surprise. I've been missing you." She picked up the little wiggler and brought him back to the counter area.

"Another surprise," she said when she saw me. Her smile was the best gift and surprise I could have hoped for. We even hugged while Lincoln jumped and barked at us.

"I'm hungry," said Trey. "What have we got here?" We unwrapped the food on the counter and dug in.

The girls were talking about an inventory and sales sheet and more decorations. Trey and I were talking boy stuff, girls, cigars, football. He was a man's man, and I liked him instantly.

While we were eating a customer walked in. He looked a lot like Wille Nelson.

"Namaste," said Audrey and Vicki in unison.

"Hey there," said Willie.

"Let us know if you need anything," said Vicki.

"Cool beans," said Willie, clearly another guy in the wrong century.

We ate and chatted while Willie wandered. I heard him laughing at one point, no doubt reliving my first experience in the shop.

Trey broke the household rules with Lincoln, feeding him people food. I couldn't object, Lincoln loved it, and the guy was six-foot-seven.

While we were still stuffing ourselves, at least Trey and I and Lincoln, Willie wandered up to the counter. "Did you find everything okay?" asked Vicki.

"Not really," he said "I was looking for rolling papers. I haven't been in the area since the late '70s but I heard you can smoke dope legally here now. Didn't this used to be the Peacock Plume?"

The girls and I laughed out loud.

"See, I told you so," I said.

Willie and Trey joined in on the joke when I told them the story. Willie gave us a "Namaste" on his way down the road.

Lunch wrapped up and Audrey invited me upstairs. "I want your thoughts on a choice between two paintings for the show," she said.

"Fine," I responded. "Should we bring Lincoln?

"No way," shouted Vicki. 'He's my love bug now. I'm keeping him right here."

"Suit yourself," I said. I followed Audrey up the steps, remembering the first time I enjoyed this view. It was even better now.

We checked out the paintings. Two portraits this time. I picked one of a young girl looking out her window into a starry sky. "It makes me think she's looking for Santa Claus," I told Audrey.

"I like that. I don't recall what I was thinking of when I did this one, but it will be Santa Claus to me now."

I told Audrey about the gun being gone for good, my Civil War connections, and my pending field trip with Darrel. "I'm going to ask the animal shelter lady, Amy, if she'd like to take Lincoln while I'm gone. I know she will."

"When are you leaving?"

"We were going to head up tomorrow evening for dinner. His friend Don insists we stay at his place. I owe them a meal for the gun sale and the appraisals. That will give us as much time as we need on Saturday and I'll be back Sunday."

"I have a better idea for Lincoln," said Audrey. "Let's go tell Vicki."

I was confused until we got downstairs and Audrey made an announcement. "Good news, Vicki. Richard has a trip he needs to make, so Lincoln will be staying with us through the weekend."

"Yay," said Vicki hugging Lincoln. "Trey is also staying the weekend. I see a dog park in our near future."

"He's a great frisbee guy," said Audrey.

"Me too," said Trey.

I did get a hug when I left but I returned home alone, missing Lincoln and wondering if he'd still remember me after the weekend.

Road Trip

S having kit, check. Underwear, check. Beef jerky, check. Trail mix, check. Water, check. Twizzlers, check.

I was just about packed for the ride. I had gathered the artifacts from the cellar and spread them on the kitchen table. I was contemplating how to transport them when I remembered my brother's old Martin guitar that was hanging in a hallway nook. The guitar case was in the attic with the rest of his memories. It turned out to be the perfect suitcase. I lined it with bubble wrap, distributed the presumed collectibles, and laid a heavy towel over the lot to keep everything secure. The neck of the case was ideal to include the sword. I was quite proud of my ingenuity, as always.

Darrel arrived at 2:30 p.m. and we loaded his small duffel bag to hit the road. He'd already plugged in the address to Don's place in his driving app. A two-hour drive and some greetings and salutations would have us at dinner around 6:00.

"I see you're bringing a guitar," Darrel said.

I laughed, "No, it just happened to be the best container I had for the Civil War stuff. I needed the neck space for the sword."

"I hope you brought lots of cash for dinner. I wasn't kidding about Don's eating habits. I'm meeting the Richmond gun guy on Wednesday and can refill your coffers then."

"No problem, credit cards cover everything, and there are no extra costs to the trip with Don offering to put us up at his place."

"I called him last night. I think he's looking forward to having the company. His wife passed away some years ago when they were in Philadelphia. Since he moved to where he is now, he says he just rattles around in a four-bedroom house. He's also really curious about what you have in the guitar case. I predict the two of you will hit it off from the start as well as Don and I did. He's an interesting guy."

"Well, we'll have widower status in common. My wife went away about a year after we moved here. It is a lonely life sometimes."

"Sorry to hear that."

"It's okay, I have a dog friend now to keep me company. That, and the ghosts of the past. How about you, are you married?"

"No, I never did. I'm a member of the 'don't ask, don't tell' generation." He laughed.

"Interesting, if I'm interpreting that correctly, so was my late brother. The family sometimes wondered about Bob's sexual orientation, but we never said such things out loud in the 1960s and '70s. That must have been tough in your line of work."

"You might think so, but oddly, it's not been a factor for my career or promotions. It never came up in the early years, and I was pretty well established when it did. Cops tend to be all brothers at work, and most are relatively mute on home life. It just works out better to keep the two apart. I've never made it an issue, and my brothers have respected that."

"Who knew cops were so accepting and inclusive."

"It's not a universal trait, but the general population is much more open-minded than we get credited for in the public eye."

"Good to know. Thanks for the trust in sharing."

We were already on 395 heading to the Baltimore Beltway and I-83 North. We should slip through Baltimore just ahead of Friday evening traffic.

"Snacks?" I offered.

"Maybe you haven't been listening to my warnings about Don's idea of a dinner."

"Just a little beef jerky and some Twizzlers to coat our stomachs?" I prodded.

"Okay, you win. How did you know I was a sucker for Twizzlers?"

We stuffed ourselves with crap all the way to York, Pennsylvania.

"You have arrived at your destination," said the driving app lady in her British accent. We pulled into Don's driveway and parked next to his Sequoia emblazoned with the Churchville University Police wrap.

"Did I know that Don was still a cop?" I asked.

"I guess I didn't think to mention it. He's the Chief of Police at Churchville University. He considers this, the Civil War stuff, and his consulting work as retirement hobbies."

Don walked out to greet us. "I've been waiting for you guys. Grab your bags, and I'll show you to your rooms."

Don was as tall as Trey and even more imposing as he carried a few more pounds. "You must be Richard," he said as his catcher's mitt of a hand swallowed mine. "I know who this guy is," he went on, dropping my hand to give Darrel a big hug. "Great to see you Darrel, I'm glad you could make the trip."

"I would never pass up the chance to eat with you, my epicurean friend, especially when Richard is buying." They both laughed wickedly at my plight.

"Come on in and get settled," said Don. He gave us a quick tour of the house, a cozy man cave of wood and leather with a faint smell of cigar smoke. "I hope you don't mind," he said showing us our rooms. "All I have to offer for sleeping accommodations is king beds."

"I'm sure we'll adjust," I said, putting down my bag and the guitar case.

"I didn't know we were having music tonight," said Don. "That will go nicely with a cigar and some brandy on the porch after dinner."

"That case is my transport for the Civil War stuff," I explained again about the neck and the sword. "Would you like to see it?"

"Tomorrow, I think. I've arranged for another expert to join us. He's the president of Churchville University and a true Civil War historian. His name is George Hunt. Let's wait and unveil it then. From the pictures, it looks like it will be an exciting surprise I'd like to share with him."

"If you two are okay with your rooms, we have about a forty-minute drive to tonight's surprise. I made reservations at Bube's Brewery in Mount Joy. We'll be dining in the Catacombs."

"The Catacombs," said Darrel.

"Three stories below street level are the stone-lined cooling rooms of the original brewery, dating from 1876. It's a unique spot and an excellent place to drop ridiculous amounts of money on a meal."

"Richard has a budget of $709," said Darrel.

"Not after tonight," said Don. Wicked laughter again.

We piled into Don's cruiser and made the jaunt to Mount Joy. We passed more than a few Amish buggies and beautiful scenery everywhere.

Bube's is an impressive brick-and-stone structure housing a hotel and two restaurants, including the Catacombs. The temperature dropped noticeably as we descended to our destination. We were greeted by pirates and serving wenches as we settled at our spartan table, the wood as rustic as the stone on the walls, definitely back in time.

"Chief Don, always a pleasure," said the sommelier as he introduced the wine list.

Don took a quick look and pointed out his choice. "Jason, this will do," he said. Make sure you have at least two bottles for us."

The serving wench also knew Don by name. "The usual appetizers?" she asked. "Scallops and bruschetta?"

"You know it, Maria," Don said. "And three orchard salads as well."

"And what are we having for entrees?" asked Darrel.

"Steak. I'm having the Brewhouse Surf and Turf, fourteen ounces of New York strip with garlic butter and a lobster tail."

"I'm in for that," I said.

"Make it three," said Darrel.

"Save room for dessert," cautioned Don. "There's a truly decadent chocolate cake with hot fudge drizzle and melting homemade vanilla ice cream."

"That ship may have sailed," said Darrel.

"That ship may have sunk," said I to the clink of wine glasses.

Darrel couldn't have warned me enough. What an amazing meal and incredible company. We talked through dinner as if we'd all been friends since grade school. The total damage for dinner was $462 plus a $100 tip. I'd still have $147 left from the sale of the gun I didn't pay for and didn't want. That will cover a nice outing for Audrey and me when she can come up for air from her work and studies.

We did finish up on Don's porch with cigars and brandy before crashing into food comas for the night. No guitar music.

The Grand Unveiling

When Darrel and I woke from our death sleep, the house already smelled like bacon. Don made us an incredible morning spread of eggs, pancakes, home fries, and every breakfast meat imaginable. Stuffed, I put the guitar case in the cruiser, and we headed to Churchville. "This is a nice little school," said Don as he gave us a quick driving tour of the campus. "It's a mostly residential campus. We had some real police issues here last year that I won't bore you with, but, aside from that, it feels like a small town where everyone knows their neighbors."

The library was open when we got there. Don showed us the way to a large room full of the Civil War. George Hunt was there to greet us.

"Good morning, George," said Don. "This unsavory character is Darrel Metz, an old friend from police life. The distinguished gentleman is Richard Craft."

"Nice to meet you," I said, glad to be shaking a normal-sized hand.

"Likewise," said Darrel. "Don speaks very highly of you, almost as highly as he speaks of himself." Polite laughter.

"I trust he's feeding you well," laughed George.

"Legendary," was my response.

"Well," said Don. "Let's get to it. What do you have in the magic box?"

I set the case on a large table and opened it, unpacking all of the contents for display. It got quiet as George and Don picked up various items, checked things with a magnifying glass and a small scale, and murmured various statements of "interesting" and "fascinating." George lined up the artifacts by some semblance of category. He then opened various display cases around the room and produced similar objects, placing them side by side with my collection. The "interesting" and "fascinating" seemed to grow increasingly profound from the comparisons.

"How are we doing?" I asked.

"Too good," said George.

"Agreed," said Don. "Wholly and bafflingly too good."

"Hmmmmm," said I.

"These are unquestionably authentic," pronounced George. "But their condition is not possible. I can tell that they've not been cleaned or polished, but they are missing the patina of over a hundred and fifty years. These are in the condition they would have been in if we saw them in the 1860s. I've never seen this level of preservation in my fifty-plus years of collecting and research. I'd be initially inclined to not believe what I'm seeing, yet here they are."

"You found these in a cellar?" verified Don.

"Yes."

"George, do you think it's possible the storage environment could have produced these results?" asked Don. "I'd be happy to go to the source and take measurements of temperature, humidity, and anything else we can think of."

"We'll need to do that and more," said George. "Richard, this is undoubtedly the most important collection I am aware of. Would you be okay if we did additional research for a paper that would document the findings for the historian community?"

"Wow," I said. "Who knew? I'd be honored to have you do whatever you think is appropriate. I'd also be honored to donate them to your collection and leave them with you for their care."

"I'll let you think that one over as we discover more," said George. "I believe that's a much more generous offer than any of us can imagine at the moment. Are there any more articles like these at your house?"

"I don't know. I found these lying on a bench in the cellar. It never occurred to me that they were that special. I've never actually searched the rest of the nooks and crannies of the place."

"Richard," said Don. "If I'm coming your way to go through the cellar, I'd like to help you look through the place. I've been through a lot of 1800s houses in my collecting hunts. Most tended to have unique features like hidden stairwells for servants. Does yours have anything like that?"

"Our family lived there for a time in the '60s when my brother and I were inquisitive youth. That we would have found for sure."

"Maybe some spaces between walls or rooms that don't add up? Hidden storage or security rooms were not uncommon in the construction of those days."

"I don't know, but I'd welcome your experience at searching the place."

"Count me in," said Darrel. "I love a good investigation."

"Richard." George Hunt this time. "With your permission, I'd like to secure your items under lock and key here in our library museum. Our location here is in the middle of some pretty fertile ground for Civil War historians. We can make these both secure and accessible to vetted experts. The more experienced eyes and minds we can bring to the inquiry, the better chance we have of solving this mystery in our lifetimes."

"Sounds like a good plan," I said. "What do we do next?"

George laughed, "I know Don will say dinner plans. Given the loan of your collection, Churchville University will be glad to pick up the tab."

Darrel also laughed, "Given the fact that Richard would need a loan after last night's forced bankruptcy, that's an excellent offer."

The group parted with plans to meet at a local favorite Mexican place later.

Back at Don's house, we enjoyed two more rounds of brandy and cigars, one before and one after dinner. Darrel and I made an early out Sunday, as early as one can muster the strength to move after another Don Weston breakfast. Don would be driving down to join us in another week. Very busy November.

Homecoming

I dropped Darrel at his car and headed straight to the former Peacock Plume.

"Was Lincoln a good boy?" I asked when I got there.

Audrey greeted me with a hug and said, "He did wake me the first night with an outburst of barking at some strange sounds."

Audrey and Vicki both giggled. Vicki said, "It was such a fun day, and I was still amped up when we all went to bed. I decided I needed some exercise to wear me out so I started practicing my mountain climbing skills on Trey. Audrey tells me I got a little loud when I reached the summit and planted my flag."

I blushed, and we all laughed out loud. I couldn't resist. "I guess I can see you celebrating a 'peak' experience," I said. Groans from the girls. "Sorry, it's all downhill from here. Okay, I'm done."

"Thank God," said Vicki. "Seriously though, Lincoln was perfectly behaved and great company. I insist you park him here anytime you go out of town."

"Nice to hear, I promise to take you up on that," I replied.

"How was the trip?" Audrey asked.

"Very productive, and more to come. The experts told us our stuff was unusually well preserved. One of them will be here next week to check the atmosphere of the cellar to see how that may have contributed to the condition. He and Darrel are also going to help me search the house for possible hidden compartments and more finds."

"That sounds exciting," said Audrey. "Maybe they'll scare up the real ghosts."

"One can only hope. But, if not for the weirdness of the ghosts, you and I might never have met. They can't be all bad."

"True. We do seem to be serendipitously linked by weirdness, but I thought it was due to your bad jokes." Smile.

"Will I get to see you at all this month? We had an awesome dinner while I was in Pennsylvania, and the guys fleeced me pretty good on the proceeds of the gun sale, but I still have enough left for us to do something special. We've not had a real date."

"No, we haven't, and if you're asking me out, I suppose I would accept but not this month. The MFA show will be done in early December. You can try to sweep me off my feet when I've swept that off my mind."

"Then we will be officially dating in December?"

"Slow down, Romeo. I still need to do a background check on you." Vicki was giggling again, amused by our awkward courting exchange.

"I'll see you at school," I said. "I've just got two more grades to enter for my classes as the final exam and assignments come in, and I'll be free after that."

"By the way, you don't need to attend the last few paranormal classes if you have other things going on. You already got an A for your haunted house journal."

"Thanks, teacher, but I think I'll drop in anyway if it's the only time I'll get to see you in person this month. I'll be the one winking at you."

Lincoln and I grabbed our stuff and headed home.

Cat Scratch Fever Strikes

I had forgotten that we were in the new moon phase.

On the drive, I commented to Lincoln that he seemed rather smitten with the girls. He didn't disagree. "I think you'll be seeing a lot more of them." He seemed okay with that too.

Coming to the end of the driveway I was pleased to see that the few lights I'd left on were unchanged. I unconsciously checked the location of the basketball, also unchanged. A quiet night would be nice.

As we hopped out of the car and I grabbed my bag, the yellow cat emerged from the darkness of the fenced yard and stared at us. Lincoln barked, and the cat ran like it was scalded. Lincoln was right behind, disappearing into the night in the direction of the pear orchard. I dropped my bag to join the chase.

Running, tripping, falling, I stumbled well behind the speed of the animals. I couldn't see a thing as I got to the orchard, but I could hear the gnashing, barking, howling, and clashing of an epic battle nearby. It was over in less than a minute, and all fell silent.

"Lincoln," I yelled. "Come." No response. I waited a few seconds and continued calling for him as I kept walking in the direction where I had heard the fight. Why didn't I have my daylight flashlight?

Approaching the burial pit, I began to see the outline of Lincoln's white mane, feet, and the tip of his tail. He wasn't moving. I dropped to my knees at his side and noticed the red among the white. He was conscious and seemed somewhat alert, but he was also inert. The yellow cat was nowhere in sight.

I scooped up limp little Lincoln and talked softly to him as he bled on my shirt and we headed to the house. "Come on boy, I've got you, everything will be okay." I didn't know that to be true, but I wanted him to believe me.

The kitchen table became the triage site. I spread a towel and laid him down to stretch him out and examine the damage. There were open wounds near one eye and all over his muzzle. His nose looked like a black olive that had been sliced in half. The hair of his mane is so thick that I couldn't assess much there but it was obvious his attacker had been able to penetrate that defense from the blood dripping free. I was crying.

I had a cell number for Amy. If I could talk to her, she'd know what to do.

Amy answered on the second ring. "Richard, good to see your name on my screen. What's up?"

"Lincoln's been hurt, attacked by a cat. He's pretty beat up and bloody. I think he'll need stitches and I don't know what else. You were the one person I could think of who might know what to do."

"Oh my God," she said quietly. "Wrap him in a blanket and don't move him. I'm on my way." She hung up, and I did what I was told, telling Lincoln everything was under control and help was on the way. I had to stop crying before Amy got here. She arrived in less than ten minutes. I was still trying to dry my eyes.

"Let's go," she said, gathering the swaddled Lincoln. "Get in the back seat and I'll put him on your lap. We're taking him to the emergency animal hospital in Annadale. I use them all the time for the shelter. I promise you can't get better care."

"I trust you," I said. "Thanks so much. I didn't want to bother you, but I'm glad you can help us."

"This call would never be a bother to me. This is what I do. I already talked to the hospital on my way here. They'll be ready for us when we get there."

And they were. Lincoln was taken from my lap and whisked away on a gurney.

"Now we wait," Amy said, taking me to a reception area. "Lincoln is in the best care possible, so don't worry. Can I get you anything? Water, coffee?"

"Water would be good," I said, still trying to hold back tears.

Amy knew all of the doctors and staff. She let them tend to Lincoln, and they let her take care of me.

"Richard," she said. "What happened?"

"I've been out of town for a couple of days. I picked him up at his sitter. We had just gotten home and out of the car when a cat showed up in our driveway, and Lincoln took chase. I heard a fight, and this was how I found him."

"I'm so sorry. I promise the doctors here will do everything to make him better." She hugged me.

It was another hour before someone came to see us, a doctor in scrubs.

"I have good news," he said. "Despite initial appearances, your lad had only fairly superficial injuries. We were able to get to all the wounds with minimal shaving. I try to do that to keep their dignity intact." He laughed. "I put in a total of twelve stitches. They're self-dissolving so you won't need to come back unless something new comes up, which I wouldn't expect. You'll leave here with antibiotic pills. Force them in daily until they run out, and all should be good."

"He's going to be fine?" I asked.

"The stitches on his face and nose will look funny for a while, but in a month or so you'll never know this happened. He won't even have to wear the 'cone of shame.'"

I started crying again and blubbered out, "Thank you, can he come home now?"

"Yes, I only used local anesthetic, so he's awake and alert. I think he'll be happy to see you now."

"What do I owe you for taking care of him?"

"Don't worry, we won't forget to bill you." He laughed again. "I'm not sure what the charges will be, but it should be hundreds rather than thousands, if that helps."

Amy hugged me again, both crying now. Lincoln was happy to see us. He was back to his old self and seemed to have forgotten the whole incident as he jumped into the car. I put a leash on him when we got out, just in case.

Amy came in with us. "I can spend the night if you two need some comfort and company," she offered. I was glad she was wearing a sweatshirt and jeans tonight. With no skin and no wink, I was able to resist the temptation, but it was close. I sent her away with another hug and thanks.

After she left, I chatted up Lincoln in the kitchen. "You'll have a big story for your girlfriends after this one. Chicks dig scars."

Turning out the lights I heard ping, ping, ping.

"Fuck you!" I shouted at the top of my lungs. "Fuck you, Tom, and fuck you, Yellow Cat. Fuck you, strange noises. We're not afraid of you. Shut the fuck up and leave us alone!"

It was quiet the rest of the November new moon.

Hunting for the Past

I called Audrey the morning after the yellow cat incident to give her an update on what she missed by skipping the November new moon. She and Vicki were quite upset with the tale. I assured them that Lincoln's damage turned out to be fairly insignificant and fully recoverable. They made me promise to bring him by the store next week for healing hugs and kisses. Chicks dig scars.

The following week, as promised, I brought Lincoln by the store for the girls to love on him and his battle wounds. The day after, Don and Darrel arrived a couple of minutes apart for our next date.

"What a great spot," said Don as he unloaded bags from the car. "It's an absolute time capsule."

"It's been in the family since it was built. This was originally home to my great granduncle, Dr. Richard Eugene Craft, my namesake, and his wife Dorothy, or Dottie as she was usually called. Richard and Dottie never had children, and the property was willed to my great grandfather, Richard's brother, upon the doctor's death.

I wish I had more detail on the history for you. We know it was 1850s construction with updates from then and into the 1960s, mostly infrastructure, AC, heat, plumbing, and cosmetic upkeep, and we know the hospital legend during the war years. Dr. Craft lived here alone after the war. He died in 1903, and the period between the Civil War time and then, which probably would have been the most relevant for your search, is a blank."

"Since we last met, George and I have done some additional research specific to this area. We were curious how it became a hospital site as it wasn't an especially convenient spot for any of the major battles. Digging into the less documented history of troop movements and skirmishes, we found many minor scrapes surrounding this spot. Very close by was activity at Burkes Station, Pohick, several minor dust-ups in Annadale, and a lot of fights in the Fairfax area. Not too far afield were a couple of Occoquan River skirmishes and several DC skirmishes, including the White House in 1864. Those all made it an attractive spot for a doctor with a big house to be drafted into hospital status."

He went on, "Another component here may have been the Underground Railroad, which would have brought both troop chases and bounty hunters nearby. Several circumstances made Virginia a place where the Underground Railroad flourished. It had the largest enslaved population of any state and a large free Black population. It also bordered the free states of Pennsylvania and Ohio."

"Funny you should mention that," I said. "We do know that two escaped slaves, a brother and sister named Tom and Betty, lived here and helped out with the hospital during the war. There's no record of them after that."

"You should also let Don know that the place is haunted," laughed Darrel.

Not laughing, Don asked, "Have you documented any of that?"

"I've been keeping a journal of odd notes after a couple of strange events. I haven't been a believer in the haunted house lore, but I also can't find facts to refute some of the unexplainable occurrences here."

"Such as?"

"The usual old house noises, sometimes what seems like voices, a monthly ritual of the sound of a basketball dribbling in the night, lights turning on and off, and an apparition that must have been a bad dream. I signed up for a Paranormal Research class to see if I could learn anything more. The teacher from that class, also a skeptic, has isolated the main events to new moon cycles. Last week was one of those. The basketball noises were present, and my dog Lincoln was roughed up pretty good by a yellow cat, another mysterious visitor."

"Is Lincoln okay?" asked Darrel.

"He suffered some bruised pride and a few stitches, but he'll be fine. Grab your bags and come see for yourself."

Lincoln greeted the guys with his usual barking and prancing. Darrel knelt to take a look. "Oh Lincoln," he said. "You look like the guy who brought a knife to a gunfight."

Lincoln licked Darrel's nose and bounded over to meet Don.

"Sorry for your troubles, little fella," said Don. "I hope you gave as good as you got. Don't worry, I got that same nose wound in a Philadelphia brawl, and I still recovered to the handsome face you see now."

Darrel laughed. "Come on Don, we should be encouraging him, not scaring him."

"It's okay," I said. "Little Lincoln has a great sense of humor. Isn't that right, Scarface? Don," I continued. "You're in charge here. How would you like to proceed?"

"I'm going to leave the museum bag of tricks here on the table to go through later. Maybe we could dump the rest of the stuff in our rooms?"

"Follow me. I'm afraid you have to settle for queen beds here." I showed them the rooms. "I'm on the left here, you're welcome to pick from the other three." Don took the other room on the left and Darrel set up in the one with the bed where both Amy and Audrey had chosen to sit.

"Now," said Don. "Before we look at any more of the house, I'd like to get a buildings and grounds tour in daylight. How much land do you have here?"

"Twenty acres total. The rest of the original farm is now a housing development, strip mall, and a school. The cleared area around the house is roughly eight acres with several small structures and its own graveyard, actually the communal burial pit from the hospital."

We stepped out into Lincoln's fenced area so he could run and bark while we toured.

"I love this," said Darrel, pulling on the pump handle to release a gush of well water. "I guess this was how everyone got their water back in the day. Very cool that it still works."

I pointed to the edge of the cleared area. "You can see the surrounding woods are pretty thick but easily navigated. There are some trails and clearings scattered throughout if you want to see any of it."

"I might take a morning cigar stroll through some of that," Don said. "For now, the grave area and buildings would be my biggest interest, ending up with the cellar, of course."

We left Lincoln in his enclosure and walked a few hundred yards out the back gate to the gravesite. "This is where Lincoln had his scuffle last night."

"Have you ever thought of digging into this mound?" asked Don.

"Not at all. I imagine one could find some more collectibles in here, but I wouldn't relish the idea of searching through the human debris field to find them."

"If you ever get to wondering, let me know. There's no shortage of amateur and professional historians that would like to be the first ones to do an archeological dig into a treasure chest like this."

Duly noted. We moved on to the smokehouse, outhouse, and horse stalls/storage shed. Darrel remarked that the outhouse was perfect for Don. "Conventional plumbing has a difficult time with the amount of food Don processes. This pit might just be deep enough to handle the volume."

"Richard," said Don. "I'm impressed with the condition of all the structures here. It's hard to believe they are all original to the time of the home construction."

"They are, as far as I know. They were a little worse for wear back in the '60s when my dad settled our family here for a few years. He drafted my brother and me to learn manly skills, helping with some wood replacement and painting. When my brother became the sole resident in later years, he found a handyman to bring everything back to what you see now. That same guy still does all of the upkeep on the property for me. I'd be lucky just to keep up the mowing, but he does everything. Lincoln and I pray for his continued health daily. I don't think he could be replaced."

"Impressive," repeated Don as we walked around to the pear orchard. Darrel almost tripped over the grave marker.

"Good job, Lincoln," Darrel shouted. "Look guys, Lincoln already got his revenge and even cleaned up the crime scene."

Laughing, Don chimed in, "Sure would be nice if all perps were so tidy."

I told them about the great granduncle and Yellow Cat legend. "Just another odd circumstance that we started getting yellow cat sightings after Lincoln arrived. It seems Lincoln and I each have our own apparitions to challenge us. Fortunately, I haven't had to fight mine."

"Yet," said Don. "It seems we're back to the front yard. Have we covered all the essential outside grounds and buildings?"

"Except the cellar," I said.

"Except the cellar," Darrel repeated, making spooky ghost sounds with a smile.

I took them behind the front shrubbery and down the stone steps to the root cellar door. It still had my lock on the hasp.

"I'll be right back. I need to get the key and a flashlight. Don, do you need the bag of stuff from the kitchen?"

"Not yet, let's see what we got here first."

From the house, I heard ping, ping, ping and shuddered. When I got back out front, I discovered Darrel and Don playing at the basketball hoop.

Into the Cellar and Beyond

They put the ball back and joined me at the cellar door as I unlocked it and pulled it open. "One of you will need to watch his head in here."

"Always," said Don.

I turned on the mega flashlight to oohs and aahs. "Wow," said Darrel. "Why don't we have flashlights like that at work? Where can I get one of those?"

"Amazon special, I'll send you the link." Proud of my manly torch, I ventured ahead to see if anything had changed. It hadn't. The hay pile seemed untouched, and the military blanket still sat neatly folded. We walked through the space in silence as the visitors took it in.

"Richard," said Darrel. "Could we still eat the stuff that's canned here?"

"I think so. I wouldn't doubt that the hundred-plus-year-old meat in the smokehouse is probably edible as well. I'll let you try it all out in case I'm wrong."

Don was studying the ceiling as he was so naturally close to it. "I've been in more than a few of these," he said. "They're quite common in the old Pennsylvania farmhouses. I wouldn't call this one a root cellar. A true root cellar would be for crop storage and would need to be deep enough to maintain thirty- to forty-degree temperatures. It is quite cool down here, but I don't think it's that cool. I'd call this a canning cellar. The walls and floor are dug through Virginia clay, which effectively insulates any outside heat transfer. The ceiling is the usual weak spot but not here. I can see through the gaps in the wood that someone packed the space from here to the joists above with a foot or more of clay as well.

"Another best practice," he continued. "Is ventilation. These ceiling gaps have outlets to the foundation for some air exchange. I also noticed a small gap at the bottom of the door. In a true root cellar, you would seal that to keep rodents out. In a canning cellar where all the stored products are sealed, a couple of small mice is not a big deal, providing that they don't chew open the base of the door, inviting larger friends inside, which they haven't here. The total insulation and ventilation design is among the best I've seen."

"What now?" asked Darrel.

"Now," said Don. "We dig into the bag of tricks supplied by the museum guys and set up our monitors."

By habit, I locked the cellar door on the way out, and we headed to the kitchen. In the kitchen bag, we found three digital thermometers and three digital hygrometers. Don explained that we'd have the results of temperature and moisture that would give us a baseline for the environment. The instruments would read out on his laptop and he could pass them on to the library/museum guys to do a relative humidity calculation. "Assuming the measures are in line and remain stable, we'll capture everything the guys back at Churchville University need for a fairly complete atmospheric assessment of the cellar."

Returning to the cellar, we placed a thermometer and hygrometer side by side on each of the workbenches to cover the whole room.

"That's it," said Don. "We'll take initial readings after we've sealed this up and let it sit for an hour or so. We'll then take three more readings while I'm here, one tonight, one early in the morning, and the last one around noon tomorrow before I head north. Time to check out the inside of the house while we make dinner plans."

We started in the attic. Don took an immediate interest in my brother's footlocker and duffel. "Do you mind if I go through this?" he asked.

"Not at all, that's where one of the mysterious unexplainables originated. The military blanket in the cellar was originally in that pile. It ended up disappearing from here and found its way into the locked cellar somehow."

Don dumped out the contents of the duffel bag, all pieces of military uniforms, and one clunk. The clunk was another pistol.

"This is a 1911," said Don. "The same sidearm I carry today."

"Would you like another one?" I asked. "It's yours if you want it. I promised a friend there were no guns in the house after Darrel sold the other one for me."

"If you want Darrel to sell this one, it probably has a value of $1,000 to $1,500."

"I'd rather gift it to you if you'd like to have it. It seems small compensation for your help on the other stuff."

"Okay," said Don. "But I'm also buying dinner tonight to honor your generosity."

"Done deal."

The rest of my brother's war chest was fairly unremarkable, but Don said it still had market value for collectors of that era. I thought I'd leave it sit for now.

We didn't find any more Civil War collectibles and no hidden spaces in the attic, so we moved down one flight to the bedrooms. The two on the right were smaller with no closets. They did have window seats with storage for blankets and pillows. No surprises in either one.

Moving to the rooms where Don and I were staying, Don asked, "Was one of these Dr. Craft's?"

"Yes, I'm not positive, but I believe it's the one you're staying in. That's the room my brother used when he lived here. It's a little bit larger than mine." There were no window seats or other storage spots in these rooms, with one giant exception.

Don walked back and forth between the two rooms. "Would you know if these two were ever one large room?" he asked.

"I don't think so, but I don't know."

"The reason I ask is I think there was some construction here after the original structure was built. Both of these rooms have closets, which wouldn't be a part of home building in the early to mid-1800s but is a typical upgrade."

"My brother and I thought there were monsters in the closets," I laughed. "And under the beds."

Don laughed, "Didn't we all, and who's to say there aren't in a haunted house? I'd like to do some measurements and maybe even destroy a little of your plaster if you don't mind. Let's look at the rest of the house first."

"Demolition is not my preferred method, but if it provides any answers, it would be worth the mess."

"Darrel," Don asked. "Any observations on your part?"

"So far just along for the ride."

Downstairs on the main level, we went through all of the drawers and cabinets of the kitchens and the built-ins of the great room. Darrel noticed Audrey's picture on the floor. "Did you leave that down there for Lincoln's viewing?" he said, smiling.

"Not exactly. That's an Audrey Welsh original. She's my paranormal class instructor. She's become a friend and my occult investigation partner. She's also a really gifted artist."

"I'll say," said Darrel. "But that still doesn't explain why it's on the floor."

"The last time Audrey was over, it fell off the wall. I thought it was another supernatural event. Audrey thinks it was an example of my poor picture-hanging skills. I had to replace the damaged frame, and Audrey made me promise to leave it right there until the next time she visits. She's going to give me a class on care, handling, and proper hanging and display of real art." I laughed.

We didn't find any suspicious spaces in our main floor inspection.

It was time to record our first readings from the cellar instruments and send them to the Churchville folks. "What's your wi-fi password?" asked Don.

I hesitated and blushed. I had just changed it very recently. "Audrey."

The two men looked at me and then at each other. "I hear she's just a friend, Don," said Darrel. They looked at me again and burst out laughing as Don typed in A-u-d-r-e-y and accessed the wi-fi.

Our baseline temperature was 55 degrees and the hygrometer measured 36 for the dew point. Don emailed that to the school, and we returned to the bedroom closet inquiry with a tape measure and the he-man flashlight, just in case.

Monsters in the Closet?

D on's giant frame filled the doorway of his bedroom closet as he announced, "I think your plasterwork may be safe. The closets and walls are built with wood paneling, probably the same wood as the flooring. It's been painted on the inside of the closet, and the outside has been plastered over to match the lath and plaster finish on the rest of the room."

"Does that tell us anything?" asked Darrel.

"It was likely added pretty early in the 1900s. In the 1940s, drywall became available. That would have been a much easier build."

"If the wood is the same as the floor," I added. "That's elm. I can't imagine they had planks of wood left from the original build, so this had to be new wood when the closets were built. Elms were lost to Dutch Elm disease in the 1930s so it can't be newer than that."

Darrel summed it up. "I'm keeping notes, guys. It sounds like the closets had to be added in the 1920s or before."

"Get ready to take more notes," said Don. "Where is our tape measure?" I passed it to him. "The door opening is three feet, with a foot of wall on either side of the frame. The depth is seven feet. We'll measure the closet in the other room next."

"Five by seven," noted Darrel. The other closet was the same.

"Now the length of the total wall." Said Don. That was nineteen feet. "Does your math agree with mine, note keeper? I come up with an unaccounted-for space between the closets of a nine-by-seven-foot vacuum."

We looked at each other in silence. I broke it with, "I guess we're in for some plaster carnage after all."

"Not necessarily," said Don. "If I were building a secret room, I'd leave a secret access point. The small gaps where the wood panels are joined are painted shut." He produced a good-sized pocket knife. "While I'm opening them up with this, can you think of anything you might have that would be thin, flat, rigid, and long, something that could probe deeper than just a knife?"

"Like a sword maybe?" asked Darrel.

"Too wide, it would ideally be maybe a sixteenth of an inch wide."

"I think I've got just what you're looking for. I saw it when we were going through the kitchen cabinets," I said while Don was using his knife to rip the seams of paint between the boards. "Be right back." I returned with a couple of eighteen-inch flat kabob skewers.

"Bingo," said Don. He had opened up one of the gaps, fully cleaned of paint down to the bare wood. The skewer slid through the opening with a little effort, continuing to disappear to its full length. "Aha, the empty space I was hoping for. Now to find the way in."

As the gaps continued to get cleared of paint, three boards in the center were clearly wider than the surrounding panels. "Would one of you guys go look in the other closet and see if you notice the same thing?" Don asked.

The boards in the other closet were uniform in size.

"I'm guessing," said Don. "This side was your great grandun-cle's bedroom, and we're looking at the way in. We've still got more scraping to do to clear the paint."

"I volunteer to help if you'll get your massive self out of there and let someone else in," offered Darrel.

"Happy to oblige," said Dan. "It is getting a little claustro-phobic in here."

"Ha, if we were working in a two-car garage, it would be claustro-phobic for you."

"Concentrate on all of the edges of the three larger boards," instructed Don.

Don sat on the bed for a break and I was able to fit in the closet with Darrel to watch the progress. Darrel asked if I had a cordless drill and a wire brush. I did. "Can you go get it? The gaps are just about freed up and I think I see a big clue on this bottom molding."

When I returned, Darrel and Don were engrossed in conversation about the top and bottom moldings of the closet's side wall. It appeared they were nailed to some sort of backing board. It also appeared there were no nails where the three larger panels sat in the moldings and joined them. A quick burn across them with the wire brush exposed the nail heads on the outer boards and confirmed their absence on the three larger panels.

"I think these may lift out," said Darrel as he plunged Don's knife into the bottom of the center board and lifted. It moved. After more digging at the paint, Darrel was able to raise the board over the level of the molding and pull it out. With the center removed, it was an easy task to grab the sides of the other large boards and lift them free. "Ta da!" pronounced Darrel.

Don observed, "Simple, but effective. The moldings finish off the floor and ceiling design, but for these three panels, they act as channels to guide them up and out. Very clever. Richard, it's your haunted house, it's only fitting that you should be the first witness if we have anything here."

Darrel had set the three boards to the back wall of the closet. I entered as he exited and turned the mega flashlight to the interior of the new space. I'm pretty sure my jaw dropped when I looked in. "Wow, wow, wow," was all I could initially say. "It's like a miniature library in here." Floor-to-ceiling bookshelves lined the two long walls, all in unfinished lumber. The middle one of those on the left side had a small built-in desk space with two candleholders on it and a small stool tucked in below. The upper shelves were filled with books and many medical references. The lower shelves had a couple of presumed doctor's travel bags and an array of surgical and other medical tools of the time and the trade. Everything looked as if the room had been last used yesterday.

I stepped out and handed the flashlight to Darrel. He came out with a look of shock and awe. Don had a harder time squeezing into the opening. Don was in there for several minutes before joining us back in the bedroom. We just stood there and looked at each other with surprise, excitement, and bewilderment. What had we discovered?

"Dinnertime celebration," Don announced. "This has been closed up for a hundred years or more, and it will be here when we return."

Into the Evening

I had a dinner plan, a Korean BBQ buffet in Annandale. I figured Don could make it a bargain and Darrel and I could eat somewhat responsibly. I figured it wrong. Don made us try everything he was having, and we all ended up stuffed anyway.

During dinner, Don got an email from Churchville. Our relative humidity was calculated at 48.64. According to the school, the combined numbers were excellent for the long-term storage of the artifacts.

"I guess that explains the condition," I said, both a question and a statement.

"Not really," said Don. "The main factor will be consistency. Our first cut at the numbers is a favorable environment, but fluctuations in temperature and humidity are the biggest culprit in the aging process. If our numbers remain the same, that would be part of the explanation. Still, George had never seen such perfect condition on these old pieces. I think it's still going to be a bit of a mystery."

Heading back to the house, we took the next readings on the cellar. They were identical to the first ones. "Good news so far," said Don. "Is anyone up for some reading before bedtime?" We took the big flashlight back to the hidden library.

Don and Lincoln entered the room first, and we all packed into the small space. Lincoln had been a big help throughout the investigation, alternately running and barking and jumping on all participants. That sounds like a nuisance, but it was a good source of comic relief, regularly breaking the tensions of the moment.

I was operating the flashlight to Don's directions. He insisted on pictures to document the exact location of every article and book title before we would remove anything. That process took about an hour. When that was complete, Don assigned us our evening readings. He and Darrel were taking a couple of the larger medical reference books, specifically looking for any notes by Dr. Craft or any assistants that might shed light on the hospital history.

There were four unmarked journals, completely handwritten, presumably by my great granduncle. "These are for you," said Don as he handed them to me. Lastly, Don found a see-through onion skin envelope as the sole contents of the one desk drawer. The envelope was closed with sealing wax and pressed with a crest of the caduceus, the historic medical symbol. The wax and the stamp were still on the desk, near one of the candles. "Also for you," said Don. "The handwriting appears to match the journals."

We trudged down to the kitchen table with all of our treasures. Don and Darrel started on the journals while I made us a pot of coffee. We might be here a while. They were sharing notes on the medical breakthroughs of the time, like piercing veins and arteries for blood-letting instead of using leeches. The handwritten hospital notes related to things such as how to apply chloroform for general anesthesia and for how long.

I delivered our coffees and focused on the envelope. As I broke the seal and unfolded the contents I was impressed with the perfection of the cursive writing, a lost art today. I can't even read my own signature. The date on the top of the page was March 28, 1903.

"To Whoever may find this,

"My name is Richard Eugene Craft. I'm 69 years old and close to my maker as I write this. I've been alone in this house since my last friend, a cat, passed on in 1868. Over the past several years, I built this room and stored all of my life's work here. I've been blessed with love and prosperity in my life. I've also been cursed by my weakness, mental and physical. As a doctor, I know that I have developed cancer in my body, and I'm choosing to end my life painlessly while I still have a presence of mind. I believe my God will welcome me and forgive me of this and my past sins. I've made my confessions in my journals and I leave this world now, in peace. Dr. Richard Craft."

"Guys," I said, passing the paper to Don. "This is a suicide note."

Darrel looked over Don's shoulder as they read the letter. "It certainly is," said Don. "I think it would be prudent to put the medical books aside for now and work on the journals." Nodding heads. "Richard, it's your family history. How would you like to proceed?"

The books were labeled by year, 1861, 1862, 1863, and 1864. "Why don't you two take the '61, '62, and '63? I'm most curious about Great Granduncle Craft's end times."

Flipping through the 1864 book, I found that the early entries were a wrap-up of hospital details as the war was dying down. After that, it was used as a personal diary continuing through time to the last pages from 1903. I started at the back, which covered his cancer discovery and known outcome but no mention of his end plans. Backing up a few years, I found he had worked from 1873 to 1894 with the Alexandria Infirmary. With Lincoln nipping at my heels, I remembered the cat and backed up to 1878. It took some digging through pages, and I found much more than expected on July 29, 1878.

"Yellow Cat left me today. He's the only company I've had at home for the past twelve years. I had a stone made for him. I thought it was fitting to bury him in the previously unmarked grave where I buried my last love, Betty."

Brain exploded. What did I just read? Wasn't Betty the slave sister of Tom? I couldn't think straight. I had to pull out my phone calendar to do 1878 minus 12, 1866. I dropped the book as I was trying to flip back to 1866.

Don noticed my fluster and asked, "Are you okay over there?"

"Not at all," I said. "I just read about the end of Yellow Cat and my great granduncle's last love, Betty, not Dottie. I need a breather and some more coffee." I poured us all a fresh cup and, vaguely composed, asked, "What are you two finding?"

Don said, "An amazing first-hand chronicle of how this piece of the local field hospital network developed. The Northern Army took over Alexandria in 1861 and commandeered a local hotel to be commissioned as the Mansion House Union Hospital. Dr. Craft's house was set up as one of the field units attached to that hospital for overflow or quick access, depending on need. He kept very legible and complete records on the number of patients, surgeries, deaths, supplies, and day-to-day operations. This is important history. What are you finding, Darrel?"

"The 1862 journal started mostly the same. It was pretty redundant, so I started fast-forwarding. I had just found an important personal note when Richard had to break. It's about your great grandmother," he said. "Your namesake was devastated and grief-stricken when she died April 25, 1863, from consumption. He cursed the fact that, as a doctor, he couldn't fix her but, oddly, thanked God that he could still save her."

My brain exploded again. I was blinking back tears in my eyes as I stared at the two men and mindlessly petted the dog. Quiet. I never had properly grieved Gwen and my son Steven. All of that was flooding through me as I imagined my great granduncle's loss.

"I vote you try to lay down and take a break," Don said. "That's a lot of information to process. Darrel and I will speed-read the rest of this and fill you in."

"I second the vote," said Darrel. "Anything special you'd like us to look for?"

"Anything more on Dottie and the whereabouts of Tom and Betty," I sniffled. "But I'm not sure I'm prepared for whatever you find."

Lincoln and I went for a long walk, Lincoln on a leash this time. He could tell I was not at my best and stayed close to my leg as we strolled. I was crushed by memories of Gwen and Steven and wondered why I didn't get us a dog when we first moved here. If Steven had lived, he would have loved playing with him, and Gwen would have loved the company.

We didn't see or hear anything supernatural in our outing. Thank God, I was emotionally spent. When we came back, the guys were engrossed in the journals. Lincoln and I went upstairs and lay down on the bed. I guess I cried myself to sleep.

Morning Has Broken

D on had found my breakfast stash as I woke once again to the smell of bacon. Lincoln and I joined him in the kitchen.

"Darrel is still asleep, we stayed up a little later than planned. I'm going to let this sit in the oven and take that morning cigar walk in the woods. Would you care to join me?"

I really, really would, I thought. It would be a pleasant transition. "I'll get us a couple of travel coffee mugs."

I looked for Lincoln. He had gone back upstairs and was lying on Darrel's bed, both asleep. I pulled the door closed.

Don and I headed out through Lincoln's yard and into the woods as he lit a cigar. It was cool and a little foggy. "Great way to start a new day," he said cheerily.

"Agreed, I needed a new day."

"I took the morning readings on the cellar. They're still stable. So far so good there. I'll check again around noon."

We wandered, Don occasionally kicking at the ground, no doubt looking for bullets or coins or other memorabilia. "You should have brought a metal detector."

"I did, but there's plenty of time to play with that on return trips." He didn't elaborate. I was afraid to ask, but I did.

"I take it you two found something more to check on?"

"A lot more. But you and Lincoln were sound asleep, and we didn't want to disturb you."

"Well?"

"After Dottie died, Betty took on her nursing role. She and Dr. Craft worked very closely together, even taking some trips to the infirmary. He had kind things to say about her work, and after a year or so, that grew into a more comforting role."

"You mean like his wife would have comforted him?"

"Yes."

I had been thinking about the loneliness of losing Gwen last night. "Darrel tells me you're a widower, what happened to your wife?"

"Lung cancer. He told me you were also a widower. What happened to your wife?"

"Accidental drowning in our bathtub per the coroner. They didn't rule out suicide, but I'll always know it was a broken heart. She died only six months after we lost our infant son to a birth defect."

"That's rough. We were never blessed with kids."

"So, Betty and the good doctor became close. That's probably not a bad thing."

"Probably not," agreed Don.

"Did he say what became of Betty?"

"He did. She died from massive bleeding, a couple of months after they discovered she was pregnant. I remember it was March 27, 1865. My wife died on March 27. He went into a long depression after that."

We were quiet while we walked back to the house, breaking up Darrel and Lincoln's frisbee game. "Morning, gentleman," said Darrel. "I woke up with a strange bed partner again. That doesn't always mean I've made good choices the night before, but I think it was okay this time." Good icebreaker. Lincoln entertained us by relentlessly retrieving a toy, switching between Darrel and me to be his quarterback. We kept to small talk about the weather while Don served breakfast. As dishes were gathered, Darrel said to me, "I assume Don filled you in on the new revelations while you were on walkabout?"

"Mostly," I said. "But Tom is still a mystery to me. He was my apparition, which led to the discovery of the war stuff in the cellar. I always assumed he and Betty had moved on after the war, but now we know that wasn't the case, at least for Betty. Did you find what became of him?"

"I'm surprised Don didn't mention that to you. I found that in the 1864 book you were reading. Dr. Craft killed him."

Not Sure I Wanted to Know any More

"**K**illed him? Was it an accident?"
"You should probably read it for yourself, I marked the pages," Don said. "Darrel, I think you and I and Lincoln should go for another cigar walk."

They left me alone with my great granduncle's words.

The marked entry started on April 14, 1866.

"What good is it to call oneself a doctor when you can't make well the only two women you ever loved? I know their souls are saved and we'll meet again, but there's nothing left in my earthly life to go on. Betty was so special in taking care of me after I lost Dorothy, and now, I've lost her and our unborn child. The only love left in my empty existence is a damned feral cat that won't leave my side. I need to be alone with my God.

"I told Tom we need to put down one of the horses and he's digging a pit by the surgical dump. We've done this once before. We take the animal to the pit and put it down as we push its body into the hole. He should be done by tomorrow."

April 15, 1866

"What have I become? As night was falling, I brought the horse to the edge of the pit. Tom was holding the reins as I picked up the shovel and dealt him a mighty blow to the back of the head. The horse ran off as Tom fell into the pit. I crawled down to where he lay and swung the shovel again, hitting him with the side of the tool to crush his forehead. I sat there as he died."

April 16, 1866

"I've committed the ultimate sin against my God and my Oath. I killed a man last night. His soul will be saved, but I took his life. He was a good man, but I have to be alone now. I filled the hole in the ground today. May God forgive me for my sorrow and loneliness. I don't know why I had to do this, but I did. May God forgive me."

There were no more entries until 1871. Those started as more normal day-to-day thoughts, as if the dark period had never happened. He must have been all alone in his depression until then. In 1873, he started a new practice and social life with his work at the Virginia Infirmary in Alexandria.

When Don, Darrel, and Lincoln returned, I still sat at the kitchen table staring at the journals. I was overwhelmed with all we'd discovered in the past eighteen hours. I was also somewhat relieved that all the questions were now answered.

"Thanks for the time alone," I said. "I needed that to digest all of the family history. It's a sad story, but now that it's out there, it's all over."

"Not yet," said Don. "The documentation of the suicide is disturbing, but not legally problematic. The other disclosures need to be reported to the authorities for investigation. Two unmarked graves of former slaves are of great interest to the historical society, and a confession to murder will bring in law enforcement. There is no statute of limitations for murder in any state. Darrel, this is your jurisdiction. What next?"

"Richard, are you okay with me taking the journals? It will be just to make copies of the pertinent entries, and I'll get them back to you. I'll handle the initial report on the murder."

"Whatever you need to do," I answered.

"George Hunt has strong connections with all the historical societies, especially Virginia, since so much Civil War action was centered here. When I get home this evening, I'll touch base with him to start the discussion on their involvement. I don't need any copies to get that going," said Don.

"Is there anything I need to do?" I asked.

"Trust us," said Darrel.

"And figure out where we're going for lunch," said Don to pained laughter. "I'll get the noon cellar readings first, and we can take two cars. I'll head on north from there."

"Three cars," said Darrel. "I'm going to take the journals to the office. The sooner I get the copies, the sooner I can return them."

"Thanks," I said.

Cellar readings at noon remained consistent. Don was going to leave the instruments in place. He set up my laptop so I could continue that chore while he was gone.

Lunch was all guy talk and camaraderie, and my friends went their separate ways. When I got home, Lincoln and I settled into a nap.

Ending November

After the nap, Lincoln and I concocted my awesome spaghetti sauce in a large pot. I planned to freeze the excess for ready provisions through the next month or so. Around 4:00 p.m., Darrel called to let me know he was done with the journals for now and offered to bring them back this evening.

"Can you stay for dinner?" I asked. "It's spaghetti with my secret sauce."

"Will I have to eat a lot?" he laughed.

"I need a Don break myself, so no."

"See you soon."

Dinner conversation was naturally centered on secret rooms and the mysteries of the house. I'm glad he was there. I was beginning to unwind from the enormity of our discoveries, and it was nice to have some friendly company who already knew the story.

When Darrel left, I called Audrey.

No "namaste" since the shop was closed. "What's up?" she said. "How are things going with your grand inquisition?"

"Overwhelming. How are things going with your gallery show?"

"Also overwhelming, but it's over next week. Can you come as my date?"

"I can't begin to express how much I would love to do that. Can Lincoln come too?"

"You know better than that, I think."

"Oh well, it was worth a try. When and where is it?"

"Gillespie Gallery on the George Mason campus, 7:00 to 9:00 on Tuesday."

"Should I pick you up?"

"No, meet me there. I'll have a lot of last-minute things to do before it starts."

"I'm in."

"Any new discoveries at the house?"

"More than you can imagine. The highlights are multiple deaths, a murder, and a suicide here."

"Yikes. Anyone we know about?"

"Yikes for real. We know all of them. I'll save the details for you to read in Dr. Craft's journals. Our next new moon date is December 12, but I insist you come over after the gallery show is done so I can show you the secret room library."

"Secret room. How did we miss that?"

"I'm not sure, but it was pretty obvious when our guy from Pennsylvania pointed it out. He has a lot of history in old house exploration and picked up on it pretty quickly."

"I'm excited to see it, and I'll bet Vicki would be too. She's never seen your place, and of course, it's always a pleasure to see Lincoln in his natural habitat. I don't think I can wait until the show. Would it be okay if we popped over tomorrow after we close the shop at 6:00?"

"Does the visit include a class on picture hanging? I put a new frame on your art."

"I'm glad you reminded me. I'll bring what I need and introduce you to the ferrule."

"Would you two like to join me for dinner here tomorrow? I have a load of homemade spaghetti sauce."

"I'd love that."

"Although it occurs to me it's not a vegan sauce."

"Vicki will either have to eat what you have or she can bring her own hippie food." She laughed. I love that laugh.

"Lincoln and I will look for you around 6:30."

Lincoln and I had a little housework to take care of before company. I picked up my drill, wire brush, and kabob skewers from the closet and put them away. Lincoln was helpful as always when I got the vacuum to clean up the paint chippings. His job is to jump and bite at the nozzle whenever the machine is activated.

Our last task before bed was to check the readings from the cellar. The temperature had dropped to 40 degrees, a full 15 points colder than all of our previous tests. I emailed the result to Don and the library people at Churchville. I guess we'll find out tomorrow what that means, if anything.

My rant from the new moon night of the yellow cat incident must be working. We haven't heard a sound since then. Lincoln and I slept well. We awoke refreshed and looking forward to seeing our girl-friends tonight.

I found a note from Don in my inbox. "Interesting numbers. The science folks calculated the new relative humidity at 85.49, which would be out of range for best storage. Doubtful that all of the ther-mometers would have failed in the same way. Keep sending the read-ings, and we'll let the pros worry about the results. On another note, I went over the events of the past couple of days with George. He's taking on the historical society contacts and will probably like to join us on the next visit to see everything for himself. Don."

I did 1,000 words or more of writing today. It was therapeutic to step out of today and immerse in prohibition-era Chicago. I'm playing with some twists that intertwine the bad guys with the good guys. I'm also diving into research like I haven't done since the dissertation. I lost track of time and it was after 5:00 when I hit the final "Save."

Lincoln and I put the big pot on the stove to start slowly warming and made some garlic bread. Now it was time for Frisbee to wear him out before our company got here. He had just given me the "no mas" signal of lying exhausted on the frisbee when the girls pulled up. Suddenly he was an alert ball of fire when he saw them. I opened the gate to the driveway and let him go. Everyone was hugs and wiggles, and one barker.

"Namaste," yelled Vicki over the din.

"Cool beans," I responded.

"Here's the picture-hanging stuff," Audrey said, giving me a small nag and a hug. "I'm taking Vicki on a quick walk around the grounds, if you don't mind."

"Don't mind at all. That will give Lincoln and me time to start the spaghetti water and get the garlic bread in the oven."

"Oh no," said Vicki. "Lincoln comes with us."

"On a leash," I said, and got one for them.

The house smelled pretty great when they returned. I was looking forward to another spaghetti dinner with friends. I could eat spaghetti every night.

"Did you see it all?" I asked.

"Even the Yellow Cat grave," said Vicki. "That's a little creepy."

"Far from the creepiest," I spoke.

"Well, there was the burial ground," she went on. "It's hard to imagine what went on here and easy to imagine why the place would be haunted. Do you mind if I look around the house?"

"Not at all. Let me get the flashlight so I can show you the secret room."

The girls fit much better in the room than the guys had.

"This is amazing," said Audrey. "I'm still surprised we never noticed this space between the closets. It seems pretty obvious now."

"I grew up here, and I've been back a few years now. I never gave it a thought. I felt pretty stupid when Don went right to it."

"I get the feeling of a presence and a sad vibe in this space," said Vicki. "Can you feel it?"

"I'll never not feel it," I said. "Now that I know what took place here. My great granduncle penned his suicide note at that desk before he closed the room in 1903. That, and other secrets, slept here in the darkness for well over a hundred years. I almost wish they'd kept sleeping." I had to change the subject. "Too much going on in life to dwell on old deaths right now. I'll let Lincoln and Audrey show you the rest of the place. I've got kitchen duty."

They wandered through the attic and all the rooms while I did my best Bobby Flay imitation. Lincoln strolled in first, followed closely by his fan club.

"I love this place," gushed Vicki. "It's homey and happy and scary and spooky all at once, everything I hope to find in a home."

"Can we help with anything?" Audrey asked.

"Nope. The spaghetti water is ready whenever we are. Everything else is done and on hold. Do you want to do some picture hanging?

The guys kidded me about the location of your masterpiece and kidded me more when they heard why it was there."

"Well let's fix that so it doesn't embarrass you further in front of the guys."

Audrey restrung the wire and introduced the ferrule. When I watched her crush it on the wire ends I completely understood why my technique was "less than."

"Thank you, my dear," I said as she hung it. "Now let's never speak of this again." We all laughed and returned to the spaghetti water. In ten minutes, everything was ready to throw on our plates and we sat down.

"Vicki," I said. "Are you going to be okay with this? The sauce is far from vegan."

"I think it's okay to break the rules every so often. It's not an allergy, it's a choice. I do like non-vegan food, but I haven't put any meat in my body for some time."

"Vicki, that's not true," said Audrey. "Trey stayed over just the other night." We all laughed so hard that I thought spaghetti would come out of my nose.

Dinner conversation was light, catching up on each other's activities of the week. Vicki shared that she thought Trey might "pop the question" for a Christmas present. "He's been acting a little odd, extra touchy-feely. I also think he borrowed one of my rings from my jewelry box."

"That's a pretty significant clue," I agreed. "I trust you're looking forward to the surprise?"

"It seems like the next logical step. We've been together for a few years. I'll act surprised of course, but I'll also accept immediately." She laughed.

"I hope you're right," said Audrey. "The two of you are really special together, but what if he's just buying you another ring, not the one you're hoping for?"

"Or fitting you for Chinese handcuffs?" I added to groans.

"Fingers crossed," said Vicki. "By the way, who are these guys you've been hanging out with, Richard?"

"One of them is a guy by the name of Darrel Metz. He's an Arlington County cop who is a student in my Marketing class. The other is Don Weston, an old friend of Darrel's. He's our Civil War expert. They're both career law enforcement veterans and really interesting new friends. Based on our findings this week, they'll both be back for more, possibly with other reinforcements. Hopefully, the two of you will get to meet them."

"That would be nice," said Vicki. "But remember we're both already spoken for. I should be a fiancée in a few weeks, and Audrey has been steadily sneaking up on you." Giggling, Audrey visibly blushed but didn't respond. I like that.

"It's okay, I think they're both confirmed bachelors."

Audrey changed the topic. "Tell us about the journals you found."

"I can do better than that. They're right here on the counter. I need to clear the table, wash some dishes, and take my nightly reading on the cellar. You're welcome to go through them while I do that. Darrel needed to make some copies from them, so the most telling entries are all marked with tabs."

"As your paranormal guide," said Audrey. "What is the nightly reading on the cellar?"

"The condition on our Civil War stuff was too good to be true. Don wanted to assess the conditions of storage in the cellar to find out why. There are several thermometers and hygrometers planted down there, and they get recorded three times a day. We had one aberration of a big temperature drop last night but, aside from that, conditions have been favorable and consistent."

"Neat," Audrey said as I handed her the journals and the suicide note and tended to my tasks.

The kitchen was cleaned and cellar readings were back to normal. I sent my email report to Don and joined the girls at the table. They were still reading and looked engrossed.

"This could be a screenplay," said Vicki.

"Or a Greek tragedy," added Audrey. I noticed she had a couple of pages of notes. "Guy loves girl, guy loses girl, guy finds love again, guy loses girl again, guy falls apart and commits unspeakable acts, guy kills himself. Oh, and the cat. Maybe not a Greek tragedy, maybe a country song. This is too much and too sad to take in all at once." She dropped the book and came over to hug me. "I'm so sorry, Richard."

Here I go with tears again. This is about the time when Lincoln or Vicki would break the tension with something goofy, but all were quiet as I flashed in my mind through Gwen and Steven and the story of my great granduncle again.

"Sorry," I said, wiping my eyes. "I thought I was coming to grips with all the news but it's still too fresh."

"Would you like me to stay with you tonight?" asked Audrey.

"I could pick her up in the morning," said Vicki.

"No, no, no," I said softly. "You two have too much going on with the shop and the show. Lincoln has been taking good care of me, and we'll be fine." At any other time, I would have jumped at that suggestion, but I was still with Gwen and Steven in my mind and not ready.

Vicki took off her necklace and handed it to me. "I know you're not a believer, but take this anyway. It's a pink opal. I believe it attracts love and warmth, especially when my mind is troubled. You need this more than I do right now. I want you to hold onto it at least until you're feeling its peace."

"Vicki, I can't take this."

"You can and you will," she said firmly. "I promise your darkness will pass, and you can return it then."

When the girls were gone, I put the necklace on. Lincoln and I went to bed. I clutched the stone as sleep arrived. When I blinked my eyes, it was morning. I hadn't dreamed, I hadn't moved, and I still held the opal. I did feel much better.

December

The next week passed quickly, and still not a sound from the poltergeist clan. I should have cursed them early and often, I thought. Lincoln and I can deal with the quiet just fine.

Tuesday at 7:00 p.m. was Audrey's show at the George Mason Gallery. I arrived fashionably late at 7:20 to find a pretty packed house. I knew this was a big deal for Audrey, but I had no idea what an event it was for the art world at large. I was greatly impressed and very happy for her.

Walking through the exhibit, I entered a second room, and there she was. Stunning. If anyone remembers Kandi from that TV show Two and a Half Men, that's what I saw. Knowing that Audrey was really smart and the Kandi character was really dim made it even more special. It occurred to me this was the first time she'd worn a dress and makeup since we met. Stunning. I don't believe I've ever been near such a beautiful woman. When she saw me, she broke off her conversation and greeted me with a hug.

"Great turnout," I said. "Congratulations."

"I'll be glad when it's over and I can get out of these heels" was her practical response.

"I like the look. I always like your look, but you're positively radiant tonight."

"Aw, thanks. I'm looking forward to getting the NVCC class and grading done later this week and taking a real break from all of this."

"I imagine you are. It's been a tough semester for you at both schools. I already have my grading done except for the final project entries. By next week I'm hoping we're both available for unstructured time together."

"Me too, December 12 can't come soon enough." That was our next new moon date.

"Do you need me to rough up any judges here?" I asked, laughing.

"We're all good," she said. "The truth is they won't let you do the gallery show until they're quite sure you'll pass with flying colors. Once they scheduled the date, I knew I was in the clear."

"So now you're a woman of letters. Audrey Welsh, MFA. Good job."

"Thank you, Dr. Craft. I've still got a few more letters to catch up with you, but I'm not rushing into that."

"Cherish the moment. The biggest days of our lives are few and far between."

"Stop," she said. "You sound like a Hallmark movie, all noble and deep and promising of a happy ending."

"When I'm with you, every moment is a real-life Hallmark movie," I said, playing along. "Okay, I'm done now. Where's the bar?"

As we changed rooms to hit the bar, Audrey asked, "Is Vicki's opal helping?"

"I'm wearing it now. I have been since she gave it to me. Things have been very much at peace in the house and in my head. I may have to become a believer in getting stoned." Frown from Audrey. "Does that mean I have to become a believer in the noises and apparitions?"

"Let's just stay on the skeptical dream scenario for now. More to be revealed."

We picked up a couple of glasses of wine and walked through the gallery. A lot of the visitors knew her or wanted to meet her. She politely engaged with each and every one. That interaction would have been just one more stressor in the past couple of months, but I could tell she was now relaxed and genuinely enjoying it.

"They like you, they really, really like you," I said as the crowd began thinning around 8:30. "What's next, DaVinci?"

"Teardown tomorrow and wrap up the NVCC stuff the rest of the week."

"Do you want help with teardown?"

Big laugh. "If I wanted your help for teardown, I'd have enlisted you at setup. With your expertise, most of the paintings would have already been down." I feigned hurt. "Don't pout," she said. "I know I'm quite anal about how things get packed and transported. I'm not good company at that stage, so it's better if I go it alone."

"A nice dinner outing one night?"

"Not a chance. The big event seems over, but there's a lot more to do. After the cleanup here, I still need a couple of days to wrap up school stuff. While that's happening, we're in peak gift-shopping mode at the store. I forbid you to see me again until I arrive at your place on Sunday. And don't cook dinner, I'm bringing something."

"Home cooking?"

"Maybe for some Chinese family. Trust me, you'll like it."

"Will you be wearing the heels?"

She punched me in the arm. We hugged and parted as she whispered in my ear, "Just till Sunday."

December 12 New Moon

Audrey arrived earlier than usual, around 5:00 p.m. A light snow had been falling for a couple of hours, and the driveway was starting to get covered. Lincoln and I met her on the porch, snowflakes in her hair. I put her bags on the kitchen table and we hugged, ending with a light peck on the cheek.

"Would you like a glass of fine-aged Costco wine?"

"Definitely. I'm pretty sure I'm not driving if the snow keeps up as forecast. Trey and Vicki can come and get me in his manly truck."

"You're welcome to stay over. Lincoln and I run a top-notch B&B here."

"I must confess, that little purple bag is an emergency overnight kit just in case of a true blizzard and closed roads. The paper bags are our dinner, and the big one is a Ouija board."

"Do we believe in Ouija boards?"

"Not really, but if we drink the whole box of wine, who knows? And it is period correct, hailing from 1891."

"Are you fully relaxed now that everything is behind you at both schools?"

"Pretty much. The store is quite busy but that's normal this time of year. All in all, I have to say I'm more light-hearted than I've been in a couple of years."

"Good to hear. Me too, despite the secret room and the journals and the more house activity to come. Between Lincoln and the pink opal, all seems to be good."

"I think I know what to get you for Christmas," she laughed.

"Another dog? I don't think Lincoln would approve."

We had hot and sour soup with Singapore noodles. The fortune cookies were profound. I got "Follow your heart and you will find happiness." Audrey's was "All things are difficult before they are easy."

As we cleaned up, I let Lincoln out in his yard. It was a blizzard. The flakes were gigantic in the light of the floods and we already had another three or four inches over the initial ground covering. "The weather outside is frightful," I reported.

"A fire would be delightful," Audrey responded.

"Since we've no place to go..." I set about building a bed of paper and kindling from the storage by the big fireplace in the great room. It didn't take long before the fire was prepared for the big logs. We sat down on the couch, the three of us, Lincoln in between. We were having a nice conversation about our recent events, and making great progress on the box o' wine when Audrey brought out her notes from the journals. "I had some time between shop hours after all the school stuff was done. I think you'll be interested in a distinct pattern of events."

"I would be interested in anything you would say," I said, a little buzzed.

"I charted the major human events from the journals and did some research. Dottie dies April 28, 1863. Betty fills the void to 1865 and dies March 27, 1865. Tom was killed on April 15, 1866. Cat dies July 29, 1868. Dr. Craft commits suicide on March 28, 1903."

A tear leaked down my cheek. Would I ever be able to deal with this without crying? Right now, I couldn't imagine it. "And?" I asked

"That's the research part. Every one of those dates is a new moon." The wine dulled the shock. "Richard, this may be a stretch, but do you remember the dates of your wife and son's deaths."

"I'm sure I'll never forget, March 6, 2019, and September 28, 2019."

She consulted her phone. "When did your brother die?"

"Bob died in 1998, October 20."

"All new moon dates. Every family death in this house aligns with the new moon. That can't be a coincidence."

Tears again. Gwen and Steven were only the latest in a long line of the Craft family legacy. Why did I bring them here? Losing myself in my loss made me think of Audrey's loss that I'd not asked about. "Audrey," I said. "Tell me about your friend who was killed."

She seemed surprised at the shift in conversation, but she spoke, "My fiancé, Clyde Francis."

"What happened?"

"We were within a couple of weeks of the wedding date, and went to meet some friends at a club downtown. It was a celebration." I could see her slipping back to that time. I felt guilty for asking. "As we were leaving, there was an altercation out front. A club security guard was being confronted by a couple of drunks he was sending out. They rushed him and he pulled his gun. In the scuffle it went off, shooting Clyde in the face."

"Audrey, that's horrible."

"Clyde's family was in Ohio, so I had to go to the coroner's office to officially identify the body."

"By yourself."

"No, a couple from our party stayed with me that night. We all loved Clyde. I think the medical examiner was trying to give some comfort when he told me Clyde would have been dead before he hit the ground." Now we were both crying.

"I certainly understand your feelings about guns, you'll never see or hear anything about them from me."

"Thank you for having that removed before you even knew the story. And thank you for asking about it now. I wasn't sure how to bring it up, but I wanted to share that loss since you're dealing with so much of your own." I was never going to mention the second gun that Don took with him.

Lincoln was getting antsy. "It's time for his out," I said. "And it's time for me to take tonight's cellar reading for Don."

"How is the box o' wine holding up?" she asked.

"We're making a pretty good run at it. No worries, I have two more behind it." I laughed.

"Show me your cellar readings."

We moved to the kitchen and let Lincoln out in the yard. He was a great comic intermission as he bounded like a hopping bunny through what now appeared to be at least a foot of snow. The temperature had dropped to 40 again, with the dewpoint remaining at 36. "That's not good," I said. "That's the second time we got a 15-degree temperature drop to an unfavorable range."

"Could it be the snow?"

"I got the impression from Don that everything was so well insulated that it really shouldn't change. If anything, I'd think deep snow like we're having would be further insulation. Plus, it wasn't snowing or even this cold when we got the last low temperature. We'll see what Don and the Churchville folks have to say in the morning."

We let the snow-covered Lincoln in and toweled him off. He was a happy guy in the winter wonderland.

"It's getting late," I said. "Do you still want to try the Ouija thing?"

"I do, and we have all the time in the world. I texted Vicki to let her know I was staying over."

"I trust she's okay with that."

"I think so," she laughed. "She texted back 'You go, girl!' She and Trey are probably already celebrating having the place to themselves, I swear they must have both been rabbits in a previous life."

"There could be worse lives than that."

"Amen, let's see what Ouija has to tell us about that."

Séance

We chose the hidden library for the setting. I brought in an extra chair and we sat, knees touching, with the board on our laps. The only light was from my great granduncle's two candles on the desk. It was romantic and sufficient. Lincoln lay down on the floor next to us, puzzled but content.

"Have you done this before?" she asked seriously.

"My brother and I played with one when we were kids in this house. I thought we were in touch with dead soldiers all the time until Bob confessed he was moving the thingy to goof on me. I was crushed."

"I always put it down to New Age hocus pocus, but Vicki believes it. I've been surprised at things it told us that I'm pretty sure neither of us could have known."

"Such as?"

"Simple things like the date on the milk in the fridge or how many receipts we wrote that day. I suppose it's possible we knew those things at some level but we didn't know that we knew them. I still have a hard time believing it's a true channel to the occult, but I'm a little more open to it now as possibly illuminating some subconscious thoughts or memories."

"Fair enough. Let's do it. Fingers lightly on the thingy? "

"Don't make me laugh, it's called a planchette."

"Sorry, I'll be serious. Who goes first?"

"It's your house and your ghosts. Ask it something."

"Ouija, what was Lincoln's name before I got him?" Testing myself for movement on that one I all but hovered my fingers over the thingy.

It moved very slowly picking out letters. It started and stopped and made big loops along the way, eventually spelling A-T-L-A-S-T. Then it was quiet.

"Well," asked Audrey.

"His name was Atlas. I'm interested. I'm certain I didn't move the thing, and I know you didn't know the name. That's pretty close. You go."

"What is Vicki's middle name?"

Another slow start, it moved sporadically and seemingly aimlessly. Eventually, it came up with R-E-N-E and stopped.

"And?"

"It is Renee but with two es."

"Maybe it's just a shitty speller?"

"Had you heard her name before?"

"No, and if I had I would have added the other e. How sure are you that you didn't guide the answer?"

"As sure as I can be. Should we try a question from the house?"

"Ask away."

"Are we here alone tonight?"

Less hesitation this time. The answer was NO.

"Who is with us?" she continued.

Fits and starts, landing on B-O-B. I expected almost any name but that one.

"Thoughts for questions?" she asked.

I did have one. I wanted to ask him how many guns he'd left in the house, but I was afraid he'd get it right and I'd have to explain it to Audrey. "What was Dad's pet name for Mom?" I swear I didn't move it and it quickly came up with P-O-O-K-I-E. "That's correct," I said. "Your turn."

"Bob, was this house haunted when you lived here?"

YES

"Were you ever in this room that we're in now?"

NO

"Did you ever see a ghost?"

T-O-M

I jumped in, "What was he wearing, scratch that, bad question. Was he wearing only shorts?"

NO

"Was he fully dressed?"

YES

"Did he talk to you?"

T-O-M

"Yes, Tom. Did he talk to you?"

T-O-M

"Is that what he said? Tom?"

YES

"Nothing else?"

D-E-A-D

"He was dead?"

H-E-A-D

"Where did he appear to you?" asked Audrey.

P-I-T

"Did he disappear after you saw him?" I asked.

YES

"He disappeared after I saw him too."

Back to Audrey. "Is anyone else with us?"

YES

"Who are you?"

T-O-M

"Tom," I asked. "How did you die?"

N-O-T-N-O-W

"Not now?"

K-N-O-W

"Not know, you don't know?"

YES

I stated the obvious. "He never knew what hit him."

Audrey: "Is there anyone here that has ever been in this room?"

NO

"Is there anyone else with us besides Bob and Tom?"

YES

"Who are you?"

S-T-E-V-E-N

"No," I said. "That's not possible."

YES

"Steven," Audrey asked. "How old are you?"

4

"Are you alone?"

NO. M-O-M

"Is your mom here?"

Through my tears, I watched the planchette drag our hands and arms across GOODBYE.

We tried more questions without response. The candles were almost burned out. It seemed like minutes, but we had been in the small library for almost two hours. I had to stand up. "Let's look at the snow," I spoke.

We blew out the candles, and I poured more wine in the kitchen. I did some math while draining the box. Darrel and I had started it on our spaghetti night, but this last trickle still came down to at least six glasses each for Audrey and me. My pleasant buzz from the fireside had faded with the passing hours. I was hoping this glass would renew it. Tears were already gone. I was also hoping I was cried out for good.

We stood on the covered front porch, holding each other in the cold, watching the snow still falling. I don't know that Trey's he-man truck could have rescued Audrey at this point. We could only stay out a few minutes, and I threw some kindling and a log on the bed of coals in the fireplace. We sat fairly close, but Lincoln was between us as usual.

"Are you okay?" asked Audrey.

"I should be," I said. "The presumed appearance of Bob and Steven was a surprise, but we didn't learn anything new about our cast of players. You've been on most of this journey with Lincoln and me. Are you okay?"

"I think we'll all be okay. It's been so much so fast, but I think we'll all be okay. A good night's rest on a snowy night will be nice. I'll be the girl looking out the window for Santa."

She picked the room where she had sat before and where Amy almost seduced me. It must be magical, I thought, but I had Steven on my mind. Four-year-old Steven and Lincoln would have been best friends for sure. I kissed her at her door. No tongue or lingering passion, just a kiss, but it was our first on the lips.

Really

M orning came, and the snow was still falling. When Audrey came down for coffee. she wore only the long flannel shirt she had borrowed as a nightgown the evening before. A couple of buttons left open shared some cleavage to complement her long nude legs. Lincoln and I couldn't help but notice the informality, the new-found familiarity, and the sensual tension in the room. She sat down to coffee as if none of that was present and started in on small talk about the weather.

"Looks like I may be trapped here another day if that snow doesn't let up. There looks to be about a foot of snow on the driveway."

"We'll see how it goes." I said. "I was about to send Lincoln out to shovel the walk and check things out."

"I'm not in any rush to go. I already called Vicki. She's closing the store today because of the weather. Our customers would be more inclined to stay at home with their crystals on a day like today."

"How did you sleep?"

"I started slow, just resting comfortably, pondering what a night would be like in your haunted house. It's a very comfy bed, and the temperature was perfect. There was that little interruption of entertainment that roused me quite nicely. After that, I was dead to the world."

"Lincoln and I had a similar night. I was wondering if you heard what we heard. The footsteps in the halls are pretty common to us, but there were other unusual sounds beyond the normal voices that we've come to know. I was going to get up and take a look around, but it was over quickly and then all went quiet."

"This may seem a little forward, but I did enjoy the visit last night, and it doesn't have to be over so quickly this time."

"Hmmm. I'm not following. What visit?"

"Our little relational icebreaker when you came into my room and ravaged me. It brought me out of a long drought in an unexpected, but very welcome, way. I'm still feeling quite amorous and a little greedy for more. I'd be happy to thank you in a very special way if you would like to join me again."

Quiet.

"Audrey, I didn't come to your room last night."

She laughed out loud. "I love your sense of humor."

"I'm not kidding. I never left my room. Maybe you had a dream?"

She laughed again. "If I did it was one hell of a wet dream. The bed is probably still as soaked as I am."

"Audrey, this is serious. You're a beautiful woman, and I'm very attracted to you. I haven't been with a woman since my wife died. I'd love to share a bed with you, but I promise I didn't last night."

Quiet.

"Silly boy, acting all polite this morning." She stood up and undid the remaining buttons on the flannel shirt, pulling it back to let her breasts hang freely above her flat stomach and bare shaved body. She wasn't kidding about being soaked, I could see the glistening moisture of her damp vagina in the morning light. "Come with me," she said with a smile. "We need to do some further investigation."

I took her hand as she led me up the stairs to her bedroom. Lincoln sensed this wasn't his playtime and retired to my room.

She closed the door behind us and drew me in for a deep passionate kiss as she let the flannel covering drop to the floor. Audrey slowly undressed me, alternating kissing and licking as she moved up and down my body, settling on her knees to pleasure me with her soft hands and her warm mouth.

We ended up on the bed together. Soft kisses and warm hands and murmurs of mutual pleasure as we explored each other's bodies. We stayed together in this shared foreplay for a long time when Audrey said, "Lie back and get comfortable, it's my turn to drive."

She climbed on top of me, and I was instantly inside of her hot wetness as she forced her hips down on mine. Her eyes were very wide open as she rode me slowly and firmly, keeping us tightly coupled. Her moans of passion were glorious. Her body above me was perfect. She stared deeply at me with a look that showed both arousal and confusion. I probably wore the same face, not believing that I could be so lucky to be inside of this amazing vessel. She came loudly, as did I, and then collapsed upon me with more kisses.

"Richard, I'm so glad you're here right now," she spoke, breathing heavily.

"Me too, Audrey, me too."

"I'm scared," she continued. "I love what we just started, but I'm scared."

"What's to be scared of?"

"You're not the man who was in me last night."

"Audrey, it had to be a dream."

"I can't say that, it was so real."

We lay there in silence for a long time.

"What can I do?" I asked.

"Anything. I don't want to think right now. Light a fire. Tell a joke. Throw frisbee to Lincoln in the snow. Anything mindless to make some distance from this. I'll think later."

"Did you know that if you give a man a fire, you keep him warm for a day, but if you set a man on fire, you keep him warm for the rest of his life?"

"That did it," she said. "I shudder to think that mindless is my new normal prescription for dealing with fears. You're my rock of mindless." She laughed now.

Winter Wonderland

Lincoln wore out quickly fighting his way through the deep snow to entertain Audrey with the most awkward frisbee display ever. When he came in, he was caked with the white stuff, snowballs hanging everywhere. Rather than pull out all his fur with the snow removal we laid a blanket in front of the fire to let him thaw and drip. He seemed content and took a nap while he dried.

The blizzard was now barely flurries, but the accumulation was impressive. It wasn't any kind of a record but it crested eighteen inches, enough for a standstill in Northern Virginia. We had plenty of firewood, and all the utilities were hanging in there. It could be a good day for a puzzle, something we had plenty of.

Audrey called Vicki to see how the shop was holding up while I was retrieving the laptop to take morning readings. I took it as a good sign that I was hearing giggles from the next room. No doubt the girls were exchanging conquest stories. It seemed Audrey had blocked the dream for now. It had to be a dream.

The numbers in the cellar were back to normal, but news from Churchville was not. Don had sent an email an hour ago with pictures from that morning. Somehow, overnight, our artifacts had acquired the patina of a hundred-plus years. I had to call him.

Don answered on the first ring. He didn't even say hello, he said, "I don't know Richard. George and I are as stumped as we were when we saw the stuff in its original condition. I'm glad we have a lot of pictures to document both states."

"Bizarre," I commented. "Like so many other things that relate to this house."

"No explanation for it, that's for sure. George is still wandering around muttering to himself."

"Should I keep doing the cellar readings?"

"Might as well, since the tools are already there. It won't give us any answers to the sudden change in the artifacts, but the fluctuations are still a curiosity."

"Seems like curiosities are the continuing norm here. I doubt that we'll find any more journals with real answers."

"Speaking of the journal answers, George made some headway with the people with the Virginia Department of Historic Resources. Since you don't have an official cemetery, just journal references to unmarked potential burial sites, the director of the department can issue a permit for excavation. George has already made that application, and it appears it would go forward without any real reservations. We will still need to circle back to Darrel and get the local law enforcement position on whether or not they want to pursue a murder investigation. I'll handle that for you. I'd be surprised if they would, given the age and circumstances."

"Should I expect a visit from the historical people?"

"No. They have declared themselves as an interested party, but they have no resources for actual disinterment. Any college with anthropology and archeological assets would jump at the chance to put students in the field to handle that. I'll do some research on that as well. I know Penn State has the skills, as we defer to them all the time here, but there may be more local schools preferable to your area. We have plenty of time for that. I'm pretty sure it would be springtime before any digging would happen, assuming you'd want to take that step. It's entirely your call."

"I do want to follow through. I'm still a ghost skeptic but, if we did find remains of Tom and Betty, I think they deserve a proper end spot somewhere."

"Sounds good," said Don. "I'll keep you up to date as I know things. Right now, I have to console George."

"Thanks."

As I hung up, I heard the sounds of a big diesel churning up the drive. We don't get snow plows here, so I walked out to the porch to see what was happening. The wet but newly unencumbered Lincoln barked his way to the front of the house with Audrey in tow.

"Surprise!" yelled Vicki, standing through the sunroof of Trey's monster truck. "We're the only thing on the road, and it's a blast." They jumped out into knee-deep snow and broke ground to the porch.

"How bad is it?" I asked.

"Without four-wheel drive and pretty significant ground clearance, it would be hopeless," said Trey. "Even this guy struggled at times, but here we are."

"How did you get here so quickly?" Audrey asked Vicki. "I was just on the phone with you."

"We were stopped at the gas station just down the road when you called."

Vicki wanted to know if we had a fire going. We did, and Audrey took her there. Naturally, Lincoln followed his girlfriends.

"Would you like some coffee?" I asked Trey.

"Beer please, a lot of beer." We heard giant whooping and laughter from the girls.

He waited on the beer and took a giant swig as I stood quizzical. "You'll know why in a second," he said. We walked into the great room to two hugging girls and a jumping dog.

"Look," said Audrey, dragging Vicki's left hand to my face. Trey must have dipped deeply into his NFL retirement funds for the Super Bowl equivalent of an engagement ring. I happily joined the group hug.

"You guys get out of here," Vicki said. "We demand some girl time. Lincoln, you can stay." Trey and I retired to the kitchen.

Trey was ready for a second beer. "I'm not sure yet if I'm celebrating or mourning."

"The bachelor's dilemma. I think you're okay with this one. You and Vicki are a unique and special couple who deserve each other. I mean that in a good way."

"You and Audrey seem to be getting along well. Should we make it a double?" he laughed.

"Too soon, I'm not sure we're sure we're even a couple yet."

"That's not what Vicki told me this morning." Punch on the arm and an evil laugh this time.

"You and Vicki are a unique and special couple who deserve each other. I mean that in the other way now."

"Hey, Vicki told me about your secret room. Can I see it? It sounds awesome."

"It is awesome," he said when we got there. "Look at all these saws and sharp things. It's positively medieval."

"State of the art medicine in the late 1800s."

Trey was especially interested in how Don was able to envision the space and the whole mechanical process of digging and scraping paint to figure out the entry.

"Are you sure this is the only secret room?"

"I think so, but this one sat undiscovered for over a hundred years, so who knows?"

"Can I get a tour of the rest of the place?"

We started in the attic, as usual.

"Audrey talked about this room as the perfect artist's studio," said Trey. "I'm not an artist, but I think I see why she would like it."

"She said the size and placement of the windows was perfect. I wouldn't know either, but I told her it was hers to use anytime."

"Who was in the army?"

"That would be my brother Bob. He was older than I was. He didn't get the luxury of passing on the draft like I did. We were close as kids, but things got more distant after Vietnam. He became somewhat of a recluse here."

We worked our way back down through the other rooms and on to where the girls were still engaged, literally and figuratively. They weren't giggling now.

"Audrey told me about last night," said Vicki.

I froze. Is nothing secret or sacred among these people?

"I know you guys don't believe in the supernatural like I do, and that's okay, but there is a difference between the explainable and the unexplainable. I think we'd all agree there are a lot of unexplainable things surrounding this house. This wasn't one of those, and it's nothing to fear. I know what it was."

"How?" I asked.

"I've done my research. There is no shortage of both myths and facts about an incubus–succubus relationship. I even dipped into the dark web a few years back trying to conjure up such a relationship for myself."

Quiet.

I couldn't hold back, it was too tense. "Is that where Trey came from?"

Tension broken, we all laughed.

"That would have been too easy," Vicki said. "The thrill of the chase is much more rewarding."

"Like climbing the mountain and planting your flag?" Audrey this time, I was glad we were all lightening up.

"Exactly," said Vicki. "Seriously though, I'm certain what Audrey experienced is something called sleep paralysis. It's well-documented and something that a lot of people experience at least once in their lifetime. It has to do with the release of hormones in REM sleep. That happens to all of us every time we sleep, but external conditions could heighten it, almost to hallucination. There are some obvious questions to consider. Audrey, have you been under a lot of stress recently?"

"Yes."

"Were you unusually tired or lacking sleep when you went to bed last night?"

"Yes."

"Had you experienced any new sources of stress just before your bedtime?"

"Yes."

I thought this was starting to sound like a Ouija board Q&A.

"Were you unusually sexually aroused when you went to bed?"

Audrey blushed. "Yes."

"I'm confident," said Vicki. "That those other factors impacted your normal hormonal response to trigger the sleep paralysis and the resulting dream. Even as an occult believer, I know there is no sustainable proof ever of a human being violated sexually by a spirit. It never happened. There's no doubt in my mind. Have we put that to rest?"

"Not quite," said Audrey. "I'm a little embarrassed to bring it up, but I was sure I'd had intercourse just from the extremely drenched state of the bed when it was over."

Vicki laughed loudly. "Maybe you guys need to leave again. It seems I have to start with the birds and the bees and the history of erotic dreams to convince Audrey of the existence of squirting orgasms."

"But I've never had one before."

"Welcome to the waterfall, Audrey. Trust me, you'll want one again," laughed Vicki. "Would you agree Trey?"

"Completely, but I've had a very good surfing coach." More laughter.

The jury is in. There is nothing secret or sacred among these people. I guess I fit right in.

Paralysis Analysis

We set up a puzzle on the big coffee table in the great room and played with it for a while. The girls were sitting on the floor while Trey and I occupied the couch. Lincoln sucks at puzzles, so he napped again. I opened a fresh box of wine for three of us; Trey stuck with beer. By the time we finished the borders, Vicki and Audrey drifted off to borrow my laptop. I asked Audrey to send Don the midday cellar numbers, and they went to Audrey's room. Vicki was going to give her an internet crash course on sleep paralysis and squirting orgasms to put her mind at rest. I hope someone gets a chance to clear my search history before I die.

I asked Trey if he and Vicki wanted to stay over. Snow had stopped, but it was still quite daunting from our limited view.

"No thanks," said Trey. "I'm pretty sure my fiancée will desire an Aquaman roleplay after today's discussion. I could go for an early dinner though. How about pizza delivery?"

We jokingly called the local pizza place for fun to hear them stammer through an apology for not having delivery, but there was someone there, and they were making pizza. We ordered up a large meat and a large veggie and assured them we'd be picking up in thirty minutes or so. We'd do a little cruising first to assess the roads. Trey told the girls what we were doing, and we set out as fearless explorers.

"Nice ride," I said as we climbed into the cab.

"If you ever need a truck for tearing down trees or hauling wood, let me know. I love to do that stuff. It's also exactly what you need on a day like today. I use it to tow the boat and for various projects, but if I didn't have a boat or projects, I'd still want one of these anyway."

"Who wouldn't." I was already having truck envy.

"People who ever look at a fuel gauge and the price of diesel," he laughed. Truck envy has a larger barrier to entry than flashlight envy. I was over it now.

When we got to the road, we could see a plow had been through. It looked like they'd just knocked off the top layer. The streets were still white. The plow had made a large raised bank at the driveway, which Trey enjoyed crashing through.

"This is all good out here for us," said Trey as we traveled. "No traction concerns, but ground clearance was even a challenge for me earlier. When we drop below freezing overnight, none of this will be good for anybody. I imagine everything will still be closed tomorrow so they can make a solid run at plowing and treating. No snow and a pickup in temperature should make this a memory after that."

Street after street was the same or worse.

"Are you keeping Audrey for the night again?"

"Only if she wants to be kept. She could always hitch a ride with you and Vicki."

"I'm willing to bet neither of them will bring that up." He gave me the guy-to-guy-about-girl grin. "I know she likes you a lot, and she hasn't made any romantic interests that obvious for a long time."

"Did you know Clyde?"

"Vicki did. That was very shortly after she and Audrey had become friends, which was a little before my time. That's a sad story we try to forget. How did you hear about it?"

"I'm an idiot, I asked. I knew she had a strong aversion to guns, and she mentioned someone close had been killed with one."

"How did that go?"

"It came up when we were talking about my late wife and son, so I think we were on fairly common ground."

"Wow, I hope the two of you have some better topics planned for the future."

"Me too, we'll probably start with you and Vicki." We both chuckled.

Back home with pizza. The girls and Lincoln greeted us on the porch. Audrey gave me the biggest hug ever, declaring, "I'm all better. Vicki fixed me!"

"Hallelujah," shouted Trey. "Can you fix me next?"

"I'll fix you good when we get home," said Vicki. "After a few hours of incubus and orgasm class, I have some new ideas."

"Promise?" Trey said.

It was time to conquer some pizza and libations so our guests could get home before the roads froze. Trey was right, neither Vicki nor Audrey mentioned her joining them for the ride. Lincoln and I didn't either. A little more fireside puzzle time after dinner, and they were gone, leaving the couch and the wine to Audrey and me, with Lincoln sitting in his middle place.

"Tell me how Vicki fixed you."

"I always knew she was into the supernatural, but she's way deeper than I ever imagined. She pulled up some fascinating research articles, a number from peer-reviewed journals, on this whole world of spectrophiles and alleged paranormal intercourse."

"What's a spectrophile?"

"Someone desirous of a physical ghost relationship."

"Demi Moore?"

"Movie references did come up, but Vicki showed me more and more serious research that debunks any possibility of such a thing and confirms, at least for me, the science of the sleep paralysis explanation. I feel so much better. And normal again."

"There go my fantasies of trysting with Glynda the good witch."

"Seriously Richard, I have to give Vicki a lot more credit for doing her homework and understanding her craft. I'm going to pay a lot more attention to her crystal talks and other new-age stuff from now on."

"I have a hard time admitting it, but since she gave me that pink opal, I'm positive I've been better at dealing with the world of this house. Did you tell her about our séance?"

"I did, and she thought it was a valid experience. Maybe we should repeat with her as a guide."

"I'm in for anything at this point. I haven't told you about my phone call with Don this morning."

"Something new?"

"Something old. Our pristine Civil War artifacts woke up this morning with the proper hundred years of patina that would have been expected."

"Are you serious?"

"I can't make this stuff up. It's all beyond my tiny imagination. By the way, what was the cellar temperature this afternoon?"

"It was 50, is it time to do it again?"

The laptop was on charge in the kitchen. When we checked it was 50 again.

"Since we're here, we should probably let Lincoln out," I said. He agreed in the usual way when he heard the word "out."

The night was beautiful, crisp, and very clear. Audrey pointed out a number of constellations I had heard of but never known how to see. I was embarrassed by my previous attempts to regale her with my amateurish celestial knowledge of Orion's Belt and the Big Dipper. Feeling quite small in the universe, I knew I could learn a lot from this woman and her friend Vicki.

Audrey slept in my bed tonight. I have to get a king, I thought, Lincoln needs more space. I think Lincoln read my mind, as he hopped to the floor. They are sensitive beasts.

Tonight was all slow passion for both of us, wonderfully beginning to learn the things that please each other. I asked her if she had gotten any pointers on the squirt thing from Vicki.

"Maybe, but I hear it's best with a willing and patient partner."

"I'm all yours and ready to dive in. Guide me on a new journey." She did.

No Snow Today

W e slept in until almost 8:00 a.m. The morning was as crisp and clear as the night had been. Bright sunshine greeted us with our morning coffee. Cellar temperatures were still at 50, and I sent that on to Don.

"Vicki texted me that the shop is closed again, so you're stuck with me at least for most of the day," said Audrey.

"After last night, my little mermaid, I think I could be happy to be stuck with you forever."

"You are turning out to be a straight-A student in my new class." She laughed that wonderful tinkling laugh.

"I'm up for some extra credit as soon as you are."

"I can see that happening."

We settled back in front of the fire, until we heard the sound of sirens out front.

"That's odd," I said. "Lincoln, let's check it out."

"Let me know if we're on fire," said Audrey. "Otherwise I'm good right here with coffee." I was happy to see her that relaxed.

The siren stopped, but the flashing spinning lights were still on as Lincoln and I found a police truck in our driveway. When Darrel hopped out, Lincoln ran to him and I put up my hands. "Are we in trouble?"

He laughed. "Just the usual. I'm not even working today," he said, which explained the jeans and sweatshirt uniform. "Since we got these new Explorers, I just love going out to play in the snow. And the lights and sirens are always fun when there's no one around and you just need to be a kid."

"How are the roads?"

"Still shit, but everything is closed and plows are out in force. The sunshine will help. I used you as an excuse for a destination, knowing you'd be trapped. Did you get another car, or do you have company?"

"Per your astute observation skills, Lincoln and I are enjoying the company of a lady friend, Audrey."

"Did the wi-fi password grant you access?"

"Funny guy, do you have time to meet her?"

"I've got all day, my friend. I wanted to give you an update on some conversation with Don, but we can do that later."

"We can do it with Audrey. She's been my paranormal partner through this whole thing, and I forgot to tell her about my conversation with Don about pending excavation possibilities."

"Great, that's part of my update."

On the way through the kitchen, I filled the big insulated coffee pot to take with us and found a mug for Darrel.

"Audrey Welsh, meet Darrel Metz. Darrel, meet Audrey. Darrel is our local constable, but he's just a friend today since he's off duty."

"Hi Darrel, you didn't sound off duty."

"Oh shit, I forgot to turn out the lights. I'll be right back." We all laughed as he sprinted to the car and back.

"That's embarrassing," he said. "Let's start over. Very nice to see you, Audrey, Richard talks about you often, and I'm glad we got to meet."

"Likewise. He's talked about you as well. He hasn't come right out and said it, but I know he's been enjoying his guy time with you and Don, who I also hope to meet."

"I have no doubt you'll be meeting Don soon. That's actually why I stopped by to go over some things with Richard. Meeting you was a bonus."

"Audrey," I said. "When I told you about the aging on the Civil War stuff, I forgot to mention that Don thinks there could be some disinterment in our future."

"Speaking of the aging artifacts, are you planning to sue Churchville for mishandling your no longer priceless finds?"

"I hadn't thought of that. That might be fun to prank George with while he's in mourning over it."

"Yeah, Don said he was deeply disturbed over the change."

"I guess I would be too," I said. "But on the scale of disturbances around here, that news was about a one-percenter. I think the murder, other deaths, and suicide take the top billing. So, what's today's update?"

"Good news and good news, I think. I took up the murder case with the police chief, and he's covered it with the city manager. It's not something they feel a need to criminally pursue. Per Don and George, we're also getting clearance from the Virginia Historic Resources people. That would put the ball in your court on how to deal with Tom and Betty."

"Were you concerned about a possible murder investigation?"

"Not really, just doing due diligence. Had it been an election year, you never know what a candidate would seize on to stir things up. But we're in normal times right now, so this comes across as just an interesting piece of ancient history. Now the question is whether or not you want to pursue it."

"I feel like I have to, knowing what we know. What do you think, Audrey?"

"I'm pretty new to your family history, but I feel like I've been steeped in its intensity forever. I know how it affects you, and it's not always in a good way. I think anything that brings closure to the past is good for you."

"I agree with Audrey," said Darrel. "I'm also new here, but after watching your reactions in going through the journals, I think you'd benefit from being able to take some action. Since there is no criminal investigation, I have no official role here, but I'd offer to follow through with you as a friend. I know Don feels the same way."

"What's next?" I asked.

"Based on my conversation with Don, the paperwork from the historical folks giving the blessing to dig, finding a college that has the resources to do it, and probably sitting and waiting until springtime," said Darrel. "You can pull the plug at any point until the first shovel is in the ground. Don and I can handle all the details for you. Just say the word."

"Word," I said.

The Next Séance

T he snow was gone. Over the next week, Audrey vacillated between
nights at my place and back at the shop. She and Vicki were staying
close, sorting out possible wedding plans and dates. Since Audrey and I
were now considered officially coupled, we spent more time with Vicki
and Trey. Audrey still wanted to do a secret room séance with Vicki,
and the opportunity came up quickly when Trey invited me to a football game. He dropped the girls off when he picked me up.

I like football, but I let him know I've never been a student of
the game. I can't name most of the positions, and I know nothing at
all about game plans and strategy. We were going to a Sunday night
game in DC between the Commanders and the New York Giants, both
currently floundering teams. The girls brought some "séance candles"
from the shop and were making their evening plans with Lincoln when
we guys headed out in the big truck.

"I played with the Giants for five years, my entire NFL career,"
Trey said.

"I'm embarrassed that I didn't know that."

"Don't be. I was a defensive tackle, not a glamour position."

"I'm embarrassed again. What does a defensive tackle do?"

Trey laughed, "You really aren't a student of the game."

"I told you so. I enjoy watching, though."

"A defensive tackle is a line position. My main job was to get in the way of the offense. That's why you never hear of us. All those boring plays where someone runs up the middle and gains nothing are our successes. Not generally highlight reel events."

"Still pretty important."

"We defensive tackles like to think our role is very important, just rarely recognized. That's pretty true for most linemen. Our biggest respect comes mostly from ourselves."

It turned out that wasn't the case. When we got to the game, we had special parking and went to the sidelines first. I discovered that Trey Roadcap had a lot of respect from a lot of people and was, in fact, quite a celebrity. For the game, we joined other retired players in a special booth right next to the announcers.

As I listened to the real students and participants of the game, I learned that Trey was better than most at getting in the way. He also had a better-than-most record of sacks, interceptions, and even a couple of touchdowns, all above and beyond his basic role of getting in the way. I felt like a celebrity just standing with him. He was also a very gracious host to me, introducing me to everyone and making sure I had access to all the amenities.

The game itself was not a stellar performance for either team, but the Giants won, so we left happy. In a former life I had been a Washington Redskins fan, and the Giants, Eagles, and especially Cowboys were our hated rivals. But the Commanders were never the Redskins to me, so I was fine with the Giants' win.

We found the girls with Lincoln in front of the fireplace. "Good game?" asked Audrey.

"Not so hot, but the team we were rooting for eked it out, so it was okay. The most fun for me was finding out what a defensive tackle did and how Trey was a luminary hero at that position."

"That's my mountain of a man," said Vicki.

"Any luck with the ghosts tonight?" I asked. Things turned a little somber and quiet.

"Steven came back," said Audrey.

"And we met Gwen," joined Vicki. "She really loves you and Steven."

Goddamned tears.

"They're happy together," said Audrey. "Part of their souls will always live with you." Probably intending to make me feel better.

"That's nice," I said. "Anything from brother Bob?" I still had a hard time with Gwen and Steven. I guess I always will. I didn't know what else to say.

"No Bob tonight," said Vicki, "But Tom dropped in. I didn't sense any darkness in his presence. I think he wants you to know something. He told us to look in the books."

"The journals?"

"He just said books. We lost contact after that."

"Did you look in the books?"

"No," said Vicki. "It was getting too late, and three of us need to get some sleep so two of us can work in the morning. Kiss your boyfriend good night, Audrey." She headed out with Trey.

I frowned as Audrey picked up Lincoln and gave him a big peck on the top of his little head. She made it better by putting him down and drawing me close for a long and very sensual connection, making me wish she wasn't leaving.

"January 11 is our next new moon," she said. "We'll have plenty of time for reading before then. Plus, if you don't mind, I'd like to bring some painting stuff over and try out the attic as a studio space."

"Whew," I sputtered. "At first, I thought you were telling me you wouldn't see me until January 11."

"Hah, not a chance. Next week is Christmas, and we have a lot of naughty time to make up for before then. I'll be back tomorrow night with the studio stuff."

Another great kiss.

"Lincoln," I said. "I'm not sure I can sleep right away after that. I definitely wouldn't be able to roll over." I know he got the joke. "Want to see if we can figure out what 'look in the books' means?"

I got an extension cord and dragged a lamp into the library space. It seemed more efficient than candles and a flashlight to get the big picture. Studying the layout before making selections, the medical reference books Don and Darrel had looked at came from the top shelf. Everything up there was like the Wikipedia of nineteenth-century medicine, big general encyclopedias of all medical knowledge. The rest of the books appeared to follow very specific topics in detail. Anatomy had many books with topics as specific as hands and toes. The same minutiae were found in biology, chemistry, and every other medical topic imaginable. Dr. Craft took his studies seriously and invested in them deeply.

I began to notice that some of the books had other papers tucked inside. There was also another journal included in one section. I started there, randomly pulling out the journal next to an embalming book that had some papers in it. I started reading my great granduncle's thoughts and studies when I realized this couldn't have been random at all. The first page was one paragraph:

May 24, 1862

> "I have become convinced, by study and thought, that the human body and the soul are the same, separated only by the final decomposition of the earthly flesh. If it is possible to preserve the physical body, the soul will remain. I wish this for my beloved wife. She has begun to exhibit symptoms of chronic wasting disease. I don't know how much time we have."

I swear I felt the room chill and a whispered voice, "Look in the books." I was alone and feeling the same fear as the first time I heard Tom's voice. As spooked as I was, Lincoln was oddly calm, almost trancelike.

The girls had just gotten back home when I called to tell them what was happening. "Walk away from it," said Vicki. "I don't think Tom means to harm you, but you should never engage alone if it can be avoided. I'll come back with Audrey tomorrow, and we can read more. Just walk away and try to get some sleep."

I went down to the fireplace and laid on the couch with Lincoln. I was asleep in seconds, dreaming of being in a park with Gwen and Steven. Steven was a normal four-year-old boy and introduced me to his friend Elizabeth, the same Elizabeth I knew when I was a four-year-old dreamer.

The Books

I awoke, refreshed and happy that Gwen and Steven were well. I guess I still believe more strongly in the explanations of dreams than in actual ghosts, but any appearance of comfort and peace for Gwen and Steven, real or imagined, is good for my soul.

I put on coffee, let the dog out, measured the normal cellar temps, and retrieved the journal I had started reading last night. I knew the girls were coming tonight to help with the books, but I'd already seen something I couldn't leave untouched. Lincoln and I sprawled again on the great room couch to read more. The journal went on from the opening entry where I started, and stopped, last night.

> "The war has provided fertile ground for the study of human preservation. We have graduated today from arsenic treatment to arterial embalming with Holme's treatment. This has proven results but there are earlier studies science has missed or ignored that, I believe, will achieve the lasting result of maintaining the body and soul.

> "Gabriel Clauderus used a balsamic immersion technique in the last century with promise. I too have experimented with the immersion style of preservation with

some success. I have also investigated curing methods. Those results will take longer to evaluate, and I fear the time is too short for that.

"Further chemical work has been documented by William and John Hunter of the Universities of Glasgow and Edinburgh with primary components of turpentine, lavender, and chamomile. These were important advances but missed an essential piece, previously discovered. Carl Wilhelm Scheele's 1774 essay on magnesia nigra was not available to Clauderus and was not known, rejected or possibly misunderstood in value by the Hunters and Thomas Holmes. The Scheele concoction of manganese, spirit of salt, and spirit of wine produced a brew that, when combined with the Holme's elixir, can be the base of permanent preservation. This I believe and seek to prove."

I read the words of Dr. Craft's experimental trials. I had to walk away many times. I needed to process the period, his mindset, and the details that answered questions I didn't know to ask, or became increasingly afraid to ask. The journal overwhelmed me with all of these.

My great granduncle wrote that he was a believer in stoicism as a philosophy and a reality. I had to look that up and still can't fully wrap my mind around it. From the doctor's writings, it appears he believed that body and soul are the same. He saw a dichotomy between the animate and inanimate state but not a separation at death. His interpretation was the separation is at decomposition and, if that could be arrested, the soul remains with the body. He was fascinated by the concept of physical body preservation long before the war years, but it was the war years that allowed him to test his mind.

Very early in the conflict, Holme's embalming fluids were patented and distributed. The Mansion House Union Hospital received many gallons of the elixir and passed some on to Dr. Craft's field hospital. Since Dr. Craft usually only dealt with immediate needs, embalming was not a mainstay of his practice, but he did perform the embalming procedure on known bodies that would be returned to their homes.

He also had unknown bodies that would be relegated to the burial pit. These and other related pieces of discarded anatomy were his to test with his philosophical and scientific theories.

The best results were presumed to be available by working with the freshest material, taken during life or immediately after death. His initial research was with small body parts like fingers, easily cut from an arm that was about to be amputated. Eyeballs were harvested as part of the embalming preparation, and these too he kept. These began the basis of his immersion studies, based on the work of Clauderus. Subsequent experimentation involved fresh limbs, dried and wrapped in burlap for curing. As I read the technical descriptions of these experiments, the current implications became clear to me in horrific visualization. I'd been reading the entire morning and I had to stop.

Lincoln and I alternately played frisbee, napped, took a long walk, made the cellar measurements at noon, and puttered. I couldn't decide if Dr. Craft was a visionary or a demon. His writing was compelling in both theory and scientific method, but his deeds, carried out clinically and thought out with a seemingly impartial questioning mind, were unimaginable to me.

The afternoon reading continued to be both enlightening and disturbing.

"The Clauderus immersive specimens are yielding positive results after several months of storage. There is a control group row of the Clauderus chemistry alone and a second and third set of samples. One is the Clauderus solution with the added Scheele recipe. The last is the Holmes mixture with the Scheele addition. All maintain texture without separation, though the Clauderus-based jars show some minor deterioration. The Holmes and Scheele combination group appears perfectly preserved, consistent with my theory. The Holmes and Scheele combination is yet to be tested in full embalmment."

"Lincoln," I said, "I don't know if your great great granduncle is Dr. Craft or Dr. Frankenstein or Dr. Mengele, but I do know why this place should be haunted."

The good doctor's state of mind, though still clinical, seemed to become more rushed as his wife's condition deteriorated through 1862. He continued specimen collection and preservation experiments, now convinced he had the final solution in the Holmes Scheele mixture. He did some field embalmment with this formula, even though he'd never see the long-term results when the bodies were shipped home. Those allowed him to refine the mechanical aspects of the procedure to ensure maximum evacuation of body fluids and maximum introduction of the preservation chemical mix.

In December of 1862, a fortuitous visit by an ambulance wagon gave him what he had been hoping for. The wagon was on the way to the Mansion House Hospital but stopped to drop off two immediate amputation candidates. The driver also wanted Dr. Craft to take another body for his pit. It was a young unknown Confederate soldier. The man was still barely alive but quite malnourished in appearance and advanced in illness. As they offloaded the Union surgery candidates, the sick man coughed blood onto his uniform blouse. Consumption. Perfect. The journal entry read:

December 21, 1862

"God has blessed me today with the hope of preserving my dear Dorothy's body and soul. Her illness has continued to progress, and I fear she has only short weeks or months on this earth. I can't lose her."

The details of two quick amputations and the initial examination of the young Confederate came next. His body still lay in the yard where he was unloaded. The journal described covering the man's nose and mouth with an anesthetic cone and topping it with a chloroform-soaked sponge that rendered him fully unconscious and incapable.

"As the lucky young man was breathing close to his last, I started opening the arteries to begin the

138

embalmment. He was about to enter eternal life in body and soul. As his sick blood entered the dirt, the healing serum was entering his body. This was the trial that would save dear Dorothy's soul. I did my best work in skill and prayer."

The entry went on to the finishing touches of the operation. When the process was complete, the body was dragged into the root cellar for storage and observation. The final perfect experiment was over. I couldn't breathe thinking about the twisted last moments of the man's death.

The soldier's body and, to Dr. Craft, his soul lay untouched in the darkness for a week before its next viewing. Dr. Craft continued,

"As I opened the cellar door in daylight, I was confronted with the perfection of my work and studies. What should have been a rotting corpse on the body pile was a vibrant-looking youth of health and good color. Thank you, God, for your gifts and guidance."

The girls would be here soon.

Studio Time

I was greatly relieved to see Trey with the girls. After last night and today, I wanted a complete coming up for air before I dove back into the abyss of the library contents. I know Vicki and Audrey were expecting to help with the books, but I was willing, and wanting, to put it off another day at least. I thought that would be an easier escape with Trey around.

Hugs all around and Chinese food again, this time a great array of choices. "Family style tonight," said Audrey. "I got all of my favorites all at once. I also got some veggie crap thing for Vicki." She laughed. "Let's eat before we get to work. We have a lot of stuff to unload and set up in the truck."

Dinner was fabulous. I joined Trey in going the beer route tonight, an excellent choice. I even tried the "veggie crap thing" and liked it. This group was exactly what I needed to distance myself from the doctor's story. I think my intensity had dragged Lincoln down. It was good to see him hyper and zooming again. It occurred to me that I too was really happy with the company. Nice to have good friends around.

"Time to open the attic," Audrey announced after the food was packed up. I went upstairs to do that while the three of them started the moving process. I joined for the second load. Art stuff isn't very heavy, but some of it sure is bulky. Lincoln was present to get underfoot every step of the way.

Trey and I left Lincoln with the ladies in the attic setting up shop while we ventured downstairs to do the manly fireplace lighting and beers. "One more thing in the car," he said when the fire was started. "I'll be right back." He returned with a big box and pulled it open to produce a pre-lit, pre-decorated six-foot Christmas tree. In minutes it was up and beautiful. I asked "Hey Google" to start some traditional Christmas tunes, and we were immersed in seasonal festivity. We grabbed fresh beers to celebrate.

"Richard," Audrey yelled down from upstairs. "Come and see the studio." The attic had been transformed. The space had been completely opened up with the neat clearance and stacking of the previously scattered attic contents. Several easels were placed for different lighting influences, and large folding tables held displays of paint, brushes, and various other tools of the artist. Additional spotlights on stands and another table set up as a desk completed the vision. Empty and partially worked canvases were lined up awaiting Audrey's imagination and touch.

"This is amazing," I said. "Now I see what you saw when you were first up here. Is it everything you wanted?"

"And much, much more," she said with tears in her eyes as she hugged me. "I can't wait to start here in the morning light."

"Would that be tomorrow morning," I asked.

"If you don't mind driving me to the shop in the morning."

"Make it late," said Vicki, smiling, on her way downstairs to start the celebration of the new studio.

We all got refreshed drinks and settled in the great room with the fireplace, the season's music, and the Christmas tree. "I can't thank you guys enough for the tree," I said. "Lincoln and I had completely forgotten about doing anything for Christmas, and I think it's just what we needed this year."

"Yeah," said Vicki. "Especially since we're all coming here for Christmas Day. We hadn't told you that part yet. We decided to take over your house for the grand event. The fireplace is too inviting to pass up, and everything here will be especially beautiful with the forecast for a little white Christmas ground cover."

"I love it," I said. "Are you sure you want a fire for Christmas? We could end up with a Crisp Kringle."

"Stop," said Vicki. "I don't want to have to cancel Christmas for fear of dad jokes. I already bought the ham and the tofurkey."

"Okay, maybe I can restrain for one day. Can I do Christmas breakfast? I could serve up eggs Benedict on a shiny platter. There's no plate like chrome for the hollandaise. Of course, we'd also have the traditional frosted flakes and missile toast."

"No more alcohol for you," said Audrey. "Do you still want to go through some of the library books tonight?"

"It's getting a little late for that. And I'm enjoying the company too much to dampen the night with the ghosts of Christmas past."

"Good enough," said Trey. "Speaking of enjoying the company, I'm going to take my fiancée home to some strategically placed mistletoe and other reindeer games, maybe a little truth or deer."

"Oh my God," said Vicki. "It might be contagious. I vote we leave now before we all end up in the witless protection program."

Hugs and kisses all around. "See you for Christmas," I said as they drove off. "I promise I'll be better."

"Better than what?" Audrey asked as the truck taillights faded into the distance.

"Better than anything you could wish for." I followed that with a little peck on the cheek. It was returned by a smoldering liplock that would have melted a snowman. "That was better than anything I could wish for. Let's go admire your studio."

Audrey walked me through a litany of plans for the place to make it her space. I encouraged each one, from ceiling lighting to painting to floor coverings. It was wonderful to see her so happy and excited. When she was through with the tour and the vision, she asked, "A little more wine before bed?"

"Love to, we still have some fire left."

Resettled, I asked if she could surreptitiously find out if Trey and Vicki could be free the weekend after Christmas. "It would mean closing the shop early on Friday and all day Saturday. Is that possible?"

"The week between Christmas and New Year's is pretty light. We could post now that we're taking our holiday break that weekend, and I'm sure we'd be okay with the regulars. It's possible. What are you thinking?"

"Two birds with one stone. I want to do a quick visit with Don Weston and George Hunt on our pending archeological dig. I can do that myself, but I thought you and Vicki might be interested. I was also thinking about my Christmas present to the three of you as a couple of days in the Lancaster County Amish Country area. Do you think that would be fun for Vicki and Trey? I have a tentative reservation for a very unique and special property I know we'd all enjoy. And it comes with a hot tub."

"Trey grew up not far from there outside of Philadelphia. He may have been to Amish Country before, but I know he hasn't been up that way in the years I've known him. Vicki and I have never been there, and it sounds fun and romantic to me. I'll see if I can talk them into the dates."

"That would be great if we can pull it off."

We sat quietly watching the fire and holding hands over Lincoln. "Are you avoiding the books?" she asked. She already knew me too well.

"I read a lot today on my own, probably too much. When you Vicki and Trey got here, I was genuinely thankful for the interruption of company. By the way, who thought of the Christmas tree?"

"You'll probably be surprised to know that was all Trey. Behind that facade is a sentimental softy. That's what makes it easy for Vicki to love him. They're not so different in that way. He likes you, and he likes that I like you, so he wanted to do something special for us. You've changed the subject again. What are you afraid of in the books? There can't be anything new that would be more disturbing than what we've already seen."

"Sorry to say you're wrong there. I want you to know it all, but I can't do it right now. There's still more I have to read myself. I think I'm close to the end of the truth. Let's go to bed. I just want to be close to you. And you have to get up early to catch the dawn light."

"I am looking forward to that. Can you give me a hint on the reading?"

"If you promise not to ask another question."

"I promise."

"I haven't checked this yet but I have a suspicion that the sausages and pickled eggs in the cellar are not sausages and pickled eggs. And the meat in the smokehouse may not be ham."

"Richard, you can't—"

I interrupted, "You promised."

She stopped. "I promised."

Morning

I smelled coffee when I got up. I was alone in the bed and checked the clock: 7:00 a.m. A little late for me but not bad. Coffee.

The kitchen was as empty as my bed had been. With that first jolt of alertness from the caffeine injection, I realized where my bed partners had gone, and I made my way to the attic to join them. Lincoln was asleep in a sunspot, and Audrey was at one of the easels wearing only my flannel shirt from our first intimate encounter. I was aroused, but I could see she was engrossed in the morning light.

"How is your coffee?" I asked with a kiss on the back of her head.

"Good, just got a refill."

"How is your morning light?"

"The best. Michelangelo would have been jealous of this studio."

"You've gotten a lot done there. It looks similar to my Audrey Welsh seascape downstairs."

"It is. It's the companion piece of the same scene in the glow of the sunrise. You'll need another ferrule when it's complete." She giggled.

"I guess you and Lincoln have been up for a while."

"A few hours. I couldn't sleep thinking about getting up here for dawn. I did a little sketching while it was still dark and started on this canvas as the day greeted us."

Lincoln had roused and needed some petting and scratching. I sat at the desk/table with my coffee to accommodate him and watched the beautiful Audrey at work. Then I saw her pre-dawn pencil sketch. It was a portrait of a youngish Black man with the saddest of eyes. It was Tom.

I kept petting Lincoln, telling myself that petting a dog was known to reduce blood pressure and be positive therapy for troubled minds. My mind was trying to be troubled. Stay calm, Richard.

"Is this someone you know?" I asked casually.

She glanced up. "Oh, the sketch. It's just an image I had in my mind lying in bed this morning. That happens often, and I try to capture them when I have the time and materials at hand. The girl you said was looking for Santa Claus came to me in the same way."

"It's very haunting, especially the eyes." I had too much to absorb and share already. I wasn't going to overwhelm her right now and ruin her morning. She looked so happy at her work.

"Thanks," she said. "It was just a little warmup exercise, but I do like how it came out. I may consider doing something in oil with it."

I'd keep it to myself for now, but I was getting ever closer to believing in ghosts. Tom had to be real. I know I had seen him, and he had to be trying to make himself known to Audrey. Calm down, Richard. It's just a random sketch. Don't try to make every little thing part of a grand occult scheme. Still, it was the Tom I had seen.

"Have you made your plans for the day?" I asked.

"Tentatively, I'll stay on your dawn seascape for another hour or so while I have the perfect light. It's only fitting that you enjoy the first fruits of the studio. Maybe you could drop me at the store around 10:00? In between we could enjoy some other first fruits of intimate pleasure, if that's okay with you. With Christmas on Monday, I doubt I'll have time to be here again before then. Vicki and I will be swamped. Self-help books are all the rage for gifts before the New Year."

"Keep painting, I'm going back to bed to await your intimate pleasures," I said, giving her a good kiss and a quick feel on the way out.

I fell back to sleep until I was awakened by a soft tongue and a warm wet mouth exploring my nether regions. We were intimate and both had great pleasure. Audrey went to shower and dress for work. Lincoln looked puzzled when I got up and disappeared behind the shower curtain with her.

"I'll check the dates for next weekend when I get to the shop," Audrey said as I helped soap her magnificent breasts. "We'd be closed on New Year's Eve and New Year's Day anyway. I think checking out early on Friday and skipping Saturday would be a nice vacation for all. Can you tell me more about this cozy vacation rental with the hot tub?"

"I don't think so, that may be the biggest fun surprise of the weekend. I want you to be surprised too."

"I do love surprises," she said with a small shiver as I soaped some other parts of her anatomy.

"Is Lincoln coming with us?"

"Afraid not."

"Maybe your guy Buck can watch him?"

"That's a good thought, but Buck and Lincoln have an odd relationship. As nice as Buck is and as friendly as Lincoln is, they don't mesh at all. Whenever Lincoln sees Buck, he cowers and runs. Not a problem, though. We always have shelter lady Amy as a good vacation spot for little Link. I'll make a call this morning."

Toweled off and dressed for the day, we took Lincoln with us to the shop. Vicki was busy, and Audrey jumped right into work to help her out. Lincoln introduced himself to the customers, all ladies of course, while I wandered around. When things were caught up, Audrey broached the trip idea. Vicki made a quick call to let Trey know the plan and I went home to finalize the booking plans. I called Amy on the way. She'd love to have Lincoln for a weekend.

I called Don Weston when I got to the house. "Still tarnished," he answered.

"Good," I said, "I wish everything else around here would return to its expected state."

"Still chasing ghosts?"

"I found another journal. This one is the technical aspects of embalming. It seems Dr. Craft was quite immersed in the art. I'm pretty sure we have some experimental specimens on the property here."

"Interesting, another wrinkle for the anthropology folks."

"That's actually what I'm calling about. Would you and the Penn State people mind giving up part of a holiday weekend to meet with us at Churchville?"

"Not for what we're talking about. What are you thinking of for timing."

"I've got plans for a rental near you on the Friday and Saturday after Christmas. I owe Audrey and her partner Vicki a nice Christmas gift. I'd bring them and Vicki's fiancée by your library on that Saturday morning if things worked out on your end."

"You could all stay at my place if you like."

"I appreciate the offer but I found a unique rental between you and Amish country that I think the girls will love. I've only driven through Lancaster County in my travels, and I thought the group would enjoy exploring there on Friday evening and after our time on Saturday."

"You all will for sure. It's a fascinating countryside, especially for first-timers. Let me verify that we can get the Penn State people on board for Saturday morning, and I'll get back to you today. I have no doubt they'll want to meet you."

"Good deal, we'll talk soon then."

More Reading

It seemed like a long time ago, but it was only yesterday afternoon when I left off with Dr. Craft checking on the progress of his Confederate corpse. The next entry was a week later.

> "All signs continue to confirm a complete success in the process and mixture of the preservation. There has been no degradation in the past seven days. The appearance is that of a living being in a pleasant sleep and the skin is supple to the touch. Surely, I have uncovered the secret that will save my bride's soul."

I was gaining insight into my great granduncle's mental and emotional makeup by contrasting this journal with the one that was more of a diary. It seemed he was very good at compartmentalizing his feelings between the daily reflections and the clinical trials. Entries from this same time in the previous journal were sad lamentations of the fading health of his wife and his inability to save her. The entries in the embalming book were focused on the scientific inquiry of his work.

He did reference his beliefs on body and soul, but the embalming book was meant for others to learn from. The diary was meant for his mind alone. The sadder the diary became as Dottie was dying, the more positive the embalming guide became.

I was thinking about Gwen again. If I had been a medical doctor, is there anything I could have done to save her, any clues I might have seen that she was in danger? Probably not, but it certainly would have compounded my grief to have such skills and find them of no value. Dr. Craft loved his wife deeply, and he was struggling to use his skills in any way possible to make things better. The methods seem ghastly, but the intent was noble and genuine.

I already knew that his trials were just starting. Being surrounded by dismemberment and death daily was nothing to him in comparison to the pending loss of his wife. And there would be more loss. He would move on, content that Dottie's soul was safe, to unexpectedly find love again. And lose it again, along with his unborn child. It's little wonder that he seemingly lost his mind and withdrew from the world for years.

Lincoln and I took another one of our long walks. He knows where my mind is when we do this. I can tell because he doesn't bark or pull at the leash. He looks at me constantly and stays in touch with my leg. He's a very special boy.

We were gone for about an hour and returned to see a text message on the phone. Don confirmed that Saturday morning's meeting would work for all parties and asked me to give him a call later. It was already almost an hour later so I rang him up.

"Don Weston, Amish Country tour guide, how can I help you?" was the answer.

"You already have, many times over."

"Saturday morning at 11:00 is good for all parties. We'll have anthropology and archeology veterans from Penn State and a couple of the library museum staff. George wants to join us as well."

"Is there anything I should bring?"

"Pictures. Take pictures of every site you think might be included in a search. On your phone is fine. We can link to the Smart Board here to show them."

"Should I bring the journals?"

"I wouldn't. I think you should protect those. I'd suggest locking them up with other important papers when you're not using them. You can speak to the content without them. Now for your vacation time. There is an Amish market that is only open on Friday nights. If none of you have done that before you really should try to get up here early enough to take it in."

"Why is it only open on Fridays?"

"Many of the customers only move by horse and buggy, so the market vendors set up in different sites on different days to make it easier for travel."

"Good to know. We should be settled at the rental by 4:00 in the afternoon."

"That will be perfect. Plan on eating at the market. They have butchers and bakers everywhere and a few sit-down dining options. Food is fantastic."

"I'll never pass up on your recommendations for eating."

"Wise choice. Then you won't mind showing up at my place at 9:00 on Saturday morning? I'll be serving breakfast for you and your fellow travelers before we do the meeting."

"You don't need to do that, we could meet up somewhere."

"I insist. In fact, make it an 8:30 arrival. That way we can have a cigar with our coffee before we eat. Would your other guy join us in a cigar?"

"I'm sure he would. We're all manly men here."

"Then plans are set. I'll email you the details on the Amish market. You can do me a favor there and pick up a box of Zerbe's potato chips. You'll want a box for you too, they are the best chips ever. I also recommend the frosted cinnamon buns for your Sunday breakfast needs. We'll talk over cigars about other options for Saturday evening and Sunday morning to make sure you see all the high spots."

"I'm looking forward to it."

"Me too, see you all soon."

I reflected briefly on Don's comment about locking up the journals with other important papers and chuckled to myself at my trusting but probably irresponsible nature. The only important papers I had were the wills from Gwen and me and Bob. I pulled them together so I could update my will after Gwen's death. Those were still sitting in a cubbyhole on my desk since the last time I looked at them years ago.

After a little nap with Lincoln, I returned to the body inspection. There were weekly visits and updates. The corpse remained unchanged for three months and was still pristine when Dottie passed away at the end of April.

April 28, 1863

> "Today, with the guidance of God's hand, I did the most important task of my life, the preservation of dear Dorothy's body and soul. I will stay with her for a week before proper interment in the Ivy Hill Cemetery where I can visit until I join her. I know now the Lord will see fit to keep us together forever."

That, and some details of the embalming process, essentially the same as the prep for the Confederate soldier, were the last entries in this journal until March of 1865. I knew what was coming then, and I switched back to the diary for the intervening history.

It was again hard to imagine the contrast between the positive outlook of perpetual bonds in the embalming book and the absolute crushing grief of the man in the diary. I thought back to Audrey's comments about a country song: "Guy loves girl, guy loses girl, guy finds love again, guy loses girl again, guy falls apart and commits unspeakable acts, guy kills himself."

I had been wallowing in my pity and woe about current events, but thinking about Dr. Craft's life brought my trials into perspective. Who was I to judge the doctor as a Jekyll–Hyde character? I certainly didn't qualify for a jury of his peers. Yes, I had lost a wife and child, but he had lost much more. I had to admit that most of my troubles were in my mind. The events of his life were not the events of my life. Why should I feel that family history is a burden I have to bear?

My tribulations beyond Gwen and Steven consisted of about four definable interruptions, haunted house folklore, an apparition that was probably a dream, a basketball noise, and a cat that menaced poor Lincoln. Yes, there were a litany of unexplainable coincidences and odd little revelations, but if I had real ghosts, they weren't out to harm me. My real challenges were very few. I had heat, electricity, plumbing, and all the creature comforts one could ever need. I wasn't living in a daily theater of blood and death. I had Lincoln, and I had Audrey. My great granduncle had none of those things. I'm sure he would have gladly traded his life and troubles for my trifling disturbances any day.

I needed a break in the worst way, and I took one in the worst way imaginable. I went to the cellar. The giant flashlight illuminated my path as I unlocked the door and entered. I'd brought a towel from the kitchen to engage the dust of the past and satisfy my curiosity. It wasn't fear now, just curiosity. Short months ago, I wouldn't have ventured in here alone. What was stored in the jars?

I looked at the first bank of goods to my right. Most had labels. The dirt coating of the years obscured all but soft outlines of the contents, and the labels had faded to illegibility years ago. It seems odd now that Bob and I never gave these containers a thought when we were kids. They were just dusty things on the walls.

The first jar I wiped off was sliced pears. Lincoln would have appreciated that if he were with me. Others had berries, beans, and tomatoes, all perfectly normal content for the days of a home garden and no refrigeration.

I clutched the stone on Vicki's necklace for comfort as I went to the back of the cellar. I was still somewhat skeptical about her New Age stuff, but her guidance and advice so far hadn't hurt and seemed to help. I stood the flashlight on its end on the desk so the whole area was intensely illuminated. If I was right about what I had read in the journals, the bottom jars would be the litmus test. I wiped off a container of pickled eggs. As I stared at the contents, they stared back at me. Human eyeballs.

The sausages were equally of interest, perfectly preserved fingers of dead men, complete with fingernails and visible fingerprints. The doctor's tests of the immersion embalming were perfectly suspended in time. They could have been placed here yesterday. Fearless now, I had to admire his work.

Christmas and the End of the Year

I had so much now to tell the world, but it wouldn't be today. Audrey arrived first, decked out in red plaid flannel pajamas. "Hurry up and get changed," she said, throwing a package at me as she dragged a suitcase out of the car. It was my very own red plaid flannel jammies. When I returned wearing my new outfit, she had already dressed Lincoln in the same suit. I thought it was charming. Lincoln thought it was embarrassing.

Vicki and Trey weren't far behind, bedecked in the same uniforms. Altogether we were quite the Hallmark card. Food and cars unloaded, fire started, Christmas carols playing, tree lit, I put out some fruitcake and eggnog to no takers. I don't like either of those myself, but they looked festive on the coffee table.

It was my best Christmas in memory. The last several had been completely alone, and here I was with Lincoln and some new good friends. There were nice presents for all, nothing extravagant but all thoughtful. Trey got everyone L.L. Bean Wicked Good Slippers to complete our holiday apparel. Audrey bought me a beautiful pink opal necklace of my own so I could return the one Vicki had loaned me. Vicki's gift to me was the hoot of the event. She presented me with the

"Scent of Uranus" and a tube of Fire and Ice massage cream. I was a little apprehensive about opening the jar of powder, but I have to say Uranus smells pretty good.

Time for my gift-giving. "Is anyone interested in joining me for the next steps in unearthing the mysteries of Dr. Craft's haunted house?"

"Me, me," said Vicki excitedly.

"You know I'm all in," said Audrey.

"I go whenever they go," said Trey. "And everyone loves a good ghost story."

"Great, I asked Audrey to check your calendars from Friday afternoon into Sunday so we can all go on a road trip together. On Saturday morning we'll meet with our Civil War experts at Churchville University, and we'll be joined by some anthropology and archeology experts from Penn State. I wasn't kidding when I said we'd be unearthing mysteries. You'll get to meet Don Weston and George Hunt, a couple of serious Civil War historians. We'll be making plans to disinter our local corpses. No doubt we'll also be digging into the hospital pit and checking out some other specimens I haven't even told you about. Still interested?"

Vicki gasped, feigning indignance. "You've been withholding information from us?"

"Not for long, it's some new information in 'the books' that Tom sent us to. I'm still chasing leads there. All will be revealed. The rest of the weekend will be all surprises interspersed with sightseeing and lots of eating."

"I can do this," said Trey.

"And I should mention we'll be staying in a house that may be even more interesting than this one. I don't think it's haunted but it does have a hot tub, so bring your swimming suits."

"Aw, do we have to bring swimming suits?" said Vicki.

"Yeah," said Audrey "Do we have to bring swimming suits?"

"Optional for couple's events," I said. "But if Trey and I are in the tub with you, swimming suits will be mandatory, wouldn't you agree, Trey?"

"Absolutely, I've seen my share of sweaty giants in locker rooms, but it would be awkward to be in a hot tub with a tiny naked guy."

"Tiny? Trey, I'm five-ten. That's an appropriate size for a normal human being."

"I wasn't referring to your height."

"Ouch." We all laughed at that one. Truth be told, if Trey's anatomy is all in proportion, the awkwardness would surely be mine.

Christmas was accomplished, Trey and Vicki went home, and Audrey helped me clean up. "The rest of your Christmas gift," she said. "Is I'll be commuting to work from here this week and staying with you every night. I hope you're okay with that."

"I'd be okay if you stayed here forever. Maybe that's something we can think about in the coming year."

"Maybe," she responded with a big hug and kiss. "Are you ready for a little Fire and Ice?"

Christmas day was the gift that kept on giving for several more hours.

The next morning Audrey and Lincoln were up early for a little more studio time. I joined them with coffee, amazed at the process of the dawn seascape emerging from the blank canvas. I never had the gift of any artistic ability and found it mesmerizing.

Audrey trotted off to work, and I returned to the books.

April 29, 1863

"Dorothy was beautiful today, laying on our bed in her perpetual rest. Her sickness is gone, and her soul remains in the picture of health that her body has become. I owed a gift of gratitude to the Confederate soldier who had given his life to save her soul. He too was the vision of health as Tom and I buried him behind the stables. I left him with a crucifix for his journey."

One week later there was a funeral for Dottie. Friends and family gathered to see her. Richard Craft devoted all his time and skill to hospital work while he slipped deeper into depression. He visited Dottie often and maintained her grave as he had maintained her body and soul.

June 12, 1863

"Betty has taken on all the work that Dottie did in
addition to her many chores. She has proven to be a good
student of the medical books and a very capable nurse."

August 10, 1863

"Betty joined me today on my ride to visit Dottie.
At the graveside, I told her of my studies and beliefs on
the body and soul as one. She loved Dottie as I did and
took comfort. I believe that she also believes."

January 4, 1864

"I've come to notice a beauty in the woman Betty.
Dying men that only short years before would have
enslaved her kind find peace in her care. She has a
gentle way of sensing and responding to the needs of
their bodies and spirits. She calms the unrest and fears.
Truly she possesses the right gift for our work."

March 7, 1864

"I've mourned my love for Dottie for almost a year
now. The mourning has become serenity in the recesses
of my heart. Though inanimate I know her spiritual
being is with me. I believe Dottie is gifting me a new
breath of life in my growing relationship with Betty. We
have become full partners in every way but one."

May 13, 1864

"Betty followed me to my marriage bed tonight. My
heart is full, knowing our coupling is blessed by God
and my beloved Dorothy. They have given me a gift of
renewed love that I thought was dead forever."

August 3, 1864

"Dear Betty and I visited Dottie again today. I felt the spirits shining on us and we thanked her for our love and confessed it together in her presence. My life with God is full again."

December 22, 1864

"A miracle is upon us for the new year. I had concerns for Betty's health in recent days, yet now we rejoice that her afflictions were the signs that she is now with our child. The child that Dottie and I could never conceive is now alive in the vessel of Betty's womb. Praise God, praise Dorothy, praise Betty for this confirmation of love."

February 1, 1865

"I fear for the turmoil in the mind of Tom. Betty's baby has begun to show, and he is troubled by the coming events. He loves Betty and he loves me, but he lives in fear of the time he and his sister spent in slavery. He seems increasingly disturbed and confused that the world we live in cannot accept the fruit of our love. We pray for him."

March 27, 1865

"Dear God, why have you abandoned me again?"

I stopped there, knowing the date of Betty's sudden death. It was late morning, and Lincoln and I needed another one of our long walks before we would return to the embalming journal. When we had cleared our minds, and Lincoln had cleared his bowels, I read about the body treatment for Betty as I had about Dorothy and the Confederate soldier. I can't say I was convinced about the body-soul theology of Dr. Craft, but I was becoming convinced that when we next saw these bodies they would be as lifelike as the contents of the jars in the cellar.

The next to the last entry in the embalming journal was Tom. I was impressed again by the complete difference between the angst of the diary and the scientific impersonal chronicles of this book.

April 15, 1865

"In another experiment with the Holmes and Scheele arterial embalmment, today's experiment was a young and healthy Negro specimen that had succumbed to traumatic damage of the cranium. This was a field autopsy, done where the body lay. The method was conducted as previously documented with the exception that the head wounds were widely open and presented an outlet for the fluid as it was introduced. This was overcome by the repeated wrapping of tightly drawn burlap to restrain the leakage. I won't see the results of this work as the body has already been buried, but I'm convinced the intervention was sufficient and the expected outcome will result."

There was one more entry and this journal was done. It documented the embalmment of a feline on July 29, 1868. I'd already seen the diary entries for the end of Tom. I could now account for Dr. Craft, Dottie, Tom, Betty, Yellow Cat, and the bonus body of the Confederate soldier. The family history, as depressing as it was, is complete.

Lincoln and I could nap now.

Thank God You're Here

After the nap, my mind was clear and unencumbered. I now know every bit of the Craft House history. There would be no more revelations and no more surprises. Nothing to fear but plenty to explore. I couldn't wait to tell the tale.

Lincoln and I had been all housewifely that afternoon, thawing the last of our signature spaghetti sauce and preparing some garlic toast for the oven. Audrey arrived home around 6:30. After some small talk about her day, I asked if she'd like to take a Lincoln walk with me and a travel mug of wine.

I was tentatively scouting out the photos I would start taking tomorrow for the weekend meeting while I shared the new secrets of Dr. Craft. "I'm so glad you're here. I finished the books and couldn't wait to fill you in. I'm full of energy with the relief that it's all out, and there's nothing more that can surprise or hurt me."

"And I thought it was my charming presence heightened by the rose opal. I could get used to coming home to moonlight walks with a happy man who's already prepared dinner and drinks. It's good to see you unburdened and energetic. Tell me everything."

"You already know the main plot. It's suffering through the revulsion of the backstory that's made me a free man. I know you'll want to read everything for yourself and take notes, and I encourage you to do that. No doubt small important details are still in there to consider.

The answers are in the multiple parallel worlds of Dr. Craft and his time. This house was a hospital, but it was also a science lab advancing important research in the field of embalming. The doctor was a clinical realist, but he was also a spiritualist with deep beliefs in the afterlife. I originally thought it was a Jekyll–Hyde horror story of a psycho split personality, but it wasn't. Dr. Craft was a good doctor and a good husband with only upright intent in all of his work. What seemed to be the dark side of his pursuits was compelled by a belief that the body and the soul are the same entity and that they don't part at death. They only part if there is decomposition of the body. If he could find the secret to perfect preservation of the human body, he could save the souls of those he loved."

After some thought, Audrey added, "That's a new verse in the country song. 'Guy loses girl but keeps her soul in a box somewhere.'"

"It does give a nuanced meaning to songs about 'soulmate' or 'soul survivor.' There may be a commercial jingle for Kia in there somewhere." Good to laugh.

"I remember the reference to pickled eggs in our conversation before Christmas. I made my promise to not ask any more questions about the readings then. Can I ask now?"

"The jars in the back of the cellar were Dr. Craft's experiments with different embalming mixtures. I was initially repulsed by my reading, but the success of his work is so remarkable, I'm now impressed. The pickled eggs are human eyes, and the sausages are amputated fingers. Would you like to see them?"

"A little close to dinner now, but I am interested in what you're telling me. The meat in the smokehouse?"

"I'm going to let the college folks explore that one. If I understand the journal references correctly, they'll find assorted cadaver pieces wrapped and smoked, not ham."

Her mouth dropped open a bit.

"The clinical book outlines the doctor's administration of the magic fluid with Dottie, Betty, Tom, and even the cat. There is also a mystery guest of a Confederate soldier buried behind the stable. While Dottie was still alive, he became the test case for the final elixir of soul-saving. Behind the stable should be the area that is now enclosed for storing the lawn tools. There are more jars and burlap to unwrap and four human bodies and a cat out here waiting for the historians. Not to mention that Tom's body adjoins the pit of despair. No more secrets to fear."

"I'm happy that all the family mysteries are out and explained, but we also have another new moon date in a couple of weeks and many other surprises that can't be explained. Is it okay if I tell Vicki all of this?"

"Definitely. I think her pink opal was more than a placebo. She has a lot more knowledge and experience in the realm of the unexplainable than I'll ever be able to comprehend, and I'd love to keep her on the case to challenge our skepticism. Maybe she can join us on the next new moon."

"Are we done out here? I do love that you're happy and relieved and chatty, but my wine is empty and my stomach is growling."

I lit candles for a romantic dinner. I even had her test the pasta with me in a reenactment of the Lady and the Tramp kiss. It was hours later in bed when she remarked, "I cry 'uncle.' You are full of energy tonight, but one of us has to work in the morning."

The next few days before our trip were pure domestic bliss. Thank you, God, for this woman and this silly dog who make my life special and complete.

There Was an Old Lady ...

Shaving kit, check. Underwear. Check. Beef jerky. Check. Trail mix. Check. Water. Check. Twizzlers. Check. I was ready early. Amy stopped by to pick up Lincoln. "I have a Christmas surprise for both of you. You'll get it when you come home," she teased. My inner lecher was thinking if I were thirty years younger, I would have unwrapped that gift months ago.

We're taking Trey's truck for the journey. It's the biggest and most comfortable transport among us, and the covered bed will handle any giant souvenirs we might pick up in our travels. It's the same route Darrel and I took to see Don, but we go right at Route 30 when we get to York. I sat up front and left the girls in the back to dole out road food. We left from my place around 2:00 p.m. and we should be at our mystery destination by 4:00.

I was fending off questions about the weekend by saying everything would be a surprise. After about twenty minutes they gave up. Trey started inquiring about tomorrow's meeting, which wasn't a secret, and I could overhear the girls talking about what I had told Audrey about Dr. Craft's legacy.

"I'm looking forward to meeting all your upcoming research partners. I played my college ball at Penn State and haven't gone back since graduation. I majored in business, so I'm sure I never met the anthropology professors, but I'm curious about how things have changed or stayed the same since my time there."

"You played in the Joe Paterno years?"

"I did. That's a sad story. Coach Paterno was a hero of mine, and I hated to see how things ended up there. Then again, Bill Cosby was also a hero to me as a Philadelphia boy, and he seems to have gotten what he deserved. My only Pennsylvania hero that emerged unscathed by scandal was Mr. Rogers."

"Why didn't you stay in Pennsylvania for your NFL career?"

"I never had a choice. You go where you're drafted. Pittsburgh was never an aspiration for a Philly guy, but my hometown Eagles would have been my first choice if I had one. As it turned out, the Giants were the right team for me at the right time. The Pittsburgh dynasty ended in my rookie year, and Philadelphia never made the finals my entire career. New York was a hot spot and gave me two Super Bowl rings. Purely a lucky break."

"Richard," Vicki interrupted from the back seat. "Audrey and I have decided we want to be beautiful forever. Do you think you can pull that off with Dr. Craft's magic potion?"

"We don't need a magic potion for you and Audrey to always be beautiful to us, right, Trey?"

"Good answer," he whispered.

"Are we there yet?" asked Audrey in a whiny child's voice. "Vicki's on my side of the seat again and I have to pee."

"Are you serious?" asked our driver as we exited toward Lancaster.

"Not really, but she is being a seat hog."

"We're getting pretty close, maybe half an hour," I said. "Keep your eyes open on the right side. There's a landmark coming up that you'll want to see. Don pointed it out when we were on our way to dinner last month." That quieted the children.

Trey spotted it first. "Are we looking for the Shoe House?" he asked.
"Yup."

"I was thinking about that place. We always waved at it when we were kids. 'There was an old woman who lived in a shoe, she had so many children she didn't know what to do.' I'm glad to see it all cleaned up. It needed serious TLC the last time I passed here. I was afraid they were going to tear it down."

"Wow," yelled Vicki. "That's amazing. Why doesn't everyone build fairy tale and nursery rhyme houses? How much fun would that be every day."

"Get off here," I instructed Trey. "We might as well get a closer look since we have to pass this way anyhow. It is very cool."

We exited and backtracked to 1-97 Shoe House Road. There was no traffic, so we stopped. Whatever TLC it needed had been amply taken care of. It was all fresh paint and neat landscaping and very inviting.

"Pull in the driveway," I said. "There aren't any cars here, so it must be empty. Let's look in the windows."

"I don't know," he said. "What if there's somebody home?"

"I think you can handle an old lady if she gives us any trouble," I laughed. "Seriously, people must stop here all the time. Let's take a look."

Audrey and Vicki were less apprehensive than Trey and bounded right up to the place. They were oohing and ahhing at the interior views when I walked up to the front door, announced, "Imagine our luck, my VRBO code opens the door," and stepped inside. "Welcome home," I pronounced.

The girls almost knocked me over with their hugs when they realized this would be our place for the weekend. We checked out every room and found the hot tub out back before we even thought about unloading the truck. It was a gorgeous, magical, whimsical funhouse.

"That's surprise number one, how am I doing so far?" Everyone seemed very happy with my choice.

"We'll have plenty of time to explore when we get back. Now we need to get to surprise number two, which will also be our dinner destination."

"East on 30, James," I said to Trey as we all got back in the truck. "We're heading to the town of Ephrata." Don had mapped out directions that would take us through the heart of the town on our way to the market. He had us driving past farms and fields and passing buggies along the way. This was all new to the girls and me, and we chatted excitedly about the house and the countryside.

Surprise number two was equally well received as we pulled into the lot of the Green Dragon Farmers Market. "Look at all the buggy parking," shouted Vicki. We found our spot way out in a field. The place was packed.

Don had loaded me up with resource sites on the market, the Amish, and the area. I was a confident guide as I explained the history of the market since 1934 and why it was only open on Fridays. I'd also studied the layout of the vendor stalls so I could make sure we saw everything and I could find Don's chips.

"Why do so many of the Amish guys have beards?" asked Vicki

"Those are the married ones. The ones without are still single."

"Some of the naked-face guys are pretty buff" she noted.

"A lifetime of farm work will do that for you," said Trey. "When we'd travel here as kids, we'd see even younger kids plowing fields. Some of them couldn't have been seven or eight years old, and they were out there guiding six giant horses across the farms."

We ate like Costco veterans as we walked through the stalls trying every sample offered. That was just the appetizer. I identified the vendors with the recommended potato chips and frosted cinnamon buns. I'd grab those on our way out.

Trey and I bought heavy leather belts. We knew they were tough ones because all the Amish guys were wearing the same style. They even punched the holes right there to custom-fit us. Vicki was a little chilly so she picked up a homespun super warm heavy sweater. Cozy. One building was all furniture, solid wood and handmade. That's where Audrey found her new desk.

"This is beautiful, simple, and sturdy. Would you mind if I got it for the studio?" she asked me.

"It will fit in the truck," Trey said.

"Sold" was my response, and I paid the carpenter. Something else to pick up on the way out. We found a little diner in one of the buildings, all kitchen tables and chairs from the '40s and '50s with checked tablecloths. This was not a hotbed of vegetarian delicacies, but Vicki made do. The rest of us loaded up on all the local foods, mostly fried. We did draw the line at sampling the pig stomach.

When we were as stuffed as the pig stomach, we made the rounds to pick up our treasures, chips, sticky buns, and Audrey's desk. Some beef sticks and jerky also followed us home, and I threw in a small jug of Amish root beer and a handful of Amish cigars.

More excited chatter on the way home. Surprise number two was a great success, and we couldn't wait to get back to surprise number one for a quiet evening, maybe a hot tub dip. Trey and I and Audrey sampled Zerbe's potato chips on the way and pronounced them the best. "These are extra good," said Audrey. "Look Vicki, they must also be good for us. There are no preservatives and only two ingredients," she read from the label. "Potatoes and lard."

"Keep telling yourself that rendered pig fat is good for you, and you're all going to die young."

Back at the shoe, I took a sip of Amish root beer and poured the rest down the sink, nasty stuff. I switched to wine with everyone else, and we decided we had a hot tub soak in our immediate future. Trey and I were in first with a couple of Amish cigars. Hard to believe they were worse than the Amish root beer. We retired those as the girls arrived. I'm glad the swimsuit rules were in place. Not only might I have been embarrassed by a naked Trey, I would have been even more embarrassed to be publicly sporting my reaction to the girls' swimwear, which might as well have been nothing. Trey and I are very lucky guys.

We overstayed the recommended tub time substantially, only coming out for wine refills and rest stops. After almost two glorious hours we were all wet noodles and ready for bed. I had almost dozed off when a warm naked Audrey pressed close to me and said, "I love you, Richard."

"I love you too, Audrey."

Planning the Big Dig

Surprise number three for the group was arriving at Don's house. Surprise number four was on me. Darrel Metz greeted us in the driveway.

"Hi Richard, hi Audrey, hello fellow travelers. I'm Darrel. Welcome to the finest breakfast spot in town. I hope you like pancakes, waffles, French toast, sausage, bacon, and biscuits with gravy. I believe that's what Chef Don is preparing for the first course."

"What are you doing here?" I exclaimed, hugging him. "What a nice surprise."

"I'm here to represent Arlington County's interests in the multiple murder investigations and evidential exhumations that will take place on your property." Pause, then a laugh. "I'm messing with you. Don told me your plans for the weekend, and I inserted myself into the college meeting for fun. It also gets me a couple of days with Chief Weston and his cooking."

Don heard us coming and yelled from the kitchen. "Everything is on hold, done, or waiting for final touches. You made it in time for the pre-breakfast cigars and mimosas."

We did introductions for Don as he sized up Trey. "I can't believe you brought this traitor into my kitchen," he said. "A Pennsylvania icon who sold his soul to New York for what, an illustrious career and a couple of Super Bowl rings? An absolute pleasure to meet you, Mr.

Roadcap. I forgive you for the damage you inflicted on my Eagles over the years, and I welcome you into my home."

"Nice to meet you too, Don. I've heard a lot about you from Richard. By the way, they're still my Eagles too, except for certain Sundays. You can take the boy out of Pottstown, but you can't take Pottstown out of the boy."

"Pottstown. I remember driving through there just to smell Mrs. Smith's pie factory. I grew up right down 422 from you in the Conshohocken area."

Darrel interrupted, "You guys can hug it out later. You're cutting into our cigar time."

Out on the porch, all the guys and Vicki lit up and nursed our mimosas. I didn't mind that Audrey abstained from the stinky sticks. I like the flavor of her kiss just the way it is. As the cigars and conversation were burning down, we had one of the famous Don Weston food experiences and loaded up to visit the college library.

George Hunt was there to greet us, along with Abbey Foster and Fred Muller, who were representing the Penn State anthropology department. George officially opened the meeting with the announcement that all clearances for excavation had been approved by the Virginia state historical powers and the local law enforcement. "Richard, the decision to proceed with any archeological exploration is yours alone. In conversation with our partners from Penn State, they have expressed great interest in becoming your field resource for that pursuit. I can vouch for their experience and competency, especially specific to the Civil War era. They have a virtual residency at Gettysburg and the deepest reservoir of peer-reviewed research by far on the topic."

"Let me ask," I said. "If this was your property and your decision, are these the people that you would choose above any others to do this work?"

"Without question."

"Then they're my choice too, and we won't have to waste time vetting alternatives. What's next?"

George continued with the story of how I came to contact Don Weston. He showed before and after pictures of the found artifacts. "I should note," he said. "That the house and grounds are reported to be haunted. In my years of historical research, I've never become a believer in the occult. I'm still not, but there is no explanation for the original found condition and the changes in these pieces of memorabilia. Richard, would you be kind enough to show the group your site photographs and speak to the broader history surrounding the potential targets of disinterment?"

"Gladly." In about a twenty-minute lecture with a corresponding picture show, I covered everything from the house build, the hospital years, the secret library and its contents, the three bodies (plus a cat) and their possible locations, the smokehouse, the cellar, and Dr. Craft's chemistry experiments. Everyone in the room had some knowledge of some pieces. My lecture goal was to impart to all at least a superficial knowledge of all pieces.

Abbey Foster spoke first. "This is an exceptional story and an exceptional historical opportunity. Speaking for Penn State, we are honored to even be in consideration to conduct this research, and we promise that you will not regret your selection of our resources."

"Thanks," I said. "What do we do now?"

"Since Dr. Hunt has already secured the necessary permissions, we only need to select dates for the engagement. We have all the resources, human and otherwise, to do the actual work. We would field multiple teams. Each team would be fully self-sufficient from tools and lodging to food, water, and sanitation needs. There is nothing you would need to do, but you and your people are welcome to join in any or all of the excavations."

"How long would things take?"

"It will be a few days into the work to get the scope of the entire project defined, but I would anticipate around two weeks."

"Could we do the first week of March for a start?"

"Certainly. Weather conditions should be generally favorable. That also fits well in the school schedule for access to additional student resources for labor."

"Let's book it then. I just wanted to make sure we'd be active on March 10 with the new moon."

All parties exchanged contact information for the next steps, and our Virginia group headed back to Don's house for another cigar.

"That went well, I think," I said, back on the porch sipping a brandy with my cigar.

"I'm glad you're okay to go with the Penn State group," Don said. "When I first asked them for some guidance, they were interested, but they also offered that Johns Hopkins and the George Washington University had the needed skills if you felt you wanted a closer school for some reason. I'm with George that no one is more steeped in this work specific to the Civil War than Penn State. We've worked with them here at Churchville. The people with us today, Abbey and Fred, are both field technical specialists, so you're likely to see them again as the actual project managers."

"I'm excited," said Darrel. "This will be my first hundred-plus-year-old homicide investigation."

"You have an odd bucket list," laughed Don.

"I crossed two things off my bucket list yesterday," I said. "Amish root beer and Amish cigars."

"I also fell for both of those atrocities when I first moved out this way," said Don. "Sorry, I forgot to warn you. For future reference, Shoofly Pie doesn't taste like you think it should either."

"That reminds me, I've got a box of Zerbe's chips in the truck for you."

"The holy grail of fried spuds. They overcome all of the local food disappointments combined."

"Speaking of food," said Trey. "I'm buying dinner tonight. Do we have any suggestions?"

Don and Darrel and I looked at each other and laughed out loud. Darrel said, "I'll bet the ladies would love the Catacombs."

"No doubt," added Don. "But Trey would have to hock one of his Super Bowl rings to spring for that one."

"I'm good," said Trey. "Test me."

"I guess that settles dinner plans," I said. "Don, since we're on the way, why don't you and Darrel come hang out at our rental for a bit while we plan Trey's demise?"

We converted two more Shoe House lovers that afternoon. Don mapped out an Amish country drive for us to take after cinnamon buns for Sunday morning on our way out of town, and we tested Trey's wallet mightily that evening.

Another New Moon

I called Amy on the ride back to arrange for the Lincoln transfer. She said the Christmas present was complete, and she'd drop him off to be waiting for us when we returned. Lincoln greeted us as a proud, preening new man. He was wearing a bandana that said "Merry Christmas," and he was freshly groomed and pedicured. I called Amy again to tell her how pleased Lincoln and I were with her gift.

Trey manhandled Audrey's desk to the attic and, with hugs and kisses, he and Vicki were gone.

"Welcome home, my love," I said to Audrey.

"It does feel like home," she said.

Audrey stayed over every night as we planned the next new moon date, I hoped it would be forever after. In the ten days before the new moon, Audrey had a lot of studio time around her work schedule. The desk was set up the first day.

"Can I have the pencil sketch?" I asked. It was still on the table where it was created.

"Are you going to hang it on the refrigerator, Dad?" she laughed.

"You'll see. Can I keep it?"

"Sure, I've got a million of them, and I can always make more."

"I have a role for it in our January 11 engagement. I also have a role for Vicki and maybe even Trey if he'd be interested. I'm thinking another Ouija séance, maybe back in the cellar again."

"It has been oddly quiet lately. Going back to the beginning might stir things up."

"I think I'm done being shaken. I'm ready to stir."

"While you work on your inner James Bond, I'll work on the rest of the journal readings. I need to get caught up."

"Are you ready to see the stuff in the cellar?"

"Not quite yet. Let me finish the reading first."

"As you wish."

"I've also been thinking about some changes in the house. Since you've become a frequent flier, which I love and welcome, I want to include your input."

"Is that a sexual innuendo?"

"Consider everything I say as a sexual innuendo, and we'll keep getting along just fine." I laughed. "What do you think if we move into the larger bedroom that had been home to Bob and Dr. Craft? Thinking of Lincoln, we might want to add a king bed, and a bit more space would fit it better."

"Sexual innuendo?"

"You're a quick study. On the subject of studies, I'm signing up for another three-course load. Will you be doing another paranormal class?"

"No, this semester will be all relaxation and artwork. The MFA show generated some more foot traffic at the shop gallery. Sales are pretty lucrative right now. I can enjoy the painting process and make some more inventory, and even some money, at the same time."

"Sounds like a plan. You move in and sell great quantities of art so I can quit my day job and make love to you three times a day."

"I've always wanted to have a kept man sex slave puppet."

"Really?"

"Never. No plans. We'll let the universe decide and take it from there."

In the next few days while Audrey did her work, painting and reading, Lincoln and I took care of the new sleeping accommodations and the bedroom move. She invited Vick and Trey for the 11th. They exuberantly accepted. Good. If we're going to stir the occult pot, Vicki and Trey would be my first choices as foxhole buddies in fighting the ghosts.

The night before our engagement, Audrey announced, "I'm done with the reading. Maybe you should start on some writing. This would make a great book. And I caught another new moon date."

"What's that?"

"The death and embalmment of the Confederate soldier. The more we know real stuff, the more the unreal crops up. I think I'm ready to look at your jar specimens now."

"On the front of the unreal cropping up, tonight's cellar temp is back in the 40s. We'll need to bundle up."

Well-layered and equipped with the right flashlight, we ventured out. The lock was on the hasp and I opened things up. Initially, everything looked unchanged since my last visit, but it wasn't. The many jars I had wiped clean were once again covered in their years of dust. The kitchen towel I'd left on the desk was still there, stained with dirt, but the jars were obscured.

"Another anomaly for the mystery pile, "I said as I explained the change to Audrey.

I pulled a jar of fingers and a jar of eyes from the shelf and wiped them again. The contents were unchanged, the preservation perfect. Audrey seemed hypnotized by the eyes looking into her own. Just as things seemed to be getting intense, she said, "I wonder if we could sell these at the shop?"

We both laughed at the insanity of it all. "I love you," I smiled. "Let's get out of here, it's cold."

The Return of Tom
and the Other

W e'd told Vicki and Trey about the temperature change last night so they could bring appropriate outerwear. Vicki chose her new Amish cardigan, and Trey showed up with one of those giant parkas seen on football sidelines. As it turned out, the cellar was back to 50 again, so it wasn't too bad. Good thing. I'm not sure we'd all fit in the cellar with Trey and the comically humongous parka.

"Wine everyone?" offered Audrey to our guests.

"You know it," said Vicki. "Always the best way to invite a paranormal encounter, especially since we'll be breaking in a Ouija virgin and a total non-believer tonight."

"I'd be happy to sit this out," said Trey. "I wouldn't want to stifle the spirits with my rookie status. I already had a cat cross my path coming up the driveway. Isn't that a bad sign?"

"You're just scared," said Vicki. "That I might be right about the spirits among us."

Ping, ping, ping

"What's that?" asked Trey.

"It's someone or something playing with the basketball out front," I said. "We missed it in the December snow, but it comes every month at this time. Our new moon events seem to always start that way."

"Who is it?" he asked.

"Come on, I'll show you how it goes."

The girls were veterans and stayed put while I took Trey to the front hall. It was louder here. Ping, ping, ping.

"Watch out front while I turn on the floodlights."

I did, and the basketball was sitting there right next to the hoop where it always was. The sound was gone.

"Huh," said Trey. "That's a normal thing for the three of you?"

"And Lincoln. It used to be the scary start of the night, but we're all used to it now. Think you're ready for the haunted cellar? I'll be happy to show you the eyeballs."

"Maybe another gallon of wine first."

We rejoined the girls. They were ready to go with a full box of wine and plastic glasses for the group. Audrey had already prepared the space with chairs and candles. I grabbed the big flashlight for backup and we headed down into the cellar. The candles had made it surprisingly comfortable in temperature. That's going to mess up our readings on the atmosphere, but there didn't seem to be anything more to prove on that front anyway.

"Since you've all gotten the story of what took place here, I invite our cruise director, Vicki, to take us on another journey of conjuring. Would you like to jump right in, or would you like to see the evidence here first?"

"Eyeballs, please," said Vicki.

I handed her the jar we had cleaned for the second time last night. The glass was still clear this time.

"Wow," she said, seeming to be in a staring contest with the contents. I put the jar of fingers in her other hand. She showed both to Trey.

"Help me understand here," he said. "You all think this is a normal thing that we want to try and scare up the guy that did this?"

"Trey," I said. "You're in the same head space I was months ago. There's nothing normal here. We can explain what's in the jars, but we can't explain that pile of hay over there or how that blanket and pillow came to join it. We can't explain why the temperature changes in this room, and we can't explain how these nights start with an invisible basketball game. Those are just the tip of the iceberg. There's a lot we can't explain, and even what we can explain is far from normal."

"You are a little scared," Vicki said to Trey with a smile.

"Apprehensive," he responded. "But also a little curious. We're here, so let's do it, whatever 'it' is."

"Sit next to me," said Vicki. "I promise I'll protect you." Still smiling. "Audrey, you sit across from me so we're boy-girl-boy-girl. Trey, we all put fingers on the planchette, that's the moveable thing on the board. We don't push or pull, we just barely make contact, almost floating above it. As we ask questions, it will move to provide answers to things we can't know from places we can't see. Do you believe that?"

"Not hardly. But I know you do, and I'm willing to hover along just because I like the company. I do admit, I am analytically intrigued."

"Then we'll have you start," she said. "Knees touching everyone, place your fingers." We assumed the position. "Ouija, we're back. You'll recognize three of us, and we have a new soul here, skeptical but somewhat open to your secrets. Can you join us tonight?"

We all watched Trey as the planchette made its sketchy path to the word YES.

"Trey," said Vicki. "Ask a question that no one here but you could know the answer to."

"Okay, football trivia. Do any of you know the year of the last scoreless NFL football game?"

"That sounds safely obscure to me," I said.

"Ouija," said Vicki. "What year was the last scoreless NFL game?"

Ouija stuttered a lot and did its loop thing but eventually gave us 1-9-4-3. We all looked at Trey again. His mouth was open.

"That's right," he said. "I swear I didn't touch the thing."

"You seem surprised," said Vicki.

"I swear I didn't touch the thing."

"Well, I'm not surprised," said Vicki. "That's how it works. Ouija, do you have anyone who would like to join us tonight?" It moved quickly to YES.

I whispered to Trey, "Yes and no questions work best, it's a shitty speller." We snickered. Vicki and Audrey frowned at us.

Vicki continued, "Who is it that wants to meet?"

Slow and rambling C-O-D-Y.

"Cody, is this room special to you?"

YES

I jumped in on a strong hunch. "Cody. Are you a Confederate soldier?"

YES

"How long were you here?"

N-O-W

"You're still here now?"

YES

"In this room?"

NO

"How long were you in this room?"

3 M-O-T-H-S

"I told you he was a shitty speller. He was here three *months*." I hadn't planned to take over Vicki's role, but I was on a roll of my own.

"Cody, is there anyone with you?"

T-O-M

"Can you talk to us, Tom?"

YES

"Tom, when I first saw you, you told me others were coming, one that would kill me. Is Cody one of the others you told me were coming?"

YES

"Is he the one that would kill me?"

NO

"Is anyone else here?"

NO

Vicki took over. "Do you and Cody know who would harm Richard?"

Lots of starts and stops on this answer. W-E-A-L-L-D-O-H-E-R-E

"When you say 'here,' do you mean the spirit world?"

YES

"We've met you Tom, Bob, Gwen, Steven, and now Cody. Are there more that we will meet?"

NO

"Is it one of them who would kill Richard?"

NO

"Do all of them know who would kill Richard?"

YES but it kept gliding W-A-R-N

"You've all come to warn us?"

YES

"Who would kill Richard?" asked Audrey.

The next move came swiftly: GOODBYE.

After a long pause, Vicki announced, "That's all we'll get tonight."

We packed up and sat around the kitchen table with more wine. "What's the verdict?" I asked the group.

"He is a shitty speller and he's good at football. These two things often go together," laughed Trey.

"I don't think he's a believer yet," said Vicki. "But I am, and I'm more than a little concerned."

"I'm a lot concerned," said Audrey. "I was just getting used to you." She laughed.

"Seriously," said Vicki, not laughing. "I know you're all skeptics, but I wouldn't ignore the warning if I were you."

"Point taken," I said. "There's enough weirdness around here that anything is possible. And the board seems to have known things we couldn't know. February 9 is the next new moon date. Would everyone like to repeat this party then?" They all agreed.

When Vicki and Trey were gone, Audrey, Lincoln, and I retired to the new room and the king bed.

Ping, ping, ping

"I thought we were done for the evening." I went downstairs and turned on the floodlights. Silence. I left the outdoor lights on and crawled back into bed. When I got up to pee around 1:00 a.m., all was quiet. I looked outside. The lights were off.

Finally a First Date

My new classes began on January 16 for the semester that would end on May 4. It appeared Audrey and I were officially living together, and Lincoln was very pleased with the arrangement. She worked a lot in the studio, and he was always with her. Trey was giving up his bachelor pad and moving into the store apartment with Vicki. He'd been helping with the shop so Audrey had more painting time. Her demand from the show was still strong, and it was financially good for all of them to support that.

The yellow cat began hanging around again. I'd see him every time I went to the shed for something, and Audrey often noticed him around the yard when she looked out the studio windows. He'd even become a subject in a sketch series she was working on. He seemed a pretty nice cat in the sketches, but Lincoln was still scared of him.

Over the past few weeks, we had settled into a good routine. Audrey had her work, I was now back in school, and we both had each other and Lincoln. It had been some time since I lived with someone else, and I was worried that I might have become too set in my own habits, but I was finding Audrey and I to be completely compatible in all ways. This was going to work. I could see myself asking this woman to spend the rest of her life with me.

"Audrey," I said one night in bed. "Don't you think it's time we went out on our first real date?"

"I don't know," she said, laughing. "I'm already getting the milk, do I still need to buy the cow?"

"Exactly the romantic response I was hoping for."

"I'd love to go on a real date with you. What do you have in mind for this special occasion?"

"Someplace with soft music, candlelight, exceptional cuisine, intimate ambiance, where I can gaze at your beauty."

"Ooh, Denny's?"

"Are you familiar with L'Auberge Chez Francois?"

"It does sound romantic."

"What are you doing tomorrow night?"

"Escargot for starters."

"Then it's a date?"

"Book it, Danno."

I came home from school and errands the next day around 4:00 p.m. to find a naked Audrey soaking in a lavender-scented bubble bath in the claw-foot tub. She couldn't know about Gwen. I stuffed my reaction quickly and kissed her. Audrey was alive, and I was too.

"Would you care to join me?" she asked. "I think there's plenty of room in here."

In less than a minute I was naked and in the warm bubbles. There was plenty of room in the giant tub for two wet bodies to cuddle. "I'm so looking forward to our first date and a romantic evening," she whispered in a warm breath close to my ear. Her hands went under the water, gently cupping me as I rubbed a beautifully erect nipple. She whispered again, even closer this time, "Can I serve you an appetizer?" Without waiting for my response, she slipped her tongue deeply into my mouth and her hands between my legs. I let her do all the work as I closed my eyes in sheer pleasure, quickly filling her hands and the bathwater with my release. Wow.

As I was recovering, she said, "Now get out of here, I have to do my hair and start getting dressed." She gave me a quick peck on the lips and sent me off. "I'll let you see me again when I'm ready for our evening out."

We weren't leaving for a couple of hours, so Lincoln and I did our walk thing. I had picked up some cigars on my way home and brought one with us. That Don is a bad influence, I thought as we walked through the woods. I talked out loud to Lincoln, telling him my shock and horror to find Audrey in the same tub where I had found Gwen a few years back.

Lincoln seemed to sense my anxiety. I was convinced he knew everything about human feelings and how to make them better. We walked for at least an hour, and I felt all better. It was just a tub. I did see the yellow cat out and about but only at a distance. Little Link pretended he hadn't seen a thing.

The second bathroom and tub were empty when we got back. "Audrey," I called.

"I'm in my dressing room," she answered from the small bedroom where she stayed before. "Get ready, I'll be out soon."

Lincoln and I picked out a charcoal suit, a white shirt with French cuffs, and a nice tie. I took a quick shower, did a fresh shave, and started dressing. I wanted to be the best I could be for Audrey. Around 6:00 she called from her dressing room, "Almost there, you can come in now." Lincoln and I had already been downstairs and poured two glasses of wine. I brought them in with me to see an amazing Audrey.

"Wine?" I said, trying to mask my fluster at what stood before me. The heels were back, and the dark stockinged legs disappeared under an electric blue dress. Every asset of her amazing body was showcased in the silky fabric.

"Thanks for the wine," she said taking a sip. "Can you give me a zip?"

She turned around showing off that magnificent butt and a lot of skin. I pulled the zipper up slowly, noting that she wasn't wearing a bra. I knew I'd be staring all night looking for nipples.

"You know," she said softly. "That zipper goes both ways. I hope you'll be wanting to try the other direction in a few hours." I gulped down too big a slug of wine. "You look nice," she added. "You clean up well."

"Not as well as you." The makeup was perfect and I was already thinking about smearing some lipstick. "Will you be warm enough?" I asked.

She picked up a heavy black shawl from the window seat and draped it across her shoulders. "I think so. Are we ready?"

The restaurant was as special as I had hoped, and the company was too. We talked like an old married couple about our work and projects, but we also flirted the night away like a real first date full of desire and expectation. The $147 left over from the sale of the gun fell short of our bill by $244.25. It was worth that and much more to be with this woman. It was everything that love should be.

Back at the house, I sat on the king bed as she approached, dropping her shawl on the floor and reminding me about the zipper going both ways. I reached around her and she pulled her arms from the sleeves of the dress as I lowered the fastener just enough for her ample breasts to spill from the fabric and into my mouth. I loved her light moaning sigh as I sucked and nibbled the nipples I'd been fantasizing about all night.

"There's more surprise," she said. I took the zipper all the way down as she stepped out of the dress to let me see her garters and dark stockings and no underwear.

I'm going to marry this woman.

Into the New Year

I was pleasantly surprised to find Darrel Metz sitting in the front row of my Human Resources class.

"I didn't see your name on the roster," I said.

"I added the class this morning."

"Did you need it for the MBA?"

"I don't think so, but an HR class can't hurt and it was a good way to keep in regular touch while we're planning the demolition of your property." He laughed.

Typical first classroom day, all intros, syllabus review, reading, and paper assignment dates. We wrapped up early, and Darrel joined me in the cafeteria for lunch.

"I was talking with Don last night," Darrel said. "He's thinking about bringing the Penn State folks down for a walkthrough before March to help them in planning on their end."

"Makes sense."

"They think a day trip will do it, driving down early, spending a few hours, and heading back home."

"We can do that anytime."

"I'd be happy to help in organizing things, if you'd like some help."

"I'll take all the help anyone has to give. Can I anoint you with the position of Arlington County Virginia Field Manager for the project?

You can tell me what we need to do. I think you and Don are better suited at this type of thing than I am, anyway."

"I accept, this will be fun for me."

"What do we do next, Project Manager?"

"Zoom meeting. We can get all the college folks together and join in with you and me. Audrey and the rest of the gang on this end are also welcome."

"Do we need to reserve a room?"

"No, we can use a laptop and do it from your place. That way we can walk things off and show different areas if there are any questions about the property. Morning would be better. Are people available around 7:00 a.m.?"

"You and I and Audrey are, for sure. Set it up, and we'll see if the others want to join."

"I'll get back to Don today. We have plenty of time before March."

I told Audrey about the talk with Darrel when she got home.

"I'll keep Vicki and Trey in the loop," she said. "They're getting pretty serious about wedding plans. It looks like May will be the date, and it looks like Pennsylvania."

"Pennsylvania in May should be nice. Is that for Trey's family?"

"Not really, you'll laugh," she said. "They're thinking they'd like to do it at the Shoe House."

I laughed, "I love it, what a cool venue that would be."

"I know, I love it too. We need to encourage that."

"There's less than four months before May. Is that enough time to get everything together for a wedding?"

"Nowadays you could do a wedding in a week. The invitations and gift lists all go online. If you've got your spot and your caterer, you're all set. Even the thank you notes are email."

"That somehow sounds less sentimental than the old way but a heck of a lot more efficient. Times change." We were quiet for a bit. I don't know what was on her mind, but I was thinking I wished we were planning our wedding.

"Do you want to do something different tonight?" she asked.

"Naw, we did that last night," I laughed and she joined me.

"We sure did. I hope that's our new norm and not something different."

"Okay by me, do you want to get normal again?"

Quiet. "I'm thinking about some Ouija time. We don't have to wait for new moons, and Vicki has me a little scared about you. Maybe there's more we can know."

"Okay." I didn't want her to know I was a little scared too. I'm pretty sure I wasn't fooling anyone.

The little library was more convenient than ever since it was now part of our bedroom. We went with candles again. Audrey didn't know it, but I also brought her sketch of the Black man. I put it in the desk drawer.

"Should we start with football trivia?" I asked.

Audrey was so beautiful in the candlelight, I couldn't help but stare. She had genuine concern in her eyes.

"Ouija," she started. "You've taken us to people and events in this house. We think they want us to know something. Is there anyone here tonight that would help us?"

YES

"Who is there?"

T-O-M

"Welcome back, Tom, you always seem to be here with us."

YES

"Tom," I asked. "Can I ask you to look at something?"

YES

I opened the drawer and put the sketch on the desk. "Can you tell me who this is?"

T-O-M

"This is you?"

YES

Audrey looked hurt. "You knew that. Why didn't you tell me?"

"I'm sorry. I was scared, and I wanted to see if we'd get a chance to ask Tom. Tom, would you ever hurt either one of us?"

NO

"Are you responsible for Audrey seeing this image and drawing it?"

YES

"Why?"

P-R-O-V-E

"To prove you were really here?" asked Audrey.

YES

"I believe you. Now, can you tell us more about who would kill Richard?"

YES K-I-L-L-E-D-B-4

I was impressed with the shorthand. I asked, "They've killed before?"

YES

"Do we know who they killed?" asked Audrey.

YES

"Who?" she continued. I suddenly felt a revelation that I knew. I didn't want to see the answer but I couldn't control my fingers as the planchette spelled G-W-E-N. Then GOODBYE.

I sobbed out loud, scaring Lincoln from the little room. Audrey moved the board to the desk and hugged me. "Oh, Richard," she said. "I'm so sorry I started this."

I thought my fears of the house were gone. I thought the revelations were done. I thought I was okay. I thought wrong. Audrey held me close as I sat there, an inconsolable, blubbering, lump.

We moved to the bed. I still sat, crying loudly. Audrey continued holding me and Lincoln pressed close to my other side.

"Lie down, Richard."

I could only curl into a fetal position while she and Lincoln held me close to comfort me. Through my bawling and weeping, I tried to tell myself nothing had changed, but everything had changed. It had to be an hour or more before I could compose enough to speak. "I knew she'd never kill herself," I whispered.

To Sleep,
Perchance to Dream

I finally cried myself to a dreamless sleep, waking at dawn to find myself alone. I could smell coffee from downstairs, and I found Audrey and Lincoln in the attic studio. Audrey was crying and hugged me again.

"I'm so sorry," she kept repeating.

"I found her underwater in the tub. I pulled her up, but I was too late, she was gone. There was an empty pill bottle on the floor. I threw it away before the police came. I've never told anyone that. I didn't want to believe she would take her own life, and I didn't want anyone to know, but I knew they would find out anyway. They said it was an accidental drowning. She didn't have enough of the drug to kill her, but they thought it was enough to disorient her and put her to sleep. She was so sad and so depressed and so helpless, but I never believed she would kill herself."

"You don't have any classes today, do you?"

"No."

"I can stay with you."

"No, do what you're supposed to do. I need to be alone and sort things out for myself. Lincoln can take care of me."

The hurt for Steven and Gwen was impossible to bear. Lincoln and I took one of our walks after Audrey was gone. It was an extra-long one, maybe two hours, I didn't keep track. I sat in the secret room for more hours. I looked through everything I could find that had notes and papers. They were all medical references, no other diaries or journals with new family history. Good, I don't know how I could have absorbed any more after last night.

I'd been deeply depressed before, when Steven died, when Gwen died, and, more recently, when I found out about the trials of my great grand uncle. I had gotten through all of that and emerged okay each time. But it always seems like the end when I'm in it. And I was in it now. I tried to tell myself this too would pass. Logically I knew it would. Emotionally I doubted it. The more I tried to be logical, the more I realized a new channel for my feelings. If someone had killed Gwen, I had to find them. I wanted to kill them too.

I was exhausted from doing nothing and my intermittent crying jags. I laid down to take a nap. I awoke to a scream and the sounds of a struggle. The noise stopped as I tried to get my bearings and a shadowy figure ran past the open doorway. Still groggy, I jumped up to give chase down the hall and the stairs and found ... nothing.

Retracing my steps and over the direction the shadow had come from brought me to the second bath, and the sound of running water. I saw the hair first, floating in the tub, and then the outline of the body. Oh my God, it was Audrey.

And then I sat up in bed, fully awake and drenched in sweat. It was a dream. Lincoln was sitting upright and alert next to me. He looked troubled. Still in shock, I went to the tub. It was empty and dry. I walked through the entire house from the attic to the great room. Nothing had changed. I finally sat down in the library again where I swear, I heard Tom's voice: "He'll kill Audrey too."

"Who is he?" I asked. No answer. None expected. I remembered my pink opal and pulled the necklace out of my shirt. I held the stone tightly and declared, "If I can believe in that, I can believe in this. You helped me before and I need you again. Bring me the love and comfort to make me whole one more time."

Audrey came home early. I was sleeping again and stirred as she lay down against me. She put an arm across my body and kissed me on the back of the head. I rolled over and brushed the hair from her tear-stained eyes, and just looked at her pain as my pain subsided. I told myself I had to be strong for her and said, "Wine?"

"Oh God yes."

We shared the stories of our day. Vicki is even more concerned after she heard about last night. Naturally, I still won the competition.

"I think I like it better when I'm alive in your arms than dead in your dreams. That had to be frightening, yet you seem better," she said. "Almost yourself again."

"Don't tell anyone but I think it's the pink opal."

"You wouldn't be the first to believe."

"Do you believe?"

"I believe that whatever settles your mind is a good thing. Why shouldn't it be the pink opal?"

"Chinese tonight?"

"I know a place."

The rest of the evening was quiet, inside the house and inside my head. We cuddled with Lincoln on the couch in front of a nice fire and spent the night right there.

Zooming

D arrel was already waiting in the HR classroom when I got there. "Can you do lunch again?" he asked. "I've got details on the Zooming."

"Good, I've got details on the haunting I want to ask you about."

The HR class was uneventful. At the cafeteria, we found a spot by one of the big windows but away from the crowd. "How is tomorrow morning at 7:00?" Darrel started.

"I'm good. I can call the store right now to check the rest of the crew."

"Namaste," answered Vicki.

"When will my pizza be ready?"

"I'm going to have to start calling you Dick."

"I'm really calling to check everyone's schedule for a Zoom meeting at 7:00 a.m. tomorrow."

And I'm really talking to you because Audrey filled me in on the past two days of your visitors. This is serious stuff we're dealing with."

"I believe you. Tomorrow is another step in the process. Can you do a quick survey there? I need to let Darrel know who to include."

"Hold please." She was back in ten seconds. "Have him email the link to the shop, and Trey and I will buzz in from here. Audrey says she's good to join from your place with coffee."

"Thanks, I promise we'll talk more about the other stuff."

"You bet your ass we will." She hung up.

"The Virginia contingent is all in for 7:00 a.m. tomorrow. Add an email to the shop with a link."

"Pennsylvania is already booked so I'll schedule this afternoon. Do you mind if I invite myself to your place for the Zoom coffee?"

"Not at all, in fact, I have some homework for you to start on that will be due then."

"Homework on the second day of class?"

"This isn't school, it's about your day job."

"Interesting."

"Are there any active serial killers in this area?"

"There are always unsolved murders, so maybe."

"This may sound strange, but Audrey and I believe we had credible contact with the spirit world."

"That's not much stranger than asking about serial killers. Are the two things related?"

"Yes. I think my wife was murdered. The murderer is still out there and wants to kill me too. Audrey's life may be at risk as well."

"Can you share the source of your reporting?" he smiled.

"Only if you promise you won't lock me up under a Temporary Detention Order." I smiled back.

"I promise. I'm intrigued by your insight and source of evidence, but I don't think you're a danger to yourself or anyone else."

Since we were being dramatic, I whispered, "Ouija board."

"Damn, I would have bet tarot cards or Dionne Warwick's Psycho Friends Network." We both laughed.

"I get it," I said. "It's nuts."

"Not completely. I've seen stranger premonitions matter in real cases before. I have some thoughts. Let me sleep on this one, and I'll let you know what I come up with over morning coffee."

"Thanks, Darrel."

Everyone was signed into the Zoom meeting by 6:50 a.m. so we started early. "Who's in charge?" I asked.

"I'll take it," said Don. "I promise this will be quick." He was in the library museum room with George and the two Penn State folks we met before. "The date for our field trip will be Saturday, February 3, barring any conflict on your side. We'll get there by 9:00 a.m., check out all possible investigation sites, and likely be gone by 1:00 or 2:00

in the afternoon. We won't have any heavy equipment, but I might run a metal detector over a couple of areas while I'm there. Thoughts or questions?" Nothing. "Then raise your hand if you'll be present that day." All raised. "I count five from Virginia and four from Pennsylvania. Thanks, I need the headcount so George can buy everyone lunch." Don chuckled infectiously. "Then we may be done."

"I have a question," I said. "Is there anything I can do here to make the visit more productive?"

"George, Abbey," Don said. "Any thoughts?"

Abbey spoke up. "No special preparation needed. If everything is unlocked and accessible, we'll find all we need to see and be able to work up a field plan for March from that."

"Adios," said Don. "See you on the third." Everyone waved and signed off.

"That was quick," said Darrel.

"I took a shower and everything," laughed Audrey.

"I told Audrey about our talk yesterday," I said to Darrel.

"The one about the Zodiac killer moving to Arlington and sending pasted-up messages to my office with you and Audrey as targets?"

"Yeah, that one," I laughed. "Have you solved it yet?"

"No, but the investigative approach would be pretty straightforward. I talked to a couple of long-time homicide guys, and they don't recall any patterns of concern but that doesn't mean we can't take another look. I'm going to have one of our trainees pull up every missing person or unsolved murder in ten miles of here from a year before your wife's death until now. If that yields nothing, we can expand the area or expand the crime base. Things like rapes, animal cruelty cases, and even breaking and entering have been known to be precursors to killings. I can't say we've had any of those cases here, but I also can't say we've had a reason to look for them before. My boss knows there are no solid leads, but he's okayed the time and resources to take a look."

"That would be wonderful," I said.

"No promises for any success, but your local law enforcement is on the case. We should have the first query answers in a day or two, and we'll take it from there."

"I feel better," said Audrey. If she felt better, I felt better.

On to February 3

E xcept for some more yellow cat sightings, things remain stable at the haunted house. Vicki and Trey joined us for dinner and she raised the level of caution after hearing from Audrey about my dream and the voice of Tom. "I may be the only one here who fully believes in the supernatural. I think it's good that you all question everything and look for explanations elsewhere but I'm begging you to suspend your disbelief and imagine what I see. I see Tom as a real entity. His appearance in voice and person is especially powerful. He's trapped in this place from an unnatural death, the same as Cody and Gwen. They're trying to save you, Richard, from the same fate."

"For discussion," I said. "I'll accept what you're saying. According to the books, Cody was embalmed before death. According to Tom, Gwen was murdered. How do you explain Steven and Bob's spirits coming to us?"

"Steven never had a chance at a natural life or death, and his spirit is probably so entwined with Gwen that they are one. That's my occult hunch. I don't know about Bob. His death seems to be natural, but he hangs around in the background just the same. I think there's more we don't know."

"If I go along with the natural versus unnatural death theory of lingering spirits, that would explain the spiritual absence of Dottie and Betty and all of the bodies in the pit. But why haven't we heard from

Dr. Craft? It seems suicide would be especially unnatural and troubling to a spirit."

"That one I also can't explain. Maybe the cancer took his life before he could."

"Maybe. By the way, Vicki, I do believe in your pink opal. It may be more psychological than metaphysical that it works for me, but it does work. If I'm also believing everything else we just said, it seems we have more business with Bob, and maybe Dr. Craft."

"Yes," she said. "And always Tom. You've seen him. He's talked to you. He's recognized the importance of Audrey in your life and given her his image. He's your biggest advocate and the most accessible contact. Be a believer, Richard, it could save your life."

"I'm there. Until I see some undisputed facts that change the narrative, I'm there."

"Me too," said Audrey.

Everyone looked at Trey. "I've always been a team player. I love Vicki in the quarterback position, and any other position." He smiled. "Can we eat now?"

I appreciated Trey breaking the tension. I was afraid we were heading to another Ouija event, and I wasn't ready for that.

The next morning, I went out to pick up the paper and ran into Buck. He still kept the supplies and equipment for his landscaping business in the shed. That was fine with me, as he needed all of them to take care of our grounds anyway. Buck always used the back road to come in and out when he didn't have the trailer on his truck. It was a right of way that went through the woods to the power lines where it met the main road in a few hundred yards. I never went that way. It was pretty rutted and had the nuisance of a gate at the property line. I guess that's why Buck was always in and out but I rarely saw him.

"Morning, Buck," I yelled and waved as I walked in his direction. "How are things?"

"Good," he replied. "Not time to start mowing yet, but there's plenty of branches and leaves to work on."

That was the usual extent of our conversation, but he kept standing there staring at me. "Looks like you have a new lady friend."

"I do."

"Do you like her?" Odd question.

"A lot." I played along.

"Going to marry her?"

"Too soon to tell but maybe. Why do you ask?"

"Just keeping an eye on things. If it's okay with you, I'm going to do a little raking and clear some sticks for a little bit."

"I've always said you can treat the place like you own it and do whatever you think needs to be done."

"I do that. This place means a lot to me."

I walked into the house thinking that was the longest and strangest conversation I ever had with Buck.

Audrey was getting ready to go to work. "I think you have another admirer," I told her. "Buck was asking about you."

"Aw, that's sweet. Are you jealous?"

"I don't think. He doesn't seem your type, and I guess I don't mind having another set of eyes on the place while we're working through our occult threats."

"He seems like a pretty good guy. I'm surprised Lincoln doesn't want to hang out with him."

"Lincoln is the jealous one."

Saturday the 3rd our guests from Pennsylvania arrived just before 9:00. Darrel and Vicki and Trey were already here.

"Good trip?" I asked.

"Great trip," said George. "I'm excited to be here. Don was right, it's quite the time capsule."

"How would you like to proceed?" I asked.

Don spoke up, "Why don't you do like you did with me? Give them the overview walking tour, show them the house, and then we'll go back for more detail in each prospective investigation spot."

"Sounds good. Come on group, follow me."

I took them past the cellar, pointing out the entrance. "That was the source of the artifacts that got this all started. There are some other interesting things you'll want to explore in there as well."

On to the pear grove and Yellow Cat. "This marker is purported to be the grave of the cat and Betty. That building over there is the stable and our storage shed, which was built later. Our Confederate soldier was buried behind the stable, which should put his remains in the dirt floor of the shed. Next, we have the smokehouse. I thought the hanging meat was old hams, but it may be cadaver parts. I'll let your party figure that out. The outhouse is self-explanatory and not known to be significant to us, but you're welcome to check it out if there are any coprolite collectors on your team."

"That's where we start the rookies," said Abbey Foster.

"No shit?" asked Don.

"The last major site of concern would be this mound. It was the depository for hospital waste of all kinds from limbs to bandages to whole unidentified bodies. We believe we'll find Tom at the near edge of that. I think that concludes the overview. Any questions before we do the house?"

Vicki spoke up. "I have a question for all of us," she said, raising her hand. "How many people here believe in the supernatural?" All hands went up, although Trey was a little late.

George Hunt looked at Don and the researchers from Penn State and said, "I don't think anyone could walk a Civil War battlefield and not feel a lingering something of the events that took place there. Would you agree?" He looked to our Penn State researchers, Abbey Foster and Fred Muller.

"Completely," said Fred. "We spend a lot of time with the bones of the past, and you can't help but feel they're with you, always trying to tell you something. Some sites speak to you more than others, but there is always a spiritual nature present in the work."

"I think this site has a lot to say," said Abbey. "We have an unusual amount of recorded history to follow as we begin the work here. Knowing the stories, and even the names, that we're hoping to find, I can't help but think we'll encounter some unexplainable assistance along the way. Historically, anthropologists would scoff at the notion of spirits, but there are too many documented field experiences to ignore, and it's become acceptable to keep an openness to such encounters. I think it's a good thing for the field of anthropology, and research in general."

"Thanks," said Vicki. "I know there is more at play here than will ever be explainable. Voices and spirits are trying to guide us against potential harm. I'm glad to hear that you'll not reject their attempts without consideration."

"Look," shouted Don, pointing to the woods. "Casper!" All eyes followed his finger for a second and returned to his face with mixed frowns and smiles. "Sorry," he said. "I like the topic, but the abyss was opening. We've got limited time today and a lot of ground to cover."

"Good call," said Abbey. "But Vicki, I hope I can spend a lot of time with you when we're here for the actual dig. We may be kindred spirits."

The highlight of the house tour was the secret library and its contents. George Hunt was familiar with a number of the reference books and very complimentary about the handwritten notes. "Your Dr. Craft was ahead of his peers in insight. His adjustments to existing procedures are remarkable, and many of them mirror what is still good practice today. I understand from Don that the embalming guides are especially rich in content. Would you mind if I looked through those?"

"I'd love to get your thoughts on anything here. Are you coming back in March for the excavation?"

"I wouldn't miss it."

"Then I'll give you the embalming notes to take with you, and you can bring them back then."

"Are you sure?" said George. "These are all very important papers."

"That's exactly why I would entrust them to you." George beamed.

When we returned to the yard, Don broke out his metal detector. "I'm going to give this a quick run over the burial sites as we get to them. It might be interesting."

We worked our way backward this time, starting at the pit. George worked with Abbey and Fred, taking measurements and notes, while Don scoped the area. The rest of us watched. Don had headphones on so we couldn't hear if he was finding anything, but he was.

"This is a target-rich environment," said Don. "I'd guess remains went in here buttons and all. I'm not getting anything in the Tom area, but we'll have other equipment to do that in March."

We bypassed the latrine and stepped into the smokehouse. "I'd love to cut into one of these burlap wraps," said Fred. "But we're better off waiting until we have more resources to make sure everything gets handled properly. Plus, if the rumors are true, the contents might be a little disturbing to some of you."

"I'm good to wait," said Vicki.

"Me too," said Audrey.

"I'm good to never know at all," said Trey, laughing.

In the shed, the team took more measurements and discussed a lot of options. "Behind the stable" was the extent of our knowledge of Cody's possible location. My guess was inside the current shed, but that was only a guess. Don had a lot of hits in this space, but he also remarked that every dropped bolt, nut, or washer would trigger a response, and you could have a lot of those in a workshop over untold years.

"All this equipment will have to move in March," said Fred. "Will that be a problem?"

"Shouldn't be," I responded. "I can help the landscaping guy move it over to the driveway area. I'll do that a day or two before you get here so we can check the weather and see if we'll need to cover any of it."

The last stop was the cellar. "I'm out on this one," said Vicki. Trey and Audrey agreed.

I got to impress the crowd with my flashlight again as they took their measurements. Don pointed out the finer points of the construction techniques while George used some other equipment he brought to check the calibration of the thermometers and hygrometers. All were working properly, and he remained baffled about the temperature changes.

To add to his puzzlement, I pointed out the desk where we found the untarnished artifacts. He stood and stared silently, obviously still in mourning for their now-aged condition. Then I wiped down and passed around jars of fingers and eyeballs.

"I've never seen anything like this," said Abbey. "These are perfectly preserved."

"You could lift fingerprints off of these," said Darrel.

"I don't think you'll get any hits in IIFAS," laughed Don.

"Hey, one of these eyes winked at me," said Darrel.

This was going downhill quicker than imagined. Dr. George Hunt cleared his throat to invoke decorum. "This is an unknown and undocumented sampling in all of my years of study. Richard, would you mind if I take one of each of these with me while I research the embalming notes?"

"I'd be honored to contribute to your studies in any way possible so, yes, take whatever helps. I have plenty. Is there anything else we need to see here?" I asked.

"Is there anything else here that needs to see us?" Darrel answered.

"Case closed for now," said Don. "Time to order lunch and review notes."

Over pizza, Vicki and Audrey took Abbey and Fred to the great room for bonding over the supernatural background of the place. The rest of the guys and I were being our usual irreverent selves when Darrel suddenly popped up with, "Hey, I got the first run back on your serial killing search."

Don's cop sense jumped right in, "What's that about?" Darrel and I explained. "So, what do you have?" asked Don.

"Possibly nothing, but in the time since Gwen's death, there have been three missing persons in the ten-mile radius."

"Anything in common?" asked Don.

"All young gay males. One within a year after Gwen's death, the other two more recently."

"Doesn't seem related, but it does raise a question worth following," said Don.

"My boss and I think so too."

"That seems like more than a coincidence," I said. "How did that not come up before?"

"Young males, heck, young adults, go missing all the time. It's even more prevalent among the gay community, so unless someone in the family is continually sounding the alarm, they just go by the wayside."

"But you know who they are, right?"

"Yes, but we never would have put them together before this. My next move is to see if I can find common links in their backgrounds. I'll keep you posted."

"Copy me on that if you don't mind," said Don. "That's interesting."

Lunch was consumed, and our travelers packed up to go. Vicki and Abbey were indeed kindred spirits and made a date to get Abbey to the shop in March during her stay here. I stopped Don as he was pulling out.

"Don, wait, you forgot your metal detector." It was sitting by the porch.

"No, I didn't," he said. "That's a gift for you. I have the newer model coming in a few days. Operation is self-explanatory. You'll enjoy playing with it."

There's a Bad Moon
on the Rise

Working our way up to the February 9 new moon, I did enjoy playing with the metal detector. I couldn't wait to call Don when I found buttons and coins and another belt buckle in one of the woods clearings. "You'll be proud of me," I said. "I'm now an official hunter of Civil War artifacts."

"I'm not at all surprised. You probably had several small encampment areas when units were dropping off casualties and waiting on their outcomes. That's easy pickings. I'm sure we'll find a lot more if we really get into it."

"That will give us something to do when the anthropology folks are here."

"I had a thought about that. How would you feel about enlarging the March party to include a reenactor camp?"

"How would that work?"

"George and I could invite a select group of experienced Civil War aficionados to join us. George does a great General Lee and I know a Stonewall Jackson and a Turner Ashby who would love to come out and play, along with some faux general infantry. We could pitch tents in one of the clearings."

"I think it would be a blast to have that going on with the dig. Let's do it."

"It's a good time sitting around the campfire and role-playing, but I'm also thinking we'd break character to do more metal detecting and a little spade work. These guys are all experienced dirt fishers, and I'm sure their foraging would expand your collection exponentially. They'd jump at the chance to explore an untouched site. Keep detecting and digging on your own until then and we'll show you some new tricks in March."

February 9 was upon us. Audrey woke up miserable. She'd said she was a little queasy the past couple of days and was now full-blown sick to her stomach. Vicki and Trey were coming by that evening for our next reach into the occult, and Audrey called to let them know she wouldn't be at the shop today. She was hoping to rally to be a better companion for the evening. I felt fine, but I was trying to talk myself into queasiness watching her distress and moping around. Last night's seafood was on my mind as a possible culprit. She couldn't stomach the morning coffee and just lay in bed with Lincoln the nurse by her side. Fortunately, it turned out to be a brief bug, and we were all back to normal by early afternoon.

When Vicki and Trey joined us, I showed them my metal detector finds and told everyone about my call to Don.

"Woo-hoo," said Vicki. "This is going to be a great party with all that Confederacy royalty descending on us. Why are they Confederates anyway?"

"I didn't think to ask but that does seem to be an obvious question. Maybe they're just more colorful characters."

"I'm looking forward to spending more time with Abbey when she gets here," said Vicki. "She's as strange as I am about the occult. It was obvious that she had to show restraint in her profession but she has a lot of pent-up demand to wallow in the wonders of the spirit world. We're going to have a great time weirding out everyone else with our dabbling."

"I can't wait," laughed Trey. "Does that mean we'll be playing the incubus–succubus game again?"

"Be careful what you ask for. I may be the incubus next time."

"Don't drop the soap," I said.

Ping, ping, ping

Lights on, noise stopped.

"They're calling us," said Vicki. "Let's ring up Tom and see if he can fill us in on Dr. Craft and Bob."

Back to our places in the secret library, with Audrey's Tom sketch on the desk. Vicki started. "Ouija, I know you know our thoughts. We come to you again on the new moon. We want to heed your warnings and save our friends. Can you tell us more?"

A quick YES

"Who is with us?"

T-O-M

"Do you know how to contact Dr. Craft?"

NO

"Do you know how to contact Bob?"

YES H-E-R-E

"Bob is with us tonight?"

YES

Suddenly I was cold and my heart was racing.

R-I-C-H-A-R-D

"Is that you, Bob?" asked Vicki.

YES

"Do you have something to tell us that can help Richard?"

The next answer took a long time, coming very slowly with many starts and stops.

M-Y-F-A-U-L-T

"You feel that something is your fault?"

G-W-E-N

"Bob, this is Richard. You never met Gwen, and you were gone twenty years before she died."

Slowly, M-Y-F-A-U-L-T again.

"Do you believe that Gwen was murdered?"

YES

"Do you know who killed her?"

YES

Vicki took over, "Is it the same one that would kill Richard and harm Audrey?"

YES

"Can you tell us who it is?"

GOODBYE

"Crap," said Vicki. "I'm not giving up. Tom, we lost Bob, are you still with us?'

We looked at each other for thirty seconds or, more, waiting. The planchette began to circle slowly, landing on YES.

Vicki continued, "Thank you, Tom."

YES

"Tom, I know you're trying to help Richard and my friend, Audrey. I believe your warnings, and I believe they are in danger. Can you give us something, anything, that would save them?"

YES

"Can you tell us who or what would harm them?"

GOODBYE

"Damnit," said Vicki. "Why can't they just tell us?"

Audrey's nausea continued through the weekend. "I think you need to see a doctor," I said.

"I think I just need to get back to the store and the gallery and stay occupied. This bug can't last more than a few days."

She went back to the shop on Monday. My classes were on Monday, Wednesday, and Friday. She did seem to be sloughing off her malady, and we even went out for dinner on Tuesday. It looked like she was going to be okay after all.

I came home Wednesday and prepared Cornish game hens stuffed with wild rice. I thought an intimate candle-lit dinner would be a nice celebration of recovery. Audrey showed up at the usual time, around 6:30. She changed into her flannel jammies and robe, and I offered her a glass of wine, which she uncharacteristically turned down. She was a little quiet. I hoped she wasn't feeling out of sorts again.

Dinner was nicely romantic and we ended up in our usual spot in front of a fire, with Lincoln draped on Audrey's lap. Domestic bliss.

"Vicki had a premonition today," said Audrey.

"That's hardly news," I laughed.

She pulled a little plastic thing from her robe pocket. "Vicki made me pee on a stick, and we got this," she said, handing over a positive pregnancy test. I stared at it with many thoughts crashing through my mind.

"Are you okay?" she asked.

"Only if it's mine," I said laughing and hugging her. She laughed too, obviously relieved.

"It is mine, right?"

"Entirely your fault."

"Are you okay?"

"Yes, now that I know you are."

"Lincoln, what do you think?" He looked happy, as usual.

The phone rang. Vicki. I put it on speaker and Audrey answered, "Yes dear?"

"How did it go?"

"I'll let him tell you, you're on speaker."

I'll have to call you back," I said. "I'm painting the spare room for the nursery."

"Sounds like it went okay," Vicki giggled. "I'm happy for you guys."

"We are too," I said.

"Will you be in tomorrow?" she asked Audrey.

"And the next day and the next day. Now that I know why I was sick, I can embrace it."

"Love you, see you tomorrow."

March Is Coming

The rest of the month flew by. Audrey and Vicki were inseparable between the pregnancy news and the wedding plans. I made a lunch date with Trey in late February. We had a guy talk to do, so we met up at Hooters.

"I guess you and Audrey are in a committed relationship now," Trey laughed.

"Looks that way."

"Are you ready?"

"I've been down this road before, and it didn't end well but I'm feeling good about it this time."

"You should. You've been very good for Audrey, and the two of you will be great parents."

"She's been good for me too. I think I'd like to keep her." I laughed

"I believe that claim is staked," he laughed back.

"Speaking of staking the claim, how do you think you and Vicki would feel about a double wedding?"

"Awesome, blossom, I'd love to not go to the gallows alone."

"And Vicki?"

"You know it. She loves Audrey like a sister. I'll tell her this afternoon."

"Okay, but keep it a secret for the moment from Audrey. I haven't asked her yet."

"What do you have planned?"

"I'm going to surprise her at the shop. I want you and Vicki to be there."

"What can we do to help?"

"Would you go ring shopping with me?"

"Finish your burger and we're there. I'll take you straight to my guy. Lunch is on me because you're about to be broke."

I couldn't match Vicki's ring but I picked out a great sparkly stone just over a carat and joined it with a solitaire setting. Simple, yet elegant, as Jackie Kennedy would have said. Or was it Coco Chanel? I don't know this stuff.

What now?" asked Trey.

"Keep Audrey away from the room full of crystals and put it in with the pink opals so I can find it."

"Done."

"I'll drop in at 11:00 tomorrow to see if she accepts."

"I think you're safe on that one. I certainly hope so. It would be kind of awkward otherwise."

Trey called me that night to let me know Vicki was ecstatic about a double wedding and the ring was in place.

"Who was that?" asked Audrey

"Trey."

"You boys are getting awfully close these days."

"Not as close as you girls, but, yeah, we're finding common ground."

I couldn't believe how giddy I was heading to the shop the next day with Lincoln in tow.

"Namaste," said Vicki.

"Konnichiwa."

"Audrey," said Vicki. "The Japanese guy is back with a dog." She gave both Lincoln and me a big hug as she put a "Back in 20 Minutes" sign on the door. She had shooed out the last customer, a regular, after telling them what was happening.

Lincoln and I met Audrey coming from the gallery. "What a wonderful surprise," she said. "What brings you two here?"

"We were in the neighborhood. I was thinking how much your pink opal was good to me, and I thought I might look at another for a matching ring. Would you help me pick something out?"

"I would, but Vicki is the real expert on the stones."

"But she's not the real expert on my heart. Come look with me."

"Okay," she said following me into the crystal room. I saw the ring box right away and hoped she didn't.

And she didn't until I opened it on one knee and proposed with Lincoln at my side and Trey and Vicki peeking around the corner.

"Oh my God, it's beautiful," she said, kneeling to hug me.

"Then you accept?"

"Of course, I love you, Richard."

"I love you too. I think Vicki has another surprise for you."

"Yes," Vicki screeched. "We need to amp up our wedding planning now that I get to walk down the aisle in a double wedding with my sister from another mother."

"What?" said Audrey, looking at all of us.

"That's right," Vicki said. "We're getting married together."

"Oh, I don't know," said Audrey. "I'd hate to take away from your special day."

"You wouldn't be taking away from anything, you'd be making it the best day ever."

"I'd love that, but I feel awkward about being a pregnant bride."

"No one will even know. I don't think you'll be showing anything in just a couple of more months. Plus no one expects people of your age to be celibate anyway. Stop being a Puritan. I can't speak for Richard, but I know you've had a lot of sex since I've known you."

"Maybe you shouldn't speak in front of Richard about that either," I said, laughing out loud.

"I won't take no for an answer," said Vicki. "We're going to be twinsie brides in May and that's it."

"Give me a day to be sure," said Audrey. "This is all happening so fast. I think it's good, but I should probably discuss it with my new fiancé overnight." She looked into my eyes questioningly. "We should also not forget that I'm hormonal and possibly dangerous." She laughed, and we all joined her.

"Get out of here and go home with your fiancé," Vicki said. "I need your affirmative answer first thing in the morning. We've got a lot to do, including picking out our matching wedding gowns."

Of course, the morning answer was a big yes.

February came to a close with some housekeeping tasks and another surprise. The housekeeping was in preparation for the March event. I made a point to run into Buck again.

"Hey Buck, I need your help this week."

"Sure, what do you need?"

"We need to empty the shed."

"What for?" he asked.

"I have a group of Civil War researchers coming in. They're going to do some investigation on the property to check out Dr. Craft's historical records. One of the spots to look at is thought to be in the shed, so they may be doing some digging there."

"Can't they just dig somewhere else? I've got over thirty years of my business stored in there."

"Afraid not, we need to clear the floor in there."

"What am I supposed to do with all my stuff? I need it for work."

"I checked the forecast, and it's clear and dry for the next week. I'll help you pull things out, and we can put everything right here by the driveway. You'll still be able to come and go for tools and things, and we'll put it all back when they finish that part of their work."

Resignedly, Buck said, "Alright, it's your place."

It didn't take long. We could drive the tractors and mowers. A lot of the loose stuff we put in the utility trailer to tow over. "The tools hanging on the walls are fine to stay," I told him. "We can leave those."

"What are they looking for in here?" Buck asked.

"We think there's a body of a Confederate soldier buried here. The doctor's notes said 'behind the stables.'"

"I've been working in here for years and never seen a thing."

"Well it's not like he'd be sitting up and waving at you," I laughed. "He's been dead over a hundred and fifty years."

"I guess," said Buck, not laughing.

When we were wrapping things up, he asked about Audrey again. "I notice your girlfriend is around a lot."

"She's not my girlfriend anymore, she's my fiancée. We're getting married in May."

"What?"

"Buck, I'm sure you meant to say, 'Congratulations, that's wonderful news.'"

"It was just a surprise, that's all. Congratulations."

"And we're pregnant," I poured on the fire.

"Great," he said flatly. "Great for you."

It was a new record for the length and strangeness of my Buck conversations. He drove away out the back road.

Housekeeping done, the surprise part came a few hours later when Darrel parked his cruiser in the driveway. Lincoln and I were doing our frisbee thing and stopped to greet him. Today was a work day, judging by his uniform.

"Yard sale?" he said, looking at Buck's equipment in the driveway.

"I wish, just clearing out the workshop so our anthropology friends can check it out."

"I probably shouldn't drop by unannounced, but I was passing by and had something of interest."

"I'm always ready to be interested."

"Do you have time right now to do a quick Zoom with Don? I promised to keep him in the loop on our missing persons."

"Sure. Come on, Lincoln. I think us boys are going to do some serious police business."

Don had already gotten a call from Darrel and opened up a Zoom room. Darrel checked his text message, and we joined.

"How are things going for our 1866 encampment?" Don asked me.

"We're ready for the circus to come to town. Bring cotton candy."

"And Twizzlers," added Darrel.

"Sorry guys, licorice whips, peppermint sticks, and Necco wafers are the only appropriate treats for a true reenactor."

"Licorice whips sound a lot like Twizzlers," said Darrel.

"Not hardly, you'll find out if you come and visit us by the campfire. By the way, you'll need the camp password to join us. It's 'Spangler Springs,' the same one we use at Gettysburg."

"Good to know," I said. "So, Darrel, what's the big news on our missing persons?"

"There is some common ground there. I happen to know more than either of you would want to know about how young gay guys get together. At least two of these took the route of anonymous meetings in public places known among others like themselves. Our third guy is no longer missing. He was a runaway from a conservative home and ended up in Orlando. I tracked him down, and he's doing fine."

"Interesting," I said. "How do these guys know where to go?"

"It's easy today to find any hookup you want with the internet. There are some sites like Grindr and Squirt specific to that pursuit. Back in the day, the Alexandria train station was a known haunt for stranger sex. Today a couple of the more popular places are the I-66 rest stop near Manassas and the Fairfax Hospital parking garage. Both of our persons of interest were known to have frequented the rest stop."

"How can you know that?"

"If you've been around the community for a while, you know the bars and hangouts. It's not as big a social group as you might think, and it's pretty close, being based on mutual trust. Ask the right questions in the right places and you can find what you're looking for."

Don said, "I never had that insight in Philadelphia. Those unique connections would be invaluable in many areas of investigative work."

"Absolutely," said Darrel. "Back to our two guys, Scott Marshall and Eli Dean. Scott was reported missing almost exactly a year after Gwen's death. Eli disappeared only four months ago. I don't know if they ever knew each other. Their patterns were similar but not abnormal for most closeted male youths. Both families deny any hint of homo-sexuality, also not unusual."

"How does this help to find Gwen's murderer?" I asked.

"Unfortunately, Richard, not at all. We know these guys by name. We know their hobbies and that they were exposing themselves to potentially bad actors in their lifestyle choices. Beyond that, we don't have a shred of evidence to solve their disappearances or even confirm foul play. The only coincidence relating to Gwen is the proximity of their homes."

Don said, "Sounds like you've got two missing persons, possibly by their own choice, and no other leads."

"That's where we're at, but I'm not giving up on Gwen. I'm going to have our trainee search the more common precursor crimes to murder and open up the search area to twenty miles. We're not done yet."

"Thanks, Darrel, I appreciate the efforts. You too, Don."

"I haven't done a thing."

"You've given a shit enough to stay involved. That means a lot."

March 4

I'd canceled my classes for the day so I could be home for the pending
party as the Pennsylvania Carnival came to town today. The Penn
State group had two large enclosed trailers full of supplies and equipment. By contrast, Don and his fellows had his cruiser and two pickup
trucks. The anthropology/archeology headquarters tents were going to
be set up between the stables and the smokehouse, central to most of
the work. We guided their trucks and trailers, snaking them through
the pear grove to a field beyond the stables where they could offload.
Don's guys drove down a path to a large clearing in the woods, dropped
their load, and brought the trucks back to the driveway.

The campsites started emerging with great contrast. The college
group shelters were portable dorms and offices, canvas sides but sturdy
structures as seen on travel brochures for high-end safari accommodations, spartan but seemingly luxurious from the other encampment.
They even had generators and port-a-potties. Glamping at its finest.

The Confederate camp shaped up to be one larger rustic tent surrounded by pup tents with a firepit in the middle. They used a chain saw
to cut down a dead tree for firewood and stumps for chairs before the
ban on modern equipment was imposed. A hole in the ground behind
the site would handle sanitation needs.

Audrey and I traipsed through both areas, asking questions and
marveling at the differences. One was new, and one was old school,

but both were fully functional for a week or two in the woods. Audrey asked Don the question that Vicki had pondered previously. "Why is a group of Pennsylvania guys doing reenactment as Confederates?"

Don laughed out loud, "It is unusual, but we can blame George for that. When I first took up the hobby, most of us started out as Philadelphia cops in Union roles, but we switched for two reasons. Some of the group were already transitioning to Southern personas just because we needed more of those for battlefield reenactments. We all converted after I met the esteemed Dr. Hunt. Before I got to Churchville, George had relocated from a previous college presidency in Virginia. During his time there he was well-established in the local historical society as a writer and lecturer who performed as Robert E. Lee. Now that we had our supreme field commander, we've all found it fun to play the other side in our hometown games."

"Speaking of George," I said. "Where is he? I thought he was planning to join the party."

"He'll be along in a day or so. He wanted to ride down on Traveller, so it's a slower trip."

"Really?"

"No," laughed Don. "You're too easy. He wanted to wrap up some things at school so he could clear a whole week to stay here."

"Too bad," said Audrey. "I would have loved to see him riding into Arlington, waving his sword."

"Wouldn't we all," said Don. "But we'll have to settle for the distinguished general to just be walking around like the rest of us."

Day One was used up getting the two campsites together for the guests. That night, Vicki, Trey, and Darrel joined us. Along with the college crew, we all followed the sounds of a banjo and a harmonica and sat by the campfire with the army men in their skivvies. Trey brought a couple of bottles of Rebel Yell Whiskey. It wasn't period correct, but no one complained, and the evidence of the indiscretion was fully destroyed by midnight. Vicki corralled Audrey and Abbey in serious conversation for most of the evening. I'll have to keep an eye on those three.

Day Two was all business. Don and a couple of his guys joined the college team for orientation. Abbey was the overall project manager, and Fred was the technical specialist. He'd guide the student and the reenactor volunteers in the use of their metal-detecting equipment and how each potential site would need to be prepared to allow the best conditions for the effectiveness of the secret weapon, the ground penetrating radar, or GPR.

"Alright gang," Abbey started. "This isn't a race. Everyone should be in slow-motion mode. We're going to cover every inch of suspect ground, and we're going to do it multiple times over several days. We won't break out the Bobcat or the shovels until we have the best mapping possible of what may be under the ground surface. I can't reiterate enough that, no matter how compelling you think a signal is, nobody digs anything today. If I see anyone sticking anything in the ground, a trowel, your car keys, or even your hands, I will stop you immediately and may even send you off the site.

"We're lucky to have extra hands here with a lot of experience in metal detecting specific to Civil War sites. We need to thank Don Weston, the guy over there, for that." Don smiled and waved. "Don, Fred will check all of the metal detectors in your group. If any of them are not up to the standards of our equipment, we'll issue them one of our own. We have plenty of backup units. If any of our Virginia partners would like to try their hand, we can outfit you as well, but I'd prefer you do your prospecting elsewhere on the property until you get a day or two of experience.

"You'll be working in teams, one experienced machine operator matched with one student volunteer. The students will have pre-printed grid maps of whatever area they are working. They'll mark your potential findings and keep notes on your interpretation of what they may be. By this afternoon we hope to have a preliminary assessment of what can be picked up by the metal detectors. If that is all we do today, we'll have been very successful. Okay teams, buddy up and meet with Fred for your technical overview."

An hour later, six vetted teams were at work. One team at Betty and Yellow Cat, one at the presumed Tom spot, one in the shed, and the other three traversing the burial mound. Except for some occasional beeps and team conversations, things were pretty quiet until the lunch break. The Confederate soldiers in the woods had cooked cornbread, beans, sausages, and bacon over the fire to feed the masses.

The afternoon was no different than the morning, with alternate teams going over the work of previous teams. Abbey announced the day done at 4:00 p.m. Don and I joined her and Fred in their command post to see how things were going. "I was tempted to break a little ground out there at a couple of points," said Don.

"Good thing you didn't," said Abbey. "You're the one person I wouldn't kick off the site, and you would have set a terrible example for the students."

"But I know it was two belt buckles," he said, laughing.

She laughed back, "They've been there over a hundred years, and they'll still be there tomorrow and the next day."

"I know, how is the mapping coming?"

"Quite good. As expected, the mound is the hotbed of metal, but the shed has more than its share for the size of the space."

Fred added, "I think we have a pretty comprehensive metal map established, since we shouldn't be finding any magnetite or other hot rocks here."

"What does tomorrow bring?" I asked.

"Initially some more of the same," said Abbey. "We have some areas where different teams had conflicting marks of objects and a few different interpretations from the machine operators. That's normal, and Fred will go back over those to clear them up. That will be a good class for the hobbyists at the same time. I'm spending the morning with Vicki and Audrey at their store. Vicki has the same occult curiosity I have. From what they tell me, you should too."

"I'm getting there."

"Any thoughts on scope of timing for the total project?" asked Don.

"We had originally cleared two weeks, but we won't need it unless something totally unexpected comes up."

"Which wouldn't be unusual here," I cautioned.

"True from what I hear," she said. "But we should be able to finish prep for the GPR tomorrow, and Fred can start that process on Day Three. Conservatively we have our underground maps and can start digging by Day Five. I'd anticipate wrapping up somewhere around Day Ten."

"You're the expert," said Don. "If you can get your troops assembled by 6:00, we've got pizza being delivered at the house."

"The college staple, we'll be there."

The General Comes to Town

A t 9:00 a.m. sharp, General Lee appeared in the driveway. George Hunt stepped out of his car in full military regalia. Don was having breakfast with us and saluted when we got to the porch.

"At ease, soldier," said the general, putting on his hat. "Have you a cup of coffee for a weary traveler?"

Audrey laughed out loud. "I'm glad I'm out of here. I sense a bunch of boys will be having a giant testosterone party today. Nice boots, George."

"Why thank you, ma'am," responded the general.

"Good thing you didn't have any traffic violations on the way here," said Don. "The uniform would have been hard enough to explain, and the 1851 Colt Navy Revolver might have made a state trooper a little nervous."

"I wanted to make a good first impression," said George, taking off the hat. "I am serious about the coffee, though."

"Come on in, General," said Audrey. "We also have bagels if that's allowed in whatever year you're in."

"Cream cheese?"

"And lox," Don said. "I brought some Philadelphia with me."

Abbey dropped in for a quick coffee, and then she and Audrey went off to girl stuff.

"How goes the inquiry?" asked George.

"Well," said Don. "They're going to do a once-over this morning on yesterday's metal sweep and move into ground prep for the radar. It's going very well."

"I may change before I check in with Fred," George said.

"I wouldn't deprive him," I offered. "It's not every day Robert E. Lee stops by to inspect the troops."

"First," said George. "I need to get your books out of the car and return them to you." As he brought the books in, he remarked, "I can't thank you enough for the loan. It was quite enlightening."

"I was pretty sure you'd know better than I did how to interpret some of that."

"The only wisdom I brought to the party was meeting with our science staff at Churchville. The chemistry and biology faculty had the background to pick out the finer points. Dr. Craft was greatly gifted, almost supernaturally, with an intuitive sense of medical vision beyond any research of his time. I can't say I agree with his 'save the body, save the soul' theology, but it was the driver of his embalming experiments. As much as we've discussed the occult influences on his home and family, I can't reject that he had some otherworldly influence in his insight."

"That's on the cusp of spooky," chuckled Don.

"It is almost spooky the way things evolved in Craft's work. Our faculty colleagues had to get deep in their research to break down the chemistry of the Scheele work that was added to the other potions. It turns out the Scheele mixture produces an impurity by-product of something called acetaldehyde, a precursor to formaldehyde, which is still the embalming standard base today. Dr. Craft used these formulas in high concentration, producing miraculous results. At the same time, he was unknowingly exposing himself to a cancer risk, specifically leukemia. Early-stage exposure can contribute to depression and some cognitive impact, both potentially noted in the later journals you've found. It appears that he found the gift of life, as he interpreted it, at the expense of his ultimate death."

"And you think he had some occult assistance in his work?" I asked.

"Our science colleagues can't explain how he could have known what he seemed to know at that point in history. Maybe it was pure luck, maybe it was brilliance beyond his years, maybe it was something else we couldn't define, but it did border on eerie to them."

"Amazing. Every time I think we've figured it all out, there's another question," I said.

"Another log on the fire," said Don. "Let's go see what Fred has planned for the day."

Fred had already given direction and dispatch to several teams that would re-map the anomalies from yesterday. He was working with the uncontested grid maps at a table outside the command tent when he looked up to see us coming.

"General Lee," he said. "To what do I owe this honor?"

George answered, "I just wanted to thank you for what you're doing here for our friend Richard."

"No thanks needed. It's our honor and pleasure to have this opportunity. No doubt there will be many journal papers for the academic world coming out here."

"I'm hungry," Don said. "Can we start getting into the smokehouse delicacies?" We laughed.

"Not today," he said. "But I promise you'll get the first taste when we do."

"Any digging today?" I asked.

"No, and probably not tomorrow, either. When we've got all of our maps in sync, we'll lay out the prime areas for the next steps. We think we know for sure where Betty and the cat are, based on the marker, but Tom and Cody could be ten feet or more from their presumed interment spots. We'll need everything we can get from the GPR before we break ground on any of them."

"Anything we can do?" asked Don.

"Not really. We need cleared flat ground for the radar, so that will be the biggest task today. I've got plenty of student resources for the grunt work. It's slow going since we don't want anything heavier than a rake on the surface, and there is a lot of vegetation to strip from the mound area and the cat grave. The Cody grave is in an area of clear dirt and doesn't need any radar prep. I wouldn't expect any of you to be interested in that work."

"Au contraire," said Don. "Several of our metal detecting group, including myself, had some good hits on items we think we know from experience. We'd be highly motivated to clear those for you so we can be ready to dig them out when we get the 'all clear.' Those are all in the mound area."

"Then stop by after lunch for the lecture on technique. When we're confident everyone understands the assignment, we'll issue rakes. Abbey and I would like to host lunch today if that's okay." He looked at me and asked, "Can we use the patio area and the grill outside your kitchen?"

"Sure, anything you need, me casa es su casa."

"She'll come back with hamburger and hot dog fixings to bulk everyone up for an afternoon of ground scraping."

Vicki came home with Audrey and Abbey shortly before noon, and they took on the cooking and serving chores. After lunch, the three women took me aside in the great room. "We've been talking about the new moon that's coming up," said Vicki. "We think you should let the three of us do the séance."

I guess they expected me to protest when I responded, "Great."

"We think the spirits are the most worried about you, and that may inhibit their responses."

"You don't have to sell me on the idea," I said. "I'd be very happy to sit one of these out. You and Abbey seem sympatico in the spirit realm, and a fresh set of eyes and ears might help. I'm more concerned about Audrey's well-being than my own, but I trust you'll take good care of her in your journey to the spirit world." I laughed. They didn't.

"Seriously," I said. "The more I get close to our new moon encounters, the more anxious I get about the messages we seem to be receiving. The three of you would probably have the most productive results, and I'm okay to get them second-hand. If any of our ghosts ask for me, I'll be having cigars and adult beverages in the 1860s camp."

Abbey joined Fred for the afternoon site preparation, and Audrey and Vicki went back to work. I was relieved to be off Ouija duty for the month.

When the day's work was called to a halt, everyone gathered on the patio again for dinner. There are seven in the reenactor group and six attendees from Penn State. With Audrey, Vicki, Trey, and me, a total of 17 dinner guests. It seemed like we had the entire menu of the Chinese place for our family-style feed. During dinner, Vicki and

Audrey picked Don's brain for wedding catering sources. He solved that problem for them with a call to the cafeteria at Churchville. They had already booked the Shoe House, so the big infrastructure parts of the nuptials were coming together.

The group broke up after dinner, going to their respective campfires or tents. The girls went to the studio to hang out. Trey brought his Super Bowl rings to show Don, and the two of them stayed on the patio, talking football over cigars.

George and I went to the library. We spent a couple of hours re-visiting the books and the medical instruments. George's knowledge of everything Civil War related blew me away. There wasn't a single piece of equipment or a journal entry that he was unfamiliar with in its content. He continued effusively thanking me for the access to everything here, and I kept thanking him for the education. What an interesting guy.

The next morning, I had classes to teach while the groundwork continued at the house.

March 7: GPR

W hen I got home from school, the GPR work had started. Fred was slowly rolling a cart over the area of Tom's demise. I found Don to ask him how things were going. Darrel also had shown up on his day off to hang out and play.

"Don's an expert on this stuff," said Darrel as I walked up. "He's been telling me about the Philadelphia history of water main breaks. Some of the early pipes were just hollowed-out trees, and the city partnered with ground radar experts to look for the old undocumented water works."

"How does that translate to corpses?" I asked.

"Pretty well," said Don. "Even if the corpse is gone, which is usually the case for the age of remains we're looking for."

Abbey had walked over to join us. "What's he doing?" I inquired about Fred.

"Looking for amplitude contrast anomalies," she responded.

"Is there a lay version of that?" I laughed

"When we approach a site where we believe bodies are buried, we start with a visual inspection for surface collapses. Often the contents of a grave will completely deteriorate and the ground will sink into the empty cavity. We don't see that here, so we move on to the metal detection indications and, finally, to the best tool we have, which is the GPR. That's the unit on the bottom of the cart that Fred is guiding."

"Is it like what we'd see from an airport scanner or an X-ray?" asked Darrel.

"That would be great if it was, but unfortunately no. Those would be almost like watching TV, where this is like watching static. It displays underground images that an experienced technician can decipher, but it's rare for us to find complete corpses that would give us the clear amplitude contrast anomalies I mentioned earlier. There was a fairly recent dig from the Second Battle of Manassas that produced just that, resulting in two complete and remarkably preserved corpses. We hope for similar results here, but it's way too early to tell if we'll be that lucky. Barring that, we look for areas where the soil has been disturbed and remains unnatural to its surrounding environment. Micro layers of the earth reveal clues to an expert operator about previous digs. The disturbance of those layers becomes different electrically from the surrounding ground."

"When will we see results?" I asked.

"Fred may see some useful information while he goes, but we won't make assumptions on anything until the entire area has been scanned twice, inch by inch."

The Penn State team had a fully stocked refrigerator of cold cuts and beverages, so we joined them for lunch. Fred had printed out a number of GPR displays and set them in front of Abbey. "This is great," she said. "Beyond expectation."

I was looking over her shoulder at wavy lines and bumps, not at all sure what could possibly be exciting in the images. "Is this like those Magic Eye things?" I asked. "If I squint hard, will I see something?"

Abbey laughed. "No, but if you look at these and work the digs of the results for twenty years or more, the meaning gets a little clearer. I like to think I'm pretty good at these, but Fred is the real expert. I'll let him explain."

"Step over here, guys," Fred said. "Class is in session."

Don, Darrel, and I went with Fred to one of the large folding tables as he spread out a dozen pictures in groupings. The students followed. I sensed that Fred and Abbey were quite excited, but I still saw nothing but lines and bumps.

"These are the bodies we came here to find," said Fred.

The rest of us looked at each other and at the pictures and at Fred. "I don't get it," said Darrel.

"This first grouping is Cody. I found him very early this morning behind the stable as the journal said. He's about three feet into the shed. The second set is Betty. I need Abbey to do some more site work there, as we have multiple signals I'd like to clarify. Based again on the journals, the additional anomalies should represent the cat. Lastly, we have our friend Tom. He is at the northwest corner of the mound. I know these are cryptic to first-time viewers, but I can tell you the strength of these findings is remarkable. We've done corpse recovery on known bodies buried less than two months and not gotten findings as clear as these."

"Do we start digging now?" I asked.

"We're getting close. I defer to Abbey as the project lead for the next steps. What do you think, Abs?"

"I think I defer back to you for input," she replied. "We have enough here to start working any or all of the bodies. What are your concerns about the cat dig?"

"I don't have quite the clear margins I would prefer to go after Betty without fear of some damage, and I think we have a couple of judgment calls before we put shovels in the ground. One is how much we care about the cat. If we're okay that the cat might get a little roughed up at the expense of getting the best disinterment chances of success for Betty, then that grave is possibly our starting point."

"Your call," said Abbey to me.

"Lincoln would say 'F' the cat. It sounds like that position favors the greater good."

"Okay," said Abbey. "The cat comes out first in whatever condition it comes out in. What are our other judgment calls?"

"The mound, or pit," said Fred. "Are we in agreement the scope of the project is surfacing the human remains of our three identified corpses?"

"I believe so."

"Then the mound is out of scope for us, and we can turn it over to Don and his guys to dig at will. I can mark off a sufficient archaeological site at each grave and leave the rest of the grounds open for free exploration."

"I think we can do that," said Abbey. "Provided that the body digs remain clean and there is no interference with equipment or human resources for those sites. Does that work for you, Don?"

"Wonderfully. I think you've already seen that our troop is pretty professional, and I can assure you they'll stay out of the way of the serious work. We can also take on any of the amateurs from Virginia or your student volunteers and work with them on the pit grounds to get them some experience without compromising the main purpose here. And we'll be ready sets of hands available to follow your guidance if you need more manpower on the graves at any point."

"Teamwork is dreamwork," said Abbey, moving to the whiteboard. "So we're all on the same page," she said, writing. "The rest of today has four tasks. One is the stakeout of the identified graves. No one enters the roped-off grounds from that point except the actual excavation teams. Two is the cat extraction. I'll lead that myself with two of the students. Three is backfilling Betty's grave so Fred has a flat surface for the GPR to do a clearer map for her exhumation. Four is for Fred and me. We'll go over the new Betty images and plan for tomorrow. We'll need to decide if we're doing one body at a time or if we want to work multiple. I have some thoughts, but anyone else is welcome to join us at that time to offer their own. Any questions?" None heard.

"Okay then," she continued. "If we fall short in any of that, we'll finish in the morning. Either way, we should be digging tomorrow. When lunch is done, Fred will need some hands to help with the stakeouts, and I'll be picking a couple of able bodies to help me pluck out a cat."

"Can I be one of those able bodies?" I asked.

"I'd welcome that," said Abbey.

Hello Kitty

Fred and his volunteer students measured and roped off the Betty site first so Abbey could get to work. Our cat preservation concerns were minimal, so she allowed Darrel to be the other able body. We were joined by two students who would be working the sieve.

"We're going to do an expedited dig here," said Abbey. "I'll instruct you when and where to use your shovels for the initial groundbreaking. Every bit of dirt will be put into buckets and run through the sieve. We don't expect to find anything there, but a good rule of thumb to remember is that any excavation is destructive and non-repeatable, so we'll still follow basic protocol. We take pictures now and at every step of the process. The first order of business is to move the headstone. Our subject is pretty shallow, probably a foot or less, and some of the body is under the grave marker."

Darrel and I used a shovel as a crowbar to break the stone loose from the ground. It was much heavier than anticipated. We each took an end and leaned it against a pear tree.

Abbey used a can of spray paint to mark out a rectangle of ground. "We know these lines are outside of the remains, so we'll start here and work our way in. Use the flat-blade shovels and go straight down into the paint lines. Don't dig anything up, just perforate the soil about six inches deep along the lines."

With that done, she instructed, "Now we're on our hands and knees with the small trowels. We can dig aggressively to a depth of six inches, and then I'll do some probing for our next steps."

The supplied tools were sharp and the dirt came away easily, going into buckets for sifting. When we had cleared the prescribed depth, she started poking a sturdy plastic knitting needle into the next layers following what she could see from the GPR images. It stopped within a few inches in some areas and pierced easily through others. She gave us a new paint line saying. "You can clear from here to the previous lines and go another six inches in depth." And we did.

"My turn," she said, and began working the surface with a heavy plastic spoon in an intentional left to right pattern. Very slowly, bits of fur began to emerge, and something else. She used a smaller spoon and a brush to concentrate on the something else, carefully surrounding it until she could extract the mysterious object.

"Aw," she said. "It's a ball of yarn. They buried him with a toy." The ball of yarn went into the bucket and onto the sieve. "Have you found anything in the soil?" she asked the students. Nothing but dirt, now sifted.

We all watched the master at work as she very carefully spooned and swept the covering of years from the animal's body. She alternated in very small bits across the upper surface, down the sides, and gently underneath. A full cat had emerged, claws and all. We'd been at this for hours when Audrey and Vicki showed up. I'd been so engrossed in the process I hadn't realized we'd gone way beyond the normal quitting time. Increasing darkness should have been a clue.

"You guys are going to miss dinner if you don't wrap up soon," said Vicki.

"Holy Hector," said Audrey looking into the hole. "That's Yellow Cat."

"That's what the sign said," laughed Darrel.

"No, I mean that looks just like the cat that we see all the time, the one that hurt Lincoln."

"It is uncanny," I said.

"Here he comes," said Abbey, working her fingers underneath the body to lift the cat clear of the grave. "I've never seen anything like this," she said. "If I didn't know better, I'd swear he could have been buried today."

Fred came by to check our late progress. He's been hanging out with Don and his guys and giving the additional details from the GPR that would be useful when they started into the mound digging. "That cat is amazing," he said. "If that's any indication of the other corpses, I'm going to expect them to talk to us."

"Oh, they do," said Vicki.

"The other two sites are ready for working tomorrow," he told Abbey. "I still need to backfill your work here and do more passes with the GPR to raise the confidence level on this one. I can do that in the morning."

"We'll get the hole filled now," said Darrel. "We've got four people with shovels. It won't take a minute."

"Thanks," said Fred. "Leave it level and I'll run the cart over it at dawn."

Yellow Cat joined us at dinner on the patio, laying serenely if stiffly on the wide wood railing. Lincoln steered very clear of that spot, obviously confused. Dinner was the ample leftovers of hamburgers and hot dogs from the other day's lunch. The girls, Audrey, Vicki, and Abbey went off to the studio again, no doubt planning either the wedding or their pending séance. The guys, Trey and Don and Darrel and I, pulled up stumps by the campfire for a cigar and a nightcap.

"Anything new on your missing persons?" Don asked Darrel.

"Actually, yes, Virginia State Police have been working the I-66 rest area since we gave them the heads-up on the disappearances related to that venue. They started a focus on human trafficking last year, and this fits right in. One of their interviews surfaced a guy who knew Eli. The last time he saw him, he was getting into a dark pickup truck with a stranger, no make or model, no license plate number. That was four months ago, consistent with the time he was reported missing. They also ran a statewide missing person report around the same data ranges, and we may have a 'person of interest.'"

"Did the stranger look like Trey? Trey has a dark pickup truck." I laughed out loud.

"I think I have an alibi," Trey laughed with me. "I'll check."

"Who is your 'person of interest?'" asked Don. "It certainly sounds like foul play could be a contributing factor in Eli's disappearance."

"Stan Galloway, a delivery driver that made weekly runs from a boat parts fabricator in Roanoke to a marine supply house in Arlington. He went missing shortly after Eli's disappearance. His route would have put him both in Arlington and traveling the I-66 corridor at the times of our missing guys."

"Does he have an alibi?" asked Don.

"Don't know," said Darrel. "He's still missing. Virginia State put some new focus on his case because of our inquiry. He has an address in Chester, South Carolina, but their contact with law enforcement there finds nothing. Oddly, Chester is the same small town where the Gilgo Beach serial killer suspect has some property."

"Curious but not likely connected," said Don. "Keep us posted on your guy Stan."

March 8

Four days into the circus and two days away from the new moon, I joined Team Don to work the pit. We had free rein to dig anything, as long as we didn't get close to Tom. We also had access to the mighty Bobcat and the complete assortment of quality digging tools. Fred had re-mapped Betty this morning, so all three graves were ready to go. Project manager Abbey and technical specialist Fred shared the plan for the rest of the engagement.

"Give yourselves a hand for all the good work yesterday. Today most of you can work on the fun dig for artifacts or just hang out. The exhumation of the cat was a great exercise to confirm the accuracy of our mapping and the possible condition of our targets, which is almost beyond belief. We're going to move extra cautiously from here. The potential condition of our human remains is too excellent to rush. I told my cat partners yesterday that a good rule of thumb to remember is that any excavation is destructive and non-repeatable.

"This is an important site that will get a lot of academic attention across disciplines. Anthropology. Archaeology. Chemistry, biology, history, and African American studies will all want to delve into the treasures of this dig. With that at stake, we choose not to be known as the ones that screwed it up. For that reason, we will do one grave at a time, Fred and I working together on each one.

"We've set the order as Cody followed by Tom followed by Betty. With support for soil movement and sifting, we've allocated a full day to each one. That's a fairly ambitious schedule, but with the confirmed quality of our mapping, we think it's fair. We have enough time in our engagement to double that if needed, and we'll reassess based on today's findings. If there are no questions, my team can follow me to Cody, and the rest of you can have fun."

The general had been on conference calls all day yesterday and was eager to get out into the sun with the metal detectors. He and Don teamed us rookies up with their experienced guys, and we set out to harvest the field. I guessed a lot of shoveling and sifting was headed my way.

These guys were like kids in a candy shop. Don had declared this a target-rich environment, and it was every bit of that. Every one of them had a spot they had found previously and went straight to digging those. Don was right on his two potential buckles and plucked them early. Buttons and coins were scattered everywhere. Apparently, any complete bodies or torsos were cast in the pit with uniform and all. Most had done the "ashes to ashes" thing. But not all. Bones, bone fragments, and teeth were also common.

Cody too was emerging. I dropped into the shed throughout the day. They got to his nose around noon.

On my way back to the pit I saw the yellow cat sitting on Betty's grave. I knew he couldn't be the same one. The one from yesterday was locked in one of the large travel trailers where the rest of the bodies would join him as they surfaced.

The Bobcat was making its third pass of the day, slicing off a foot or so of the mound each time. All of that was fed to the sifters with the sieve, yielding more and more buttons, coins, and teeth. It was getting to be quite a collection.

George borrowed one of the large folding tables and a chair to set up a desk for sorting the most significant finds. Those would include the belt buckles and buttons that could identify different military units. More memorabilia included bayonets, gun cleaning kits, canteens, and remnants of small arms. Today's collectibles were both common and virtually worthless in the 1860s, so everything had gone into the pit with the medical waste. There were also personal items, jewelry, small picture frames, field-eating utensils, sewing kits, pocket knives, pipes, and combs.

I was looking over the gathered items when George asked, "What would you like to do with these? They're all your legal possessions."

"Wouldn't the guys who dug them up want to keep them?"

"Yes, but they came from your property, so you are the owner. There are some museum-quality items with unique historical worth, but even the more pedestrian artifacts have a high dollar value, especially in these quantities. This is a very rich site."

"Can I give it to you and Don?"

"You can do whatever you want with it. You don't need to make a decision any time soon. I'll tally up a rough estimate when everything we can find has been extracted. You're looking at tens of thousands of dollars here."

"That could help with funeral expenses for Tom and Betty. I want to give them a proper burial near Dr. Craft and his wife. I suppose Cody can join them there."

"The Shelby Springs Confederate Cemetery in Alabama would welcome Cody with open arms. I'm quite sure their Sons of Confederate Veterans would even cover all costs of transport and burial."

"Do you have any connections there?"

"I have connections everywhere in the realm of Civil War historical obscurity," laughed George. "Would you like me to follow up to assess their interest?"

"Yes please, that sounds much more appropriate to plant him among his peers."

"I saw you were coming from the shed. How is Cody doing?"

"I saw his nose, which looks as perfect as Khloé Kardashian's cosmetic job." I laughed. "The sides of the pit were already cleared like we did with the cat last night. The rest of the spooning and brushing should be pretty straightforward with Abbey and Fred both working on it. I think they'll have him ready on schedule by dinnertime."

"They are the best I know at this. We're lucky to have them here."

"They're also good company. I think Audrey and Vicki have adopted Abbey as another sister. At the rate they're going, I don't doubt that she and Fred will be part of the wedding party in May."

Don overheard the last part as he joined us. "Am I invited to the nuptials?"

"We decided we're going to invite everyone here this week to the nuptials. None of us have any close family, and this extended group has been a lot of fun. They'll mix well with Vicki and Audrey's New Age regulars and whatever posse Trey stirs up."

"The lunch spread is out, same as yesterday. I'm off to build a Dagwood," said Don. "Do you have school tomorrow?"

"Just in the morning. Why do you ask?"

"I thought maybe you and I could partner up on the shed. If you're interested, the timing should be fine. By afternoon they'll have all the Cody cleanup done. George can handle the guys here at the pit."

"Count me in, we can leave the doors open and smoke cigars while we labor. What do you think we'll find there?"

"No idea, but there were a lot of metal hits. I don't expect any Civil War pieces, probably just nuts and bolts. It will be a good exercise for you to practice more with your new detector, and me with mine."

"I'll come find you when I get home from school, that sounds like a good time."

The afternoon saw more slices with the Bobcat, the dig now getting below the current ground level. The ground continued to bear fruit. Fred came to get me around 4:00 p.m. "Are you ready for Cody?" he asked. "I thought you should see him first."

I went back to the shed with him where Abbey and the students were preparing to pull Cody from the ground. He looked asleep, not dead, with Dr. Craft's crucifix lying on his chest. He still wore his stained white shirt with a wool jacket and cotton twill pants. Someone had attempted to pull the damaged fabrics together in as neat a fashion as possible.

"This is a first for me," said Abbey. "There are many cases of complete remains described as well-preserved, but Cody here sets a new standard for grading. I'm quite certain that a body buried this long has never been seen in this condition."

I had no point of reference for comparison, but if Dr. Craft was right about his body and soul theory, I could easily believe that Cody was still here with us. Six of us solemnly lifted him from the grave and onto a stiff stretcher. The rest of the crowd came to pay respects, and he was loaded into the trailer with Yellow Cat.

Everyone was quiet that night.

March 9

S chool went well this morning, as always. Darrel was in class and stayed afterward. "Can I borrow one of your spare bedrooms this weekend?" he asked. "I've got the weekend off. I'd like to come immerse in your grand unveilings and do a little dirt fishing, but I'd rather sleep in a bed than a pup tent."

"You are always welcome, and you'll notice I haven't sampled the fireside sleeping either."

"How are things going with the project?"

"Great, and creepy. We finished on our Confederate guy yesterday, and he came out in the same condition as the cat."

"I'll have to check him out. I've seen bodies come out of shallow graves before, but none that I wanted to look at very long. The cat was a first for me. I was wondering if Lincoln really had gotten revenge and planted the fresh one there just to goof on us." He laughed.

"That would have explained it better, but I've seen our current yellow cat since then. It's still alive and well. Cody is even harder to explain or imagine. They're going to work on Tom today."

"Count me in bright and early tomorrow. You and Don are having too much fun without me."

I changed into shorts, Crocs, and a Blue Oyster Cult t-shirt when I got home. I smelled Don before I saw him, cigar smoke wafting from the direction of the shed.

"Oh fine, you started without me."

"There are plenty more cigars in this day. I haven't touched anything here yet. I got a few minutes with Fred before they started on Tom. He showed me the GPR scans inside the metal mapping for this building. I couldn't make any sense of them, but he says they're consistent. He also said they're done with the building. Now that Cody is out and backfilled, we're free to dig whatever we find."

"Do you have anything in particular you want to start on? I know you had buckles you had identified in the pit."

"Nothing so obvious here, just small random hits. My vote is we scrap the maps, treat it like a fresh find, and establish our grid as we go."

"Lead on, McDuff."

Our canvas for the day was a freshly raked, flat soil surface. We each started in one of the corners by the open door. We would sweep the side walls first and work our way up and down to cover everything. Don brought a bunch of landscaping flags to mark the hits. We'd go back over those spots together and dig then. Headphones on, we started slowly and met at the back wall to compare notes.

"I've got nothing," I said. "Maybe I'm doing something wrong."

"I think you're okay," he said. "I only got one hit on my wall, and it's not a real strong one. Let me check your machine."

He took my detector and went over the small spot marked with his flag. "All good," he said. "You get the same strength I do. Now we walk back along the line we just created. Your range of width is the head on the detector. We give about a two-inch overlap to make sure we cover it all. Since we have freshly raked dirt, we can drag a line with our feet to mark our lanes."

Lane two was another bust for me. Don got two flags on his pass. By lane three we each had two strikes. I continued to get one or two hits while Don's path accelerated in findings.

"Can you tell me what was in this building, and where?" he asked.

"All of the equipment parked by the driveway was parked in here. The long workbenches you see in the trailer were all located on your wall."

"That explains the pattern. If this wall is the main area for work, we'd expect to find more hardware or tools that got dropped and kicked under equipment or the benches over the years."

We continued until we did the entire floor, thirty-five flags in all.

"Good work," said Don. "Now we'll each do a quick diagonal of everything just for drill."

I came up with one more flag in the area I had previously swept. Don got the same hit. "I'm pretty sure I just forgot to flag that one," I said.

"Happens all the time, that's why we do the second sweep. I'm confident we've got all our targets marked. Do you need a break before we start digging?"

"A walkabout with a cigar might be nice." We fired up our stink bombs and went to check on the rest of the activity. Abbey and Fred were engrossed in Tom. We observed from a distance to not bother their fine sweeping.

The grave was scored and dug around and below the level of the body, as we did with the cat. Tom's hands were visible and looked as fresh as the fingers in the jars. They were folded across his chest like he might have been praying. What would have been his face was also uncovered. The head was wrapped in burlap cloth. This was going well. We'd probably have Tom on a stretcher in just a few hours.

Don checked in with George. "More buttons, coins, and another buckle sifted out of the area around this one," George told Don. "The buckle is a real find, a complete two-piece CS in excellent condition."

"There's another $2,500 for your war chest," Don told me.

"Richard," said George. "I spoke with someone from Shelby Springs this morning. They'd be ecstatic to provide perpetual rest for Cody, all expenses covered."

"Good to know," I said. "I'm going to contact the Ivy Hill people and see if they can take Tom and Betty. I hope so."

"What about the cat?" laughed Don.

"I think we'll keep him right here. He already has a headstone."

We went back to the shed to start digging. "I don't believe there's anything here below six inches," said Don. "We can probably wrap this up in time to see Tom's full reveal."

We each took one of the nice sharp Penn State trowels and a small pick and started pulling up junk from each flag. As expected, modern-day hardware and small tools like sockets, driver heads, and drill bits were the stars of the show.

Don was working flags in the middle ground when he asked, "Hey Richard, what do you know about Wakefield High School?" Odd question.

"They were a football powerhouse in the '70s. Not anymore. I think they went 0–10 last year. Why do you ask?"

"I just dug up a Wakefield High School ring from two years ago. This is a local school?"

"Arlington County, yes."

"Maybe your yard guy lost his ring."

"He's way too old for high school, and I know he never finished anyhow. It can't be his."

"It's an unusual stone," Don said, bringing it over to show me.

It was very unusual. I remembered the stone from my high school days. I think it was called white spinel. I liked it because it looked like a big diamond, but it seemed a little ostentatious at the time, so I went with the more traditional red.

"I'll bet it's one of the lawn guy's summer hires. He takes on additional workers in the heavy months."

"I gift it to your safe keeping," said Don. "It's engraved 'ED' on the band. Ed would probably like to see it again someday."

I put it in my pocket. It went in the junk drawer of my dresser with all of my keepsake tidbits that night. Nothing else of value came out of the shed search.

Back at the mound that was no longer a mound, the Bobcat had cut its way about four feet below ground level. The pickings were getting slim. Still a few teeth and buttons but no more bones. They were all one with the soil at this depth.

At 4:00 p.m., Tom was ready to join the world again. Abbey and Fred directed his pallbearers in lifting him out and loading him on the stretcher. What we could see, which was everything but his wrapped head, was perfect. Abbey carefully pulled loose the stuck layers of burlap, cutting with care at the stubborn spots. When the last layer was removed, Tom was looking at us with a surprised expression. The gaping forehead wound was gruesome, and the back of the skull was intact but soft, crushed beneath the skin. Embalming fluid had trickled from the wounds and stuck to the cloth. It had the consistency of dried rubber cement.

Two down, another quiet night.

March 10: The New Moon

D arrel joined Audrey, George, and me early for a Don Weston breakfast extravaganza. "Did I miss anything in the last couple of days?" he asked.

Audrey answered him, "Just a couple of fresh bodies, nothing out of the ordinary here."

"So, my dear," I said. "Thanks again for letting me off new moon detail this month. What do you and Vicki have planned?"

"Abbey is going to join us for fresh energy. We picked out the smokehouse for tonight. It will be central to all of the activity of the past week and one of the last spots on the property with human remains from the war years."

"Are you looking forward to getting all the carpet baggers and inter-lopers off your land?" asked Don.

"Everyone has been a lot of fun," she said. "But I won't mind get-ting back to just Richard and Lincoln and I. There's a lot to do before the wedding."

"Is Lincoln participating?" asked Darrel.

"He's not allowed to stay at the Shoe House, but we definitely want him for the ceremony."

"The woman from the animal shelter, Amy, has agreed to take him," I said. "We'll need to get her a pet-friendly room nearby."

"Done," said Don. "They'll stay with Darrel and me at my place."

"That was easy," said Darrel. "Any other insurmountable problems? You can put Amy in touch with me. There's no reason we can't ride up together with Lincoln."

"See Audrey, wedding planning isn't too hard after all," I said. "I also need to do some funeral planning. I think George came up with the perfect solution for Cody. He has a Confederate cemetery that will take him and handle all arrangements. I need to set up the other two. I should probably make that call today."

"I need to get to the shop," said Audrey. "Vicki, Trey, and I will be here around 6:30. Do you need us to bring anything for dinner?"

"Dinner at the campfire tonight," said Don. "Are you up for venison and sweetbreads?"

"Pass," said Audrey decisively. "I'm not a Bambi fan, and Vicki would die from the smell alone."

"Joking," laughed Don. "We've all been too quiet the last couple of nights, so George is going to cater a Mexican fiesta with all the trimmings, including bottomless margaritas. Right, George?"

"Whatever you say, Don. I'm just here for the chips and salsa."

After Audrey left, I took Darrel to see Cody and Tom. We had used one of my locks on the trailer. It was from a set with matching keys that also fit the shed and the cellar.

"Wowee," said Darrel. "How old are these guys?"

"1862 for Cody, 1866 for Tom."

"Tom looks as shocked as I am. Nice skull fracture. No surprise on cause of death for this one."

"Feel the embalming liquid that leaked from the head wound, it's like gum."

"No thanks, I'll take your word for it. I wouldn't want to disturb him. Are we sure these aren't movie props? I hear those Hollywood guys can do some pretty freaky stuff." Darrel laughed.

"I wish, maybe that could explain some of the other freaky stuff that goes on here."

We'd already seen the start of Betty on our way to the trailer. They were still in the spray paint and square shovel stage and were now just beginning the dig and sift.

"Last one," said Fred. "She's a little deeper than the boys, but I think we'll finish today with daylight to spare."

"There's a Mexican fiesta at the house tonight. I guess we can call it a celebration of work ending," I said.

"Not quite," said Abbey. "We'll still have a good two days of cleanup, restoration, compiling records, and teardown before we're out of your hair. The celebration is freeing your former residents. We can all drink to that."

"Dr. Hunt found us a final resting place for Cody in a Confederate cemetery. I'm off to see if we can find space for Betty and Tom where Dr. Craft and his wife are buried. I think the cat will stay with us."

"Would you like us to put the cat back in here when we're finished?" asked Fred. "This ground will all be filled and leveled when we're done, and we can put the marker right back where it was."

"That sounds good, but if you don't mind, I think Audrey and I would like to join you when Yellow Cat goes back into the ground, maybe Lincoln too."

"That's a couple of days away. We'll make sure to get you for the services."

Darrel joined Don and George at the pit. I went back to the house to call Ivy Hill Cemetery. The woman who answered the phone was very helpful. One of their board members happened to be in the office at the time and we went on speakerphone. I explained to them who I was and that I happened to have the bodies of two former Civil War era slaves on my property. "I'd like to bury them near my great grand-uncle, Dr. Richard Eugene Craft, and his wife Dorothy."

"Do you know what area they are buried in?"

"No, but their deaths are 1903 and 1863. The plot would have been purchased in 1863. Does that narrow it down?"

"That pinpoints it precisely. They would be near the cemetery founder, Hugh Charles Smith. Mr. Smith would be pleased to have them join the area. He made a practice of purchasing slaves in the 1800s so that he could free them. The plots there are quite limited and quite expensive in comparison to the rest of the grounds. Have you considered having the remains cremated? That would make interment much more flexible."

"No, for sentimental purposes I'd like to keep them as is." I wasn't about to get into the body-soul theory and everything else surrounding Tom and Betty. I was afraid they might turn me down for fear of a zombie apocalypse rising on their grounds. But I did want them to end up in Ivy Hill if at all possible. "Can you check the possibilities for two whole grave sites and let me know? I'm not concerned about the price, but I am hoping we can fit them in near Richard and Dorothy." They told me again why Hugh Smith would be glad to host two former slaves and promised they'd make it happen if at all possible. They also gave me tentative pricing and a funeral home contact that could handle transportation and services. We exchanged email addresses for follow-up, fingers crossed.

I joined the guys back at the pit, which was now really a pit, probably six to eight feet deep. George was now presiding over three large folding tables of mound pickings. "You have an extremely impressive haul here," said Don. "You've advanced very quickly from lucky find status to the ranks of the elite collectors. We could fill a website with this stuff and you'd screw up your tax status for the year overnight."

"That may influence my next choices. I know where I want to put Tom and Betty for their perpetual rest, but it could cost somewhere between $20,000 and $30,000 to make it happen."

George Hunt chimed in, "I've no doubt you have that well covered."

"Is there anything here of truly unique value that I could donate for the Churchville Museum collection?" I asked George.

"All of it, of course," laughed George. "But honestly, we have most of what is represented here. There are a few unique buttons and one buckle that would fill in holes for us."

"Then pick those out and take them with you, please."

"We have a collection budget so we can still pay you for them."

"Nope, I want you to have them, and I want you to keep the original stuff from the cellar as well. How can we best sort out what we can give to the guys who have done all the work here?"

"You mean our F troop?" said Don.

"Sure, I think they all deserve some souvenirs from their time here."

"That's a generous offer. You don't have to do that," said George.

"Don," I asked. "Can you check with them individually and see what they would like to have?"

"I can, but I'm also going to put some limits on them. A few souvenirs are good and will be appreciated, but we've also had a good time here. It's rarer than you could imagine that a property owner would offer a virgin site to strangers. I promise they're pretty happy just to have been here."

"I think we'll still cover funeral costs if you'd like us to start listing everything after that," said George.

"Please," I said. "You'll save me a lot of time trying to learn how to value stuff and where to post it."

"That's what student volunteers are good for," George pointed out.

Betty joined us around 3:30 p.m. with the standard grave-to-stretcher exercise. She was, and still is, a very pretty woman. Her arms were folded across her chest, just like Tom's. It occurred to me that Tom would have been there to assist with her burial. The two men had taken great care to present her at her best for the afterlife journey.

After Betty was secured in the trailer, everyone broke off to clean up for the fiesta. The girls and Trey arrived as the catering was spread out and tequila began to flow. I knew Audrey liked a good margarita or two, but she was abstaining for pregnancy. Vicki and Abbey were less restrained and headed for a good buzz prior to séance.

Around 8:00 p.m. the girls gathered their candles and folding chairs and headed toward the smokehouse. The usual gang of Don, Trey, George, Darrel, and I went to the campfire with cigars and drinks and pending tall tales. I was anticipating drunk debauchery for all the woodsy party goers.

March 11: Aftermath

I think I was still slightly afflicted when I woke with a headache. I could see from the sheets that Audrey came to bed last night, but she wasn't there now. Faithful Lincoln was pressed hard against my side, keeping me company. He jumped up and stared at me when I stirred. I think he thought I had died.

It was 8:00 a.m. but still quiet. No sounds of digging. I wondered if everyone got as drunk as I did. I hoped so. I got cleaned up and went to look for company.

Audrey was in the kitchen and greeted me with a nice kiss. "Hello, you sleepy derelict."

"Hello back, you beautiful vision. Did we have good games last night?" I kissed her again and cupped her butt playfully.

"If the competition was performance of husbandly duties, you failed miserably. If it was world-class snoring, you took the gold." She laughed.

"Where is everyone?"

"I think most are still sleeping in like you. Trey and Vicki stayed over, and I haven't seen them yet. Don and George stopped by for coffee. I think they're out at the mound."

"Seen Darrel?"

"I think he's following your condition. I could hear him trying to compete with you in the sleep apnea Olympics. If you keep that up, you're getting a CPAP for your birthday." She smiled again. I did pick the right one to marry.

Don and George were making notes and taking pictures at the artifact tables. "P.T. Barnum is up, "said Don. Uh-oh.

"P.T. Barnum?"

"The Greatest Show on Earth," said George. Uh-oh.

"I'm a little unclear on some of the later evening events. Can you help me out?"

"You don't remember arm wrestling with Trey?" asked Don.

"No, how did I do?" They both laughed.

"Don't worry, you didn't hurt him," said George.

"We finally put you to bed when you challenged one of the soldiers to Mumblety-peg," said George. "We knew Audrey would look upon us with less favor if we dragged you home minus a foot." They were enjoying this.

"Sounds like I might have had a little too much tequila."

Still laughing, Don asked, "How did those worms taste?"

"No mas," I pleaded. "I guess I owe some apologies."

"You weren't the only entertainment," said George. "We had to talk two of our guys out of bringing Cody and Betty to the party."

"Sounds like a good time was had by all."

"All in all, it was a pretty normal reenactor event," said George, still laughing.

Darrel wandered over about then. "What's so funny?" he asked innocently.

"Memorable moments from last night's fiesta," said Don. "Your story about dressing in drag for prostitution stings made the list." They howled at that one.

"It's a historical piece. We all had to do it in the old days of police work."

"Did we?" laughed Don.

"Maybe not for you supersized tanks of testosterone, but before we had a core of female officers, we young pretty boys were always ready to don our finest fishnets in the line of duty."

"Truly noble and commendable," commented George.

"So, I don't owe any apologies?" I asked.

"Not hardly," said George, "I think we all enjoyed the show."

"Speaking of shows," said Don to me. "We put a couple of your artifacts on a Civil War auction site an hour ago, and you're already getting serious bids. You're going to easily recover the finances for the Tom and Betty arrangements."

"Good to know, what do we have on tap for today?"

"I haven't seen Abbey and Fred yet. I think they're having coffee in the main tent. We may have our guys restoring your mound today, but let's check with them first."

They were having coffee and organizing the notes and pictures of the week. "Good morning, gentleman," welcomed Abbey.

"I'd use that term lightly with this particular group," said Don. "But good morning. Do we have assignments yet? I was thinking I should get our guys to start filling the hole we made."

"It's okay to do that, including the area where Tom was. We've gotten everything we need from that part of the yard, so you won't interfere with anything by doing that. Just check in from time to time with Fred. We're a little particular about how we leave a site."

"Understood," said Don. "We'll proceed with caution."

"Richard," she asked. "Have you seen Audrey and Vicki this morning?"

"Audrey is up. Vicki and Trey were still comatose when I left the house, but they're probably into caffeine by now."

"We need to talk about last night."

"Please tell me I didn't streak the séance."

"No, but it is about the séance. I think we should get them and let us tell you how it went." She seemed serious. "I'm ready now if you are."

"Let's do it."

Vicki, Trey, and Audrey were at the kitchen table. Trey looked as miserable as I felt. Tequila didn't agree with him either. Audrey and Vicki were chatty and perky but stopped when they saw Abbey with me.

"Did you tell him?" asked Vicki of Abbey.

"Not yet, I thought the three of us should tell him together."

We settled with coffee and Lincoln in the great room to chat. "You have my full attention," I said.

"I'm new to the party," said Abbey. "But Vicki and Audrey told me about the previous encounters and the cast of characters before we started. I know I'm supposed to be an objective scientist, but I do believe in the paranormal, and last night proved to me that this place is rich in it. It also makes me a believer that you and Audrey are in danger, and soon, probably within months."

I looked at Audrey. "Are you okay?" I asked.

"Only because I've been involved from the start and I'm used to it."

"She means she's still in denial," said Vicki. "Last night we heard from Bob and Tom, and we had a new visitor. Tom is grateful to be out of the ground, and Bob is still claiming responsibility but we don't know what for. The new guy warned us that he is dead and you are going to meet the same fate as him."

"Who is he?" I asked.

"We don't know," said Abbey. "But he tells us he's been here before and never left."

"I asked for a sign," said Vicki. "And one of the sacks in the smoke-house fell to the floor. That can't be a coincidence that something hanging there for a hundred years or more would happen to drop while we're doing a séance in that room."

"Bob and Tom and the new guy all confirmed that your killer is alive, and they know who it is," said Abbey.

"Who is it?" I asked, looking at Audrey.

She said, "Just like the last time, when we got to that question, they said GOODBYE."

"I wonder who the new guy could be, and why he'd only show up now."

"Time is short," said Vicki. "I truly believe that."

"I do too," said Abbey.

"I am a little worried for you," added Audrey.

"I'm worried for you."

"I guess we don't know if the killer is something supernatural, but if it's something real and alive, they're only flesh and blood," said Abbey. "Just in case, do you have a means of protecting yourself when you're at home?"

"If you mean a gun, no, but Darrel told me Bear Mace was a better defense anyway. I do have that."

"I'd carry it with you while you're here," said Abbey. "Audrey should too. You may not have any warning when the time comes."

"I'll get it now."

The whole group gathered out in the yard to get the next instructions from Fred and Abbey. I was wearing my Bear Mace on my belt. Darrel noticed and said, "Daniel Boone, are you plannin' to kill a bear?" He pronounced it "bahr."

"Just following the advice of my spiritual advisors. They think I'm in danger. You know the story."

"I'm still a bit of a skeptic," he said. "But it can't hurt you, so I applaud your armament."

Fred went over the tasks for the day. "I'll stay with the army guys and the Bobcat to reconstruct the area of the pit and Tom's exhumation. Abbey could use some help to clean up the shed and Betty's grave. That should cover the morning. At precisely 2:00 p.m. all interested parties can gather at the Betty site for a solemn reinterment of Yellow Cat. Please dress appropriately."

Abbey added, "The goal, as always, is to leave any site in the same or better condition than it was found. Fred and I will inspect that as we go. We should be done with that today. Tomorrow, Fred and I will be compiling research, and everyone else can start breaking camp. We'll be on the road bright and early the following morning. Any questions?"

"Don wants to know what's for lunch," laughed Darrel.

"Already covered," said Don. "More cold cuts today. Pizza for dinner, no tequila."

Fred pulled me aside as we were breaking up. "Abbey told me about the dropped bag in the smokehouse. I checked it out this morning and it's exactly what we expected, smoked limbs and body parts. They're well preserved but, unlike the corpses, not pretty. Would you mind if I took those back to school with me? They don't have the same significance as the rest of the finds here, but they'd be excellent tools for student training."

"I'm happy to gift you my holiday hams, as long as you take them all."

I had a text from Ivy Hill. They thought they had space and wanted to know if I could come by to see it. "Want to go for a quick ride?" I asked Audrey. "We can take Lincoln with us."

"I'd like that very much. We haven't had time as a family for a week or more."

The cemetery grounds are quite beautiful and lush. The proposed sites were perfect, side by side and midway between the Crafts and the cemetery founder. We stopped at DeMaine Funeral Home on our way back. The Ivy Hill folks had told them our story, and they seemed truly honored to be involved. Betty and Tom would be picked up today. They also offered to handle the storage and transport of Cody if needed.

We got back after lunch to find George and Don packing the articles from the tables. "I let the guys pick souvenirs," Don said. "It didn't make a dent in the overall value of the bounty, and they're greatly appreciative of the gesture. We have everything cataloged and photographed. When we get back to school, we'll let the student volunteers do the listings and handle shipping. I wouldn't be surprised if it all finds new homes in the next two weeks."

"I don't know how I can ever repay you two for all the help," I said.

"You already have," said George. "The museum donations and your friendship more than cover it all."

"I have a funeral home that can take care of storage and transport for Cody. Do you think that would be a help for the guys in Alabama?"

"Let's call them and see."

The answer was yes. I called our funeral guy back, and he said they'd pick up Cody with the other two. That was a huge relief to know all three would be on their way to a better place soon.

The 2:00 p.m. service for Yellow Cat was an intimate, somber affair. Lincoln seemed relieved when the ground was covered and the stone put back in place.

March to May

Yesterday finished with the funeral home taking our three corpses away. It was a bittersweet goodbye. I hoped to attend all services in April, and Don and George promised to join me.

When the shed was freshly raked and pronounced done, I texted Buck to let him know I was ready to start moving his things back in. He called right back. "I'm on my way, so wait for me. I wanted to move some of the big equipment and the trailer around anyway, so I'll be there shortly."

It wasn't twenty minutes before he drove up on the back road and parked by the shed. I met him there. "I guess you'll be glad to have your space back."

He walked into the cleared building and said, "All the time I've worked in here a dead guy was watching me?"

"Sort of," I laughed. "He was right here," I said, stepping off the area inside the back wall. "How did you miss him?"

Buck guided Darrel and me as we alternately pushed and drove everything back into the designated spots. We helped put all the workbenches and tools back in place, and we were done. "Business back to normal," I said.

"Whatever normal is," he mumbled.   "Are you okay?" I asked.

He came up with a little smile, seeming to remember social graces again. "I'm fine," he said. "I've got to go." He drove off down the rutted road.

"He's an odd duck," said Darrel.

"He is, but he does great work, and he's cheap. I plan to keep him as long as he's happy taking care of the place, and I hope that's a long time."

"He's still odd."

When all the grounds were restored and the camps broken down for tomorrow's travel, we gathered for pizza. No one seemed to opt for alcohol this evening. The whole group joined the soldiers in their skivvies for the last harmonica and banjo concert. Don asked if I was going to do another arm-wrestling demonstration. I declined.

The Pennsylvania Circus planned to be on the road by dawn, so we made our goodbyes tonight.

"I'm going to miss you two," said Abbey as she hugged Audrey and Vicki.

"We're all sisters now, so you won't get away that easy," said Vicki. "Audrey and I have a gift for you."

Abbey cried when she unwrapped a large chunk of clear quartz. "The Master Healer," she said. "I love you two." They all hugged and cried together.

"We'll stay in touch, and you can always visit. We're only a couple of hours apart," said Vicki.

"And we'll all be together again at the wedding, you'll love the Shoe House," Audrey added.

As we finished our cigars, I hugged all the guys and thanked them for their service. "See you in class tomorrow," I said to Darrel.

Audrey held me close that night in bed. "This has been quite the adventure, but I'm looking forward to having you all to myself again. I have some pent-up demand waiting for your full attention."

"Should we do another formal date tomorrow? Peking Duck perhaps?"

"Mmmm, I'd like that. Can I wear heels again?"

"Only if you promise to wear not much else."

"Get your sleep. You're going to be up late tomorrow."

The caravan left us early as promised the next day. I was up to see everyone off with last hugs and promises to stay in touch on the funeral and wedding arrangements. Mission accomplished, time for everything to return to whatever normal was around here.

That night's date with Audrey was everything I needed, and I think she enjoyed herself as well.

The rest of March went by quickly, and April was upon us. I didn't see much of Audrey and Vicki, as they were fully immersed in the wedding preparations. They let Trey and me know they'd found the perfect gowns but we weren't allowed to see them before the big day. He and I picked out the wedding bands and scheduled the rentals of our morning suits with tails. Don, George, and Darrel needed the same.

I picked Darrel as my best man, and the girls chose Abbey as maid of honor. George would walk them down the aisle.

George, Don, and I made a road trip to Alabama on April 4. It was an 11-hour drive. That night we slept in pup tents with the reenactors from the Sons of Confederate Veterans. In the early morning, Cody was laid to rest with full Confederate military honors. George attended as Robert E. Lee to do the eulogy.

On the way home, we stopped at eight hours to spend the night In Lexington, Virginia. We splurged on the Georges historic hotel for the luxury of king beds to make up for the night before. We also visited Stonewall Jackson's home and the museum at the Virginia Military Institute. George was a celebrity there, with several of his books on the shelves in the gift shop.

I was home in time for the new moon on April 8. Trey and Vicki joined us for dinner that night. When nothing happened, not even a basketball bounce, we skipped the Ouija and just relaxed, reviewing wedding plans. It was a pleasant evening for the four of us looking forward to our double wedding. Don had secured a local photographer and music so everything was in place — venue, catering, and table and chair rentals. We just needed to show up in another month. The wedding date was set for May 8, another new moon we planned to skip.

On the morning of April 20, we buried Tom and Betty. This was a big one. The story had been picked up by the *Washington Post* and attracted hundreds of people. All of the Pennsylvania groups that had participated in Tom and Betty's most recent emancipation were in attendance, marking a grand reunion of the events that happened just a month ago. The ceremony was a simple graveside affair. Distinguished historian Dr. George Hunt presided, but not as Robert E. Lee this time. We made the evening news, with Ivy Hill representatives getting an opportunity to tell the story of why the event would have been so significant to their founder. The local press asked me about the history of the house, but I referred them to Abbey and Fred as the heroes of the work that led to today.

All three of our funerals felt right to me. Each of our lost souls was now exactly where they should have been over a hundred years ago. We all breathed a sigh of relief, knowing wrongs were now as right as they could be.

Wedding Bells

W e rented the Shoe House for the full week. We bridal couples were going to give it two days for setup and details followed by the main event and four days of honeymoon. We arrived on May 6 for the start of our new adventures together. The house didn't need a thing, so we took the first night for hot tubbing, with swimsuits of course. Audrey had the tiniest bump emerging, you would never know except for her barely there bikini.

"Are we ready to do this?" asked Trey, lifting a glass of champagne.

"I think you're the only one anybody was nervous about," responded Vicki. "Are you ready to do this?"

"I've never been more ready for anything in my life," he said, kissing his fiancée.

"I was nervous," said Audrey. "Thinking I'd be all fat in my gown."

"I told you nothing would show," said Vicki. "You'll be the perfect not obviously pregnant vision of loveliness and purity."

"Are you ladies comfortable with Don's musical selection? I think it's harmonica and banjo."

"Is not," said Vicki. "He promised a group of excellent musicians and singers who can do anything we want to hear, from the 'Chicken Dance' to 'Ave Maria.' I've texted my special request to him. You should all do the same."

"Did you pick 'YMCA?'" I asked. "Does Adam Sandler know that one?"

"It's a secret surprise," said Vicki.

"Don't even think of putting 'Having my Baby' on the list," Audrey said, punching me on the arm. "I think I can guess Vicki's song for Trey: 'Ain't No Mountain High Enough.'" We all snorted champagne at that one.

"Is Don doing his famous breakfast in the morning?" asked Trey.

"No," I said. "He's calling it brunch this time. Darrel, Amy, and Lincoln are expected in by 10:00 a.m. for the feast. We get to sleep in tomorrow."

When we got to Don's the next morning, the other Virginians were already there. Lincoln was happy to see everyone, especially Audrey. Darrel signaled me to join him for a private moment. "Amy is very nice, but I swear she was hitting on me," he said nervously.

"Oops, I should have warned you, she seems to have a daddy complex. She made a run at me several times. I thought you were bulletproof in that arena," I laughed.

"I am, but I didn't want to be mean. I guess I should now be hurt to know how poor her selection process is, if she tried you on." Now he laughed.

"Wear your finest fishnets to the wedding. That might slow her down. Speaking of wedding dress, have you and Don tried your suits? Trey and I fitted up last night."

"We're going to do that after we eat so we can measure them in real-world conditions. Don rented ours locally, so we'll have time this afternoon if we need to make adjustments."

Surprise guests George, Abbey, and Fred joined us for the meal. We all got to see the Don and Darrel and George fashion show. They looked quite proper.

Nerves settled in when we got back to the house. Tomorrow was the big day. The girls disappeared to do girl things. Trey and I had cigars and beers on the porch.

"Did you see the gift bags the girls made with their shop friends?" Trey asked.

"No, I didn't know about gift bags."

"Whoops, it was probably a surprise."

"What are they?"

"You'll see. They wanted to include something meaningful from each of us for the guests. Mine is a little football."

"What's mine?"

"You'll see tomorrow."

We got quiet dragging on our cigars. "Richard," said Trey. "You've done this before. How should I be feeling right now?"

"Like running off to a strip bar and never coming back." He appeared to be processing that thought when I continued, "Tomorrow is going to be the happiest day of your life, I promise. You'll smile so much your cheeks will hurt."

"Good," he said. "I think I'm ready for this."

"You are."

We had set the witching hour as 11:00 a.m. That way the visitors from Virginia had an option to do the event as a day trip. The Churchville contingent, Don, Darrel, George, Amy, and Lincoln, got to the house at 8:00 a.m. The rental people were already there, and the group helped set up tables and chairs and place flower arrangements. When Amy and Lincoln finished setting out the gift bags, everything was ready for company. I found out later that each gift bag contained Trey's football, one special stone for each of the brides, and a real Civil War button to represent me.

People started trickling in around 9:00 a.m. and by 10:00 most of the guests had arrived to mimosas and a continental breakfast. The brides and the maid of honor were secreted away in the house doing their mystical preparations. We wouldn't see them until showtime. We guys got into our morning suits and mingled with the crowd. The band started up at 10:00 a.m. with some nice background music and a couple of swing tunes to get everyone warmed up.

At 10:45 the music transitioned to traditional wedding introductions. All the guests were seated, and the guys in tails went to the stage for a quick huddle with Ethan McCallum, the chaplain from Churchville University. Amy and Lincoln took the rings and went to the back to wait for their cue.

At precisely 11:00 the band struck up the first notes of "Here Comes the Bride." We all looked at the house to see Vicki and Audrey appear on either side of George. They were dressed in matching floor-length satin gowns slit to the knee. Their headdresses were held by tiaras, faces veiled. They were stunning, carrying bouquets of fresh daisies. Abbey followed in a similar gown in robin's egg blue.

The ceremony was a quick blur. The chaplain went through the standard words, we all said yes, exchanged rings, lifted veils, and kissed. I couldn't be a happier man when were introduced as husband and wife to the applauding crowd. Audrey kissed me again and whispered a soft "I love you" in my ear. "I love you too."

And the party was on. The caterers were popping champagne corks and seating guests at tables while the bridal parties took their place and the toasts began. The caterers served a caprese salad followed by stuffed lobster rolls, and the bar was open for everything.

Trey and Vicki took the first dance to her special request song, "The Time of My Life." Possibly the highlight of the entire affair was when they did the lift to finish it off. Giant muscular Trey and tiny graceful Vicki made it look easy.

I looked at Audrey with my mouth open. "Don't even think about it," she said. She picked "Dancing Queen" for us, and the dancefloor filled. We continued with my song request "Do you Believe in Magic" followed by "Backfield in Motion" for Trey's choice. It was a free-for-all after that one.

The wedding was a complete magical success. Trey found me around 3:00 p.m. "My face hurts," he said.

"I told you so."

Around 4:00 things started to wind down, with some of the Virginia folks needing to travel. I could tell the girls never wanted it to end, hanging out with their shop regulars and Abbey. Good for them, I'm glad they're happy, I thought as Trey and I went to take care of business.

We approached Don, George, and Pastor Ethan as they sat together at one of the tables. "What do we owe you guys?" I asked.

"For what?" asked Don.

"For the band, the catering, the rentals, the flowers, the cake, and everything else you arranged."

"Already taken care of," said George. "It's Churchville University's wedding gift to you for all you've contributed to our museum collection and our research."

"I can't accept that, it's way too much."

"Too late," said Don. "Your money's no good here. It's our pleasure."

I looked at Trey. "I'm good," he said. "The girls will love the gift. Thanks."

When everyone and everything was packed up and gone, we married folks soaked in the tub with champagne and cigars, except for Audrey, who had sparkling water and no cigar. I know my marriage got consummated that night and I believe I heard the sounds of Vicki planting another flag on Mt. Everest.

The joint honeymoon took us back to the Green Dragon on Friday and two great long day trips, one to Fallingwater and another to the Pennsylvania Grand Canyon. We also swung by the ghost town of Centralia, where a mine fire has been burning since 1962.

We returned to our respective homes refreshed, relaxed, and married. Lincoln was waiting on Audrey and me, and we hunkered down for the night, happy to be just the three of us again. We never gave it a thought that another new moon had passed.

Domestic Bliss

Audrey went back to work, and I went back to school the next day. I saw Darrel for the first time since the wedding. "Knocked it out of the park," he said. "The wedding to beat all weddings."

"Thanks, I couldn't have done it without my best man. Do you have any plans for the day?"

"Just some errands, shopping, and haircut, it's my day off. Why do you ask?"

"When Don and I were digging in the shed, he found a high school ring. It's from Wakefield. I put it in my junk keepsakes drawer and totally forgot about it until I was putting my wedding gift bag in there this morning and saw it. I imagine whoever it belongs to would like to have it back. Is that something your investigative talents could solve?"

"Easy peasy. Let me have it, and I'll bet I can find out today."

"I didn't bring it with me. I was going to see if I could find Buck today and show it to him. I'm pretty sure it has to belong to one of his summer work hires."

"No problem, call me when you get home. It will have a manufacturer stamped on it. They should have a record of their sales if I can give them enough information."

"It's an unusual stone, and it has the name 'Ed' engraved inside."

"Easier yet, get me the jeweler's name, and we may be able to get it back to Ed today."

"Thanks, I feel bad that I forgot it for two months."

"We won't tell Ed." He laughed.

When I got home, there was a note on the door from Buck. "Meet me at the shed when you get back." Good, I won't have to hunt him down to ask him about the ring.

I called Darrel. "The jeweler's name appears to be Jostens. The stone is a white spinel and the engraving says simply ED, Ed. It's from Wakefield High School two classes ago. Do you think we can find Ed from that?"

"I can almost guarantee we'll have him identified in less than an hour."

"Great, thanks." I let Lincoln out and changed clothes to go see Buck.

The shed door was open, and he was puttering at the workbench. "What's up? I asked.

"It's time to move on."

I panicked. I didn't want to lose the best yard guy ever. Confused and surprised, I asked, "Where are you going?"

"I'm not going anywhere, you are."

Even more confused. "What do you mean?"

He turned from the bench holding what looked to be a small caliber revolver. "I'm going to kill you," he said, shooting me in the leg. I fell to the floor as an incredible burning pain hit me and I saw blood starting to stain my shorts.

"What the fuck, Buck."

He didn't say anything as he dragged me over to the trailer and handcuffed me to it.

"I've read the wills," he said.

"The wills?"

"The ones on your desk. Bob left everything to you but, if you didn't want it, it was supposed to go to me. I lived here all those years keeping the place nice for you and not knowing that. Then I read your will and found out that if you died without any heirs, you were leaving the place to me. I'm owed this property. You should never have come back."

"I don't understand," I said through the pain. I didn't yet.

"I killed your first wife. I thought you'd leave."

"You killed Gwen?" Tears for the pain and tears for Gwen.

"She was easy, you were off doing stuff and I found her in the tub. She'd already taken pills, and I just pushed her under the water. She struggled a little, but she was really easy. I tried to scare you off then, making noises and moving stuff around the house so you'd believe it was haunted."

"How did you make Tom appear?"

"I don't know anything about any Tom. I just know I have to kill you and kill your new wife when she gets home so I can have Bob's house back. He owed it to me."

"Why?"

"For all the time he kept me. I was only thirteen when I started mowing his yard with a push mower. He bought my first riding mower. He talked me into dropping out of school and starting a business. I was only thirteen, and I believed him. He bought me more stuff and taught me how I could hire others to do work for me. And then he taught me about how men and boys should do favors for each other. He bought me and trapped me. I owed him everything and had to do what he wanted."

"Buck, I didn't know."

"Nobody ever knew. Nobody cared."

"I care, let me help you."

"You'll help me when you and your wife are dead and I can have my house back."

"No, really you don't have to do this. Audrey and I can leave, and you can have the place."

"I know you're lying. If I let you go now, I'll spend the rest of my life in jail. It's too late to pretend you care. Your graves are already dug in the woods off this old road. I'm going to stick you and your new wife right by the two boys and you'll be as disappeared as they are."

"The two boys?"

"I had to practice. I didn't mind killing your wife, but it was too easy. I had to make sure I could kill a man. They've been out there awhile and never found. You won't be either."

I looked down at the pool spreading from my leg. I was seeing it in tunnel vision, and I could feel myself slipping away with the blood. "Please, Buck, we can get help."

"Not anymore, it's your time to go."

He raised his gun hand, pointing at my head when a loud voice behind him said, "Drop it or you're a dead man."

Buck turned, gun in hand, to see Darrel just beyond the doorway.

"Too late," were Buck's last words as he raised the gun and Darrel shot him three times in the chest. He wavered for a second or two and fell hard.

I knew I was as dead as he was when my vision stopped.

And on ...

I woke up in a hospital bed. The first things I saw were Audrey crying and Darrel smiling.

"It's alive," said Darrel, doing his best Gene Wilder imitation.

"Oh, Richard," said Audrey hugging me.

"What happened?"

"Buck shot you and Darrel saved you. The doctors said you're going to be okay."

"Walk it off, snowflake," said Darrel. "It's only a flesh wound as the knight said in Monty Python."

I was beginning to get alert and coherent. "That didn't end well for the knight."

"It's going to end fine for you. You'll be home and walking tomorrow. You had excellent emergency treatment, you're welcome."

"What about Buck?"

"He was home the second I shot him."

"Dead?"

"As three center shots from a 9mm will typically do."

"How did you know to be there?"

"The ring. I called the Jostens folks after you gave me the description, and they pulled it right up. White spinel only went in three Wakefield rings that year. ED wasn't Ed. It was initials for Eli Dean."

"Why is that a familiar name?"

"Our latest missing person from the Gwen search was Eli Dean. You had said you were going to look for Buck to ask him about the ring. I now knew he was our serial killer and you were walking into trouble, so I hightailed it over your way."

"He told me about Bob and Gwen. And the two boys."

"I heard his confession. I was going to arrest him for the murders when he turned with the gun. I put 911 on speakerphone while I was wrapping duct tape around your leg. A lot of cops and paramedics were there in minutes, and here you are."

"Thanks," I said.

"All in a day's work," he laughed. "I'm just glad you're going to be okay."

"What do we do now?" asked Audrey.

"Take care of your husband," Darrel said. "I checked with the hospital, and you can stay with him overnight. That couch is a bed. If there are no complications, you'll be out of here in the morning."

"I have to get home for Lincoln."

"No, you don't. I'm going to your place now to get with the team at the crime scene. They found your pending grave and evidence of the other two bodies. I'll stay there tonight and take care of Lincoln."

"Thanks, Darrel, for everything," she spoke.

The hospital kicked me out in the morning. I get to keep the .22 caliber bullet in my thigh as a lifetime reminder, like I'd need to be reminded. The crime scene techs had finished up overnight.

Darrel and Lincoln greeted us when we got home. "Buck earned me a few days off for administrative, so I'm available if you guys need anything."

I was drawn to the crime scene tape at the shed. "Can we take a walk?" I asked.

"I know I can," said Darrel. "But I wasn't shot in the leg yesterday."

"It's a little tender, but everything seems to work just fine," I said. "Do you want to join us?" I asked Audrey.

"Yes and no. I'm not sure. Maybe. Can Lincoln come with us?"

"Sure," said Darrel. "The crime scene is cleared, so we can do anything we want."

"Okay, I'll come with you," she said, getting a leash.

Buck's truck had been towed away. "Did you know I'd been shot when you got here?"

"No, that was a later surprise. I came in quiet, not knowing what, if anything, to expect. I saw Buck's truck, another consistency to our missing person's case. The shed door was open, so I walked off to the side of the opening, and I heard Buck talking as I got closer. I heard enough to make an arrest and walked up behind him when he turned with the gun. I didn't know you were shot until I stepped over him to clear the gun."

I told Audrey about Buck's confession to Gwen's killing and the other two. And what he said about Bob.

"Now we know why Bob was trying to tell us things were his fault," said Audrey.

"Want to see your grave?" asked Darrel. We walked a couple of hundred yards up the dirt road.

It was weird for Audrey and me to look into the hole where Buck had planned to bury us just last night. His small backhoe was parked there at the ready to fill us in. "The boys are already gone," said Darrel. "They pulled them out last night."

We went back to the house. Audrey called Vicki to let her know we were home. They had talked from the hospital after her quick departure from work, but she now filled Vicki in on the Bob story. Darrel and I talked to Don. After he heard about the class ring and Buck's demise, he simply said, "Nice job, Darrel."

"I need to go turn myself in for an interrogation," said Darrel. "So you can have your house back."

"Any concerns?" I asked.

"Just a formality. You may get a call as a witness, but I doubt it will even go that far."

"Good luck."

"I'll be fine. See you soon."

And it was just Audrey and I and Lincoln again, home safe and sound.

"I wonder how the rest of the year will go," I said.

"I wonder how the rest of our lives will go," she said. "I'm not sure we'll ever see as much drama and excitement as the past year."

"I'm sure I don't want to. Every day with you is plenty of excitement for me," I said with a kiss. "We might need to find some hobbies."

"I've already got mine with the studio and the gallery. I thought you wanted to be a writer."

"I do but it's hard to get excited about prohibition-era Chicago after everything we've experienced here."

"Maybe you could start on a haunted house story."

Maybe I could, I thought.

Acknowledgments

Thank you for reading 'Blame it on the Moon.' I'd greatly appreciate it if you could find the time to submit a review of your thoughts on the book, whether you loved it or not. It's been a very special journey for me to get to this point in my writing career. Your words and thoughts help me to continually improve in this adventure.

You're also welcome to connect with me directly through my website loupuglieseauthor.com. I read and respond to those notes personally and will continue to do so as long as I can.

My other thanks need to start with my wife, Kathy, and our dog, Mitch. They have both been by my side for every bit of this endeavor. Kathy is beta reader number one on everything I write, and Mitch is always with me and my cigars when I write.

My Mom has been gone since 1989 but she was always the largest influence in my education, career, and writing. She missed being here for a lot of the milestones, but I have no doubt she'd be proud. The rest of the family has also been a great supporting cast, giving me honest feedback. Many close friends have also served as readers and critics.

There are a lot of other aids and influencers in this work. I'll try to catch many of you, but I'll apologize in advance for those I miss. You know who you are, and you know I love what every one of you has done for me and meant to me in this journey.

The extended FWA family and contacts include Vic DiGenti, Elaine Senecal, Claudia Oltean, Linda Guecia, and the Royal Palm staff. You've all made me better through nudges and encouragement. MWA Sleuthfest was another exceptional learning experience.

Since Vic Digenti drafted me into my initial FWA service as the coordinator for the Clay County chapter, I've been blessed to meet many successful authors and make contact with other resources that have improved my knowledge and writing over the past years.

Several of those authors, Michael Wiley, Lisa Black, and Armand Rosamilia, have given me more guidance than they will ever know. That started with my first author lunch with JT and Joy Gilstrap. At the time I had an unedited and unintentionally pornographic draft that I left with John. His advice to take my time learning the world and craft of fiction writing, along with hitting the conventions and hanging out at the bar, helped immensely.

In the actual book construction and assembly, I need to thank my editor, Jennifer Ellen Cook. Jenn and I have worked together since early in this century, starting with her editing work on my doctoral dissertation at GW. Beyond her editing gig, Jenn is also an active singer, songwriter, and guitarist in the Austin music scene. If you get the chance to catch one of her shows, tell her I sent you.

My cover designer, Christine Holmes, came to me through Linda Guecia. I love how Chris started the project and how we evolved into the perfect images. My formatter, Autumn Skye, was also a gift from Linda. I'm sometimes lacking in attention to detail and Jenn, Christine, and Autumn cover that up well.

Acknowledgments

I'm hoping a lot of people will love this book and its characters. If so, there is a Don Weston prequel that is already written. I'd love an excuse to ship it by Jenn, Christine, and Autumn for the next release.

Made in the USA
Coppell, TX
03 May 2024

32004822R00163